Alexis Ascending

A NOVEL

by
Dilek Mir

MIR HOUSE • LOS ANGELES

This is a work of fiction. Names, characters, businesses, places, events, locales, and incidents are either the products of the author's imagination or used in a fictitious manner. Any resemblance to actual persons, living or dead, or actual events is purely coincidental. However, specific references to research and discoveries published in scientific journals is factual. Visit our website for links to those publications: https://mirhouse.net/science-behind-the-book

Published in the United States by Mir House™
ISBN: 978-1-953887-01-6

Cover art by: Rob House

What makes each day at the lab new and exciting is the richness of "what we know we don't know" and the possibility each day that we will discover some small clue that brings us closer to the truth. Even more tantalizing is the prospect of discovering aspects of the natural world that "we didn't know we didn't know"—discoveries that increase the breadth of the mystery.

Robert M. Hazen
The Story of Earth

1

SQUARE ROOT OF FOREVER

"Alexis, this is a very impressive application. But, today we have eighty clubs on campus. More than half of them have fewer than ten members. The last thing I'm going to do is approve the establishment of another club, if the sole purpose of said club is to pad the high school resume of the person seeking to *create* the club," Vice Principal Montgomery tells me as he skims through the twenty-page club application form on his desk. I labored over that document and I don't appreciate how casually he flips through it.

I gasp. "Mr. Montgomery! Are you accusing me of high school resume padding? Really?"

"No. No. Now, I didn't say that," Mr. Montgomery denies, shaking his head.

"Actually, you did," I insist.

"It was a purely hypothetical statement," he says.

"I am seeking to establish the Earth Science Club here at our high school to advance our understanding of the planet upon which we live. Are you not in favor of the advancement of science, Mr. Montgomery?" I accuse.

Mr. Montgomery's fingers dance across his keyboard. Is he even listening to me? From my seated position in his guest chair, I spy the keys his fingers have pounced, A, L, L, E, R, T, O, N. He scans his computer screen. I peer at the window behind his desk. It's not a mirror of course, but still, it reflects enough of his computer screen to enable me to read, in reverse, my name and my school profile page. He's sizing me up.

"Oh. I see you are a member of the Comic Book Club," he says.

"And the Debate Club," I add.

Mr. Montgomery takes his fingers off the keyboard, pushes away from his desk a smidgen and leans back in his chair. Over steepled hands he says, "Those two clubs have over twelve members each, so they are safe."

"Safe?" I ask.

"You see, during morning announcements today, we will inform the student body that the board passed a rule, proposed by me, requiring student clubs to have at least a dozen members, and not one, but two faculty advisers," he says. Then, he almost whispers his last phrase. "Or else, they will be terminated."

Mr. Montgomery, A.K.A. The Terminator, is a new Vice Principal here and I don't think he's going to last. He doesn't exactly embody the "be kind and compassionate" culture of our school.

"I can get a dozen people to join the club," I tell him. "And I can get a second faculty adviser as well."

"You do that, by October 11. Resubmit your application, and Alexis Allerton, you will be President of the newly
established Earth Science Club." Mr. Montgomery stands up and moves his hand in the direction of the door. I get the hint. I grab my application document off his desk and try not to storm out. But, I sort of do anyway.

Exiting the Main Office, with my Earth Science Club application rolled up in my hand like a holy scroll, I enter the stream of students moving through the hallways. Destination—Period One Physics class. I zig and I zag through the slow flow, darting past students less eager than me to get into their classrooms.

"Mrs. Cromwell!" I speed walk into my class and approach the physics teacher extraordinaire.

She stands up from her desk, hands on pregnant belly. Oh my. Did her belly get even bigger over the weekend?

"Mrs. Cromwell, Mr. Montgomery just told me that all clubs now need not one, but two faculty advisers!" I blurt out.

"The reason why I said no the first time, and suggested you go to Mr. Rubin, that reason, hasn't changed," Mrs. Cromwell says, rubbing her belly. "I'll be gone for three months and can't be of much use to you."

"Yeah. But, please, please, please?" I beg.

"That's a fine rational case you're making," Mrs. Cromwell says with biting irony.

"I already made my fine rational case when I first asked you, so, yes now I'm resorting to begging," I admit.

She shakes her head no.

"Come on. Earth science! I know it calls out to the astrophysicist in you. Do it for the advancement of science. Do it for your unborn child! Do it for all of the future children of Earth!" I pour it on thick.

"Alright, alright," she says. On the first alright, I had already unrolled my club application. On the second alright, I flipped to the faculty adviser page.

I grab a pen off her desk, fill in her name, and then hand the pen to her.

"Mind signing on the line there?" I ask.

She does.

"Thank you. Thank you. Thank you!" I say, as I walk to my designated lab bench and sit next to Hannah. We both open our notebooks. Interspersed among our academic notes from yesterday about the property of collisions, are notes of a more personal nature. This is our standard communications protocol during physics class. Good thing Mrs. Cromwell doesn't collect notebooks.

With the ring of the bell, Mrs. Cromwell starts the lesson.

You have to join the Earth Science Club, I write, moving my notebook closer to Hannah for her reading pleasure. She rolls her eyes at me.

You have to. They made up a new rule. I need 12 people by Oct 11 or else, nix, no go, abort takeoff! I write.

Hannah reads but gives me no response. Her eyes drift up to the guy sitting at the lab bench, two rows up and over to the right. Josh. Each time Mrs. Cromwell turns her back to the class to write on the white board, Josh turns around to look at Hannah. Over and over again. Mrs. Cromwell and Josh's motions are so synchronized, I wonder if they are jointly delivering a lesson on Newton's third law of action and reaction.

Will you stick around with me after PE for my cheer practice? Josh says he's got a surprise for me on the football field. Hannah writes to me in her notebook.

Oh please. He's got no surprises. I write back.

She sighs.

What? You're not actually into him now? That's not possible. We've known him our whole lives. I write.

You hang with me on the field during cheer practice and I'll join your boring rock collectors club. Hannah writes.

Deal! I write in agreement.

But then, I can't help but continue making words with my pencil. *Earth Science is not just about rocks...and there's nothing 'just' or 'boring' about geology.*

Stop! Before I retract my offer. Hannah writes.

In the cafeteria, I put my backpack down at our regular table and eye the shorter-than-usual lunch line. Strange. Hannah's not here. She's always here first because her fourth period class is prime real estate. It's cafeteria-adjacent. I look around.

"Hey," says Josh, as he pulls out a chair next to mine and drops his backpack in it.

"Lunching with us today?" I ask.

"Yep. And I hear you're joining Hannah today to observe football practice," he says.

"Football? Nope. Hannah recruited me to hang out during cheer practice," I respond.

"Cheer, football, you know, it's all the same," he says shrugging his shoulders. His blond curls bounce on his big broad shoulders as he makes the motion. I've seen him make that motion countless times as far back as I can remember. But it just looks different now that he's six-feet, four inches tall, and built like a tank. At some point, the boy next door turned into this.

I scan the cafeteria again, looking for Hannah.

"She's donating," Josh tells me.

"Donating what?" I ask.

I look around some more. Then, I notice it. The Red Cross blood bank posters are all over the place. Oh yeah. I knew it was blood bank day. I had pushed it out of my mind. I could just skip these bi-annual blood drive days, if only I were the type who could casually skip school. I am not that type. OK. I take a deep breath. I have to get over my fear of seeing blood. I grab my backpack and head out of the cafeteria.

"Hey, Alexis," Josh catches up with me. "You don't really want to go in there? Do you?"

"No. I don't. And that's exactly why I need to," I say, charging towards the multi-purpose room. I speed walk, because I'm not supposed to run. Josh is in lockstep with me.

"OK. Then I'm going in with you," he says, patting me gently on the back. It's the same gentle pat on the back he gave me when I got sick and vomited at the sight of blood pouring out of his cut knee. We were five years old. Emboldened by wearing his Superman cape, Josh had jumped off the very top of his swing set. That was the first time I saw blood, it was not the last time I have barfed at the sight of it.

We walk into the multi-purpose room. They've put up room dividers, creating a reception area, and blocking my view of any blood. The Red Cross rep at the reception desk greets us.

"Welcome. Thanks for your interest in giving blood today. Are you sixteen or older?" she asks, pulling together some paperwork. My eyes dart between her and the room dividers.

"Yes. I'm sixteen. But, no. I-I can't give blood. I'm . . . a hemophiliac," I tell her. It's like telling her I am an American, or telling her I am a human. It's simply what I am, my state of being, not subject to change.

"Oh. No, ahh . . ." the young woman pauses and seems to be at a loss for words. Then, she continues. "Best for you not to donate today. We can't take the chance that your bleeding would continue after the donation."

"No. Of course not. I'm careful. I'm always careful," I say. I feel like a robot saying this. Careful—it's the word I hear too much. Careful—the word is programmed into me.

"Come on. Let's leave," Josh nudges me towards the exit. I move in the opposite direction towards the room dividers.

"May I just go in and visit my friend who's donating in there?" I ask the Red Cross rep.

"Sure. Just be careful," she says. There's that word again.

I walk past the room dividers. Josh is beside me.

Dozens of students, lying on dozens of stretchers, filling dozens of blood bags with their red liquid. I take it all in. There's Hannah. Her head is turned the other way. She doesn't see me. Blood is moving from her vein, through the IV connector, into the clear tube and collecting in her blood bag.

As I watch her blood bag fill halfway, it happens.

I feel a sharp pain at my right temple, like someone just stuck a knife in there. In my mind, I see Hannah's and every other student's blood bags fill, overflow, and burst. Gushing blood pops the IV connections out of their arms, and now all of these people are hemorrhaging. The pain at my temple intensifies. It's like the knife is piercing deeper, deeper, until the image in my mind disappears.

I see the room, in real life, as it is again. Nothing but well-meaning students donating blood. No blood bath.

Momentary relief.

Then, I enter the barf phase. The sharp pain in my temple moves to my belly. The pain tells me I don't belong here, with all of these people whose bodies know how to heal. Maybe I don't belong anywhere. I feel very badly about myself. I can't stand this feeling. I put my hand on my stomach and double over. Josh instantly produces a trash bucket, into which I vomit.

Nice. This is so embarrassing. The kale and spinach smoothie I had this morning is now staining my white linen top.

Each time I see blood, in real life, and that's not often, as I usually avoid it, my reaction is almost the same. First, I imagine the person with the punctured blood vessel creating a bloodbath. Then, knowing I'm the only one who could actually hemorrhage, I vomit.

I have tried going to hemophilia support groups. But that didn't help me. Talking with a bunch of super nice, well-adjusted, normal people who have the same condition as me, only served to underscore how much I feel like an outlier. Those people are encouraged to do some physical exercise to strengthen their bodies. I'm an exception. I have a very severe case of the disease. Even the slightest injury can cause internal or external bleeding for me. Because I'm missing blood clotting factor IX, I can bleed to death. Anywhere. Anytime. My parents and doctors never let me forget this.

Physical education. It's for everyone but me. Today on the football field, my classmates run sprints back and forth from mid-field to the goal line where I stand. They are sweating on this unseasonably hot September Massachusetts day. Not me. I'm the PE teacher's assistant and my physical exertion is limited to blowing my whistle in two minutes when this set of sprints is done. Every student here runs, jumps, climbs, catches balls, and does whatever the PE curriculum requires. They are allowed to test their physical limits.

I am not afforded that luxury. I could have taken study hall, an extra elective, or even left to go home early. Instead, I choose to stand by and watch others bounce the basketball, leap over the hurdle, and swim their strokes. That's right, I can't even swim, because the possibility exists that while doing a flip turn, I might hit the wall, cut myself and bleed to death in the pool. But I always have the itch. That itch to just simply run until I fall, to see what my limits are.

Observing PE each day is my practice in resisting this urge. I've either sat out recess and PE, or been the coach's assistant armed with a whistle and clipboard during my formal schooling in kindergarten through tenth grade. By now, in my junior year, this has become a Zen meditation. Seeing the thought, the urge to run, and letting it go.

My stop watch tells me it's time, and I blow my whistle.

My whistle is followed by the PE teacher's, which announces class has ended. Sixth period PE students vacate the field and make way for the cheer squad and football team. By the time I'm done gathering our PE equipment, I see Hannah, captain of the cheer squad, followed by her teammates, enter from the south gate. Josh and his teammates come in from the north entrance. While Hannah is moving towards me, Josh makes a bee line for his coach who stands at mid-field. Josh is saying something to coach, but I can't quite make it out.

"You're what?" the coach shouts. This, I could definitely hear. I assume, so could anyone else on campus.

Josh's response is simply a shrug of the shoulders. He turns his back to coach and runs in our direction. Hannah is now standing by me at the goal line.

"Goldstein! You get back here!" Coach dials up his volume even further. "I'm not losing a player to the cheer squad!"

"I heard you were looking for a few guys to join your squad," Josh says to Hannah. "Well, here I am. Now you've got a guy."

While Hannah's jaw drops towards the field's artificial turf, I see two more football players coming our way.

"Roberts! Brown! Where do you think you're going?" Coach demands.

One of the two responds. "Coach, we're less likely to suffer a concussion on the cheer squad."

I roll my eyes and look at Josh. "I suspect this is more about you and your buddies preferring the feel of tossing and catching girls rather than pig skin. It's so immature!" I say.

He and Hannah are both ignoring me and looking into each other's eyes instead.

"How did we get from holding hands and skipping around the block to this?" I ask them.

"Alexis . . ."Josh says.

". . . shut up," Hannah completes his sentence.

"Welcome to the team," Hannah says to Josh and his two buddies.

"On one condition," I butt in.

"Condition?" Hannah asks.

"As long as the three of you guys agree to become members three, four, and five of the new Earth Science Club, then you are welcome to join the cheer squad," I say. "Right, Hannah?" I prod.

"Sure," she says. "If I have to suffer through your boring club, I may as well have company."

The guys nod in agreement. I'm five-twelfths of the way to my goal.

We walk home. South on Seaver Street, around Woodlawn Cemetery, and onto the corner of Sterling and Temple. Hannah took a right turn several blocks back towards her house. Josh and I walk up Sterling Road, towards our adjacent homes.

I see the driveway's automatic gate slide to the right along its tracks, offering entry to my house. The open invitation through the black wrought iron gate and fence welcomes my hematologists Drs. Roman, Roman and Roman in their souped-up, customized white Cadillac Escalade EXT pickup truck. The truck, equipped with the gate's remote control, roars.

"Time for your treatment," Josh says.

"I need a few more minutes before I make my passage through those gates," I say.

"Avoiding what's uncomfortable are you?" he asks.

"Totally," I respond, looking down at the green vomit stain that's been decorating my white linen top since lunch. I hold out my hand to Josh. "Can we? Like we used to?" I ask.

He doesn't say a word. He just takes my hand. We skip together up and down the street, like we did when we were much younger. This comforts me.

The Cadillac's driver door opens. The door features their logo, which is an outline of a house with Dr. R^3 in its center, and the words House Calls as the foundation of the house. Sam gets out first. He drives because he can see. Eyeing me down Sterling Road, he gives me his knowing nod. The nod is his main mode of communication, because he can't talk. The back passenger door pops open. A white cane is carefully placed on the truck's running board, and then is moved down to the surface of the driveway by Ira's hand. The rest of Ira's body follows. Behind his dark glasses, he's blind. Sam walks around the front of the truck and opens the front passenger door. Kan steps out of the truck. She says thank you to Sam, who holds her delicate hand. She can't hear his response. She is deaf. They are triplets, and they are always in their white lab coats. They are adored by my parents, my community, and me, for their courage to become practicing doctors, despite lack of sight, sound, and speech. They compensate for each other and make each other whole. Having them treat me reminds me that I don't need to feel like an outlier. Maybe each of us can feel normal and feel like we belong, no matter how different we are.

"I still wonder if they shove their medical mistakes into that hardtop covered trunk," Josh says as he lets my hand go. He's joking. He's often joking about my odd doctors.

"Don't become a medical mistake," he adds.

"Maybe I already am one," I say.

"That's not what I meant," Josh says. He pats me on the back to signal he's sincere.

"I know. Lucky you. You don't need clotting factor IX injections every other day," I say and I walk through the black wrought iron gates.

Inside, Drs. Roman, Roman and Roman prepare to treat me. My mother, lovely and ever present, holds my hand over the dining room table. As always, during the treatment, she gazes into my eyes, giving me a point of focus away from the pain of the needle.

It's like a mirror. We have the same almond shaped brown eyes, thick straight black hair, and tall slender figure with boobs. The boobs part surprised me. Since I haven't yet gotten my period, I didn't expect getting boobs would be part of my puberty experience. I quite frankly don't know what I will do about the vomit situation when and if I do get my period. My father's side of the family, the very Anglo Allertons, describe me as exotic. My opinion differs. I've been derisively called a mongoloid by a mean kid in my fifth grade class, and my nickname on the debate team is Genghis Khan. Apparently, I can sometimes be brutal. In a totally non-physical kind of way, of course. The similarity with my mother stops at our skin. She's a shade of honey-olive that just looks right. Looks graceful on her. I'm more of a sickly, cement grey. Not like an elephant, just an unhealthy pallor.

When I had first learned that hemophilia was the disease of the European royals, that made me feel like a princess, for at least a day. The Allertons, my dad's family, arrived in Massachusetts on the Mayflower. My mom's a more recent import. Her family emigrated to the U.S. when their homeland of Kazakhstan became part of the Soviet Union in the 1920s. As a merger of common folk from east and west, I get to live with the royal disease of hemophilia, without the perks of an aristocratic life.

Kan tightens the red rubber tourniquet around my right arm just above my elbow, restricting the blood below my elbow from returning to my heart. Ira's fingers, which serve as his eyes, glide around my forearm, seeking the optimal blood vessel to receive the needle. With an alcohol soaked swab, Kan disinfects the lucky spot that Ira has selected. Sam connects the needle and thin white tube to the vial of clotting factor IX, the protein that people with hemophilia B lack. Because I have less than one percent of the amount of factor IX that my body needs to form a blood clot, I'm diagnosed with a severe case. Worse, my body creates inhibitors against clotting factor IX, so most of what's injected into me is inactivated by my inhibitors as soon as the factor IX hits my bloodstream. Ira had explained, this is why they need to keep upping my factor IX dose. This prophylactic treatment is supposed to help my blood to clot, in case I have an internal or external bleed. Thus, *careful* is my mantra.

I feel like an uber-mutant female because hemophilia is caused by a mutation on the X chromosome. To be exact, on the F9 gene of the X chromosome. An estimated 400 boys are born with hemophilia in the U.S. each year. As a boy, with one X and one Y chromosome, all you need is one mutant X and you've got the disease. The Centers for Disease Control doesn't even publish the number for girls born with hemophilia. Maybe since that number might be zero, except for the year I was born. As a girl with two X chromosomes, even if you had one mutant X, the other X in all likelihood would be normal and healthy and you'd merely be a carrier of hemophilia. I hit the jackpot because I have two mutant Xs. Most people with hemophilia inherit it. Mine? My mother is not even a carrier, so it's a spontaneous mutation.

I imagine how it might have happened. Of the approximately 1,000 genes on the X chromosome, just that one F9 gene mutated on each of the X chromosomes I got from my mother and father. What are the chances? I've already asked my mother if she and my dad were in some kind of radioactive chamber at the moment of fertilization. Despite my many efforts to ask this intimate question about my conception, Mom is still mum on the topic.

"Ouhhh . . ." and there goes the needle. Sam's in. Blind Ira feels around the table, gathering the packaging and remains from the disposable supplies they just used. He places this trash into their black doctor's bag. Kan removes the tourniquet.

I exhale. Just a little. I won't fully regain my breath until the needle is out.

It takes all of three minutes. A treatment, three minutes in duration, when time stands still. I always do my best to focus straight into my mother's eyes and ignore my peripheral vision. But I still see them. Sam, Ira, and Kan. This doesn't disturb me so much anymore. I like them now. They help me feel normal.

It was different when I was younger, young enough to not be able to articulate what I saw. That's when I would witness it. As I looked into my mother's eyes during the treatment, into my peripheral vision would float three white orbs. The orbs floated around and through Sam, Ira, and Kan. In my peripheral vision, Sam, Ira, and Kan merged into one, becoming as amorphous as an amoeba. It—they—moved around me by growing an extension of their body and flowing in the direction of the growth. Were they beside me? In front of me? Behind me? Something about seeing Drs. Roman, Roman, and Roman in a form that is not solid, not human, and not having definitive boundaries, terrified me. I used to see this often. Then, as I got older, when I turned seven years old, I saw this less and less frequently, and then, I stopped seeing them this way at all. Maybe I imagined it. Maybe I've just gotten better at keeping my focus on my mother's eyes.

One hundred and eighty seconds after Sam inserted the needle, he gently pulls it out and Kan places a bandage on the injection site. She gives me a lollipop. I'm sixteen years old and my doctor still gives me a lollipop. I don't mind. They know my favorite flavor.

"Alexis, dear, you'll remember that people with severe hemophilia have a 2.69–fold increase in death rate compared to that of the general population. Yours is certainly higher due to the clotting factor IX inhibitors your body insists on producing. Keep doing what you're doing. Follow the rules and be careful," Ira reminds me.

"Good girl," Kan adds.

It's not exactly the same speech each time, but they find some kind of statistic or factoid to throw at me at each visit. Sam nods in agreement. I'm dismissed, and pleased to be so.

I make my way into the kitchen.

"Strawberry and banana today?" my father asks. He's still in business casual clothes, which are almost like a uniform for him. He's not compelled to change out of them when he walks home from Babson College where he teaches economics. This is our ritual. Smoothie time follows needle-stuck-in-my-arm time.

"I'm in more of a carrot-apple kind of way today," I respond.

"Make that two." It's Amanda's voice.

"Amanda!" I say looking around for my sister.

"My disembodied voice is coming at you from Dad's speakerphone," she informs me. "My body remains at New Mexico Tech in Socorro, New Mexico."

"Tease! My mind jumped to you being here for a surprise visit," I tell her.

"Not till Thanksgiving break," she says.

Sam, Ira, and Kan walk by the kitchen on their way out.

"May I offer you a smoothie?" my dad asks them.

"Thanks for your hospitality," Ira says to my dad. "We must move along to our next house call. So long, Dale. See you, Alexis," he says to me.

I think, OK, blind man. But when will this thought cease to be the first thing that pops into my head when blind Ira says *see you*? It feels so disrespectful, but I can't stop the thought.

"The day after tomorrow," Kan finishes his sentence in a perfect cadence, as though they were one person speaking. I credit that to her superb lip reading skills. I don't know how long she's been deaf, but her enunciation is perfect. I don't think she was born without her hearing.

Sam nods.

The sound of the front door closing is my signal to fully exhale.

"Everything good, Alexis?" Amanda asks via speakerphone.

"Yes," I respond. This feels like a half-truth. I don't like half-truths.

"I'll check in with you tomorrow. Bye!" Amanda signs off.

Tomorrow. No treatment tomorrow. That's when I go to my favorite place, the geology lab where I intern. It's a close runner up to my second favorite place, school. Being here at home, it's not my third favorite place.

This is the seemingly utopian American middle class existence where my parents love, adore and protect me. My big sister Amanda checks on me daily, even though she's more than 2,000 miles away at her university.

This is the place where I am guilty and ashamed for feeling that things are very wrong. I would call this unsettling feeling a gut instinct but it doesn't live in my gut.

It floats around different parts of my body, looking to find a place it can burrow and hide. In moments when it can't hide from my awareness, it feels like a sharp electrical current that translates into thoughts. Thoughts that don't go away. Thoughts that morph back into the feeling that I don't belong in this house. I've had this feeling for a long, long time.

It feels like for the square root of forever.

2

HOME AT THE LAB

"Ridiculous, goofy, and stupid," I declare, eyeing myself in the locker room mirror. Girls rush by, into and out of the showers following a demanding sixth period PE class. They help me out by offering other words that more accurately describe it. The abomination that I am wearing.

"Tacky."

"Idiotic."

"Sappy."

"Pathetic."

"Keep it to yourselves," Hannah snaps at the commentators. Her blonde bob cut hair bounces as she moves her head from left to right, looking at me, then me in the mirror, me, then me in the mirror again.

"He's gonna love it," she insists.

"Nope. Not doing it," I tell her.

"He won't be able to take his eyes off you," she persists.

I resist. I don't like wearing t-shirts to begin with. It's just too boy-man for me. Women have such diverse options for ways to clothe our bodies. Why choose something that originated as a man's undergarment? This particular t-shirt I'm staring at in the mirror is far worse. It's kelly green, with a cartoonish drawing of a quartz crystal and the words *Of quartz I love geology* written in all caps, in bold white font, across my chest.

"The least you could've done is find a women's cut," I complain.

"Hey, if there were demand for geeky, goofy geology t-shirts for women, then there'd be supply. One customer a market does not make," Hannah decides.

"Forty percent of Earth science PhDs are women. Hardly a market of one," I retort. Then, I reconsider. "Those women just have better taste than to create a market for this."

"Trust me. This will do the job," she says in full retail sales clerk mode.

I grab the bottom of the t-shirt and pull it up over my head. During the 1.5 seconds in which my face is covered in kelly green jersey, Hannah bolts.

"See you outside!" she says.

I see Hannah making her way towards the locker room exit with my periwinkle silk top. Balling it up, she shoves it into her backpack, and she's out the door and out of sight.

Pulling the ugly t-shirt back down over my body, I grab my backpack. By the time I catch up to her outside, she's walking with Josh towards the bumper-to-bumper procession of cars at the student pick up line.

"Nice!" Josh reacts to what Hannah is showing him on her phone.

"What?" I poke my head between the two of them.

"That's him?" Josh teases.

"Uh, huh," I shake my head.

"Where's his face?" he challenges.

I shrug my shoulders. I snuck the photo. He was at the other end of the lab bench. I had held the phone down by my hip and pressed the button repeatedly, blindly hoping to catch a decent shot. I can't have him know I took a picture of him. Since I couldn't find him on social media, how else am I to show Hannah the reason my job at the lab just got exponentially better in the few weeks since the school year started?

"This?" Josh points to the photo on the phone. The shot presents just a glimpse of the object of my interest, only the back right side of his head which is covered in thick milk chocolate brown hair and the corner frame of his tortoise shell eyeglasses.

"This is the reason you're wearing that?" he points at my t-shirt and guffaws. He amuses himself and sometimes, and just occasionally, others.

"And this," I ask Josh, pointing at Hannah. "Is the reason you're wearing that?" I glide my finger over his cheer squad t-shirt.

"True love pushes a man to do glorious things," Josh says.

This puts a broad smile across Hannah's petite features.

"Every day I've seen him at the lab, he's in one of these," I admit, showing Josh and Hannah the collection of t-shirts he's worn, which I have since cataloged on the new Pinterest page I've created dedicated to goofy science t-shirts. On my Pinterest page, the t-shirts are worn by a variety of models, not him, and therefore Hannah and Josh still have not seen his face. The t-shirts make declarations including:

Never trust an atom, they make up everything. The *o* being an atom symbol.

I wear this shirt periodically. This features the periodic table.

If it moves it's biology. If it stinks it's chemistry. If it doesn't work it's physics.

"This wardrobe would normally be a deal breaker," I tell them, putting the phone back into my pocket. "But, he's really interesting."

"More interesting than a pile of rocks? Setting the bar high there are you?" Josh mocks.

"He's a geek with just the right amount of cuteness," I clarify.

"Woah. Don't call him cute. You sound like a schoolgirl," Josh counsels me. Hannah and I shoot him simultaneous glares. "What?" he asks defensively. "You are a school girl, a high school girl. And he's what, a grad student right?"

"He's right," Hannah decides. "Hot geek. Does that sound more collegiate?"

I roll my eyes. I just want to get to the lab and leave the friendly mockery behind at the high school campus.

"BEEP!"

The horn of my mother's silver Tesla Model X startles me. The falcon wing doors silently glide up and open.

"Bye! I'll keep your words of wisdom in mind," I hop into the backseat, leaving Josh and Hannah at the curb.

"Hi Mom!" I say.

"Hel . . ." she's cut off before she can finish her greeting.

"Hi, Mrs. Allerton!" Hannah says, her body half-inside the car already.

Hannah gives me a seated hip bump. She packs a lot of power for a tiny thing. The falcon wing doors close us in. The motion of the doors is smooth and seems oddly gentle for a large hunk of metal, making me feel like an eyass. Baby falcons have a very high mortality rate when they first leave the nest. As high as hemophiliacs who have the urge to leap tall buildings in a single bound? I wonder.

"What are you doing?" I whisper to Hannah.

"Thanks for driving me to the lab Mrs. Allerton. Alexis's passion for rocks is becoming contagious," she tells my mom.

"It's not just rocks! It's geophysics and geochemistry and geobiology and . . ." I mutter through my clenched jaw.

"OK. OK. Take it easy there. I'm interested in all of it," Hannah says.

"That's great, Hannah," Mom says. "Maybe you can ask Professor Ojigwe if he needs another intern. We would love it if Alexis had a peer there, someone her own age."

"Oh, I'll be sure to think about that," Hannah promises my mom, without a trace of sarcasm in her voice. Instead, she wears the sarcasm on her face in the back seat with me.

I had met Professor Ojigwe at the Wellesley Library while doing research for my science fair project on the Earth's changing surface over the past 4.5 billion years. Lucky for me, he lives in town. He struck up a conversation with me, offering me some tips, and as a joke, he told me he was pleased to meet a future colleague. I jumped on that opportunity. I asked the professor if I could apply to be a high school intern at his Earth science lab at the Massachusetts Institute of Technology. He told me I was bold to ask and that they normally don't have high school interns.

Bold? I suppose. But, if I can't take risks with my physical body, then I figure I have to compensate by taking intellectual risks, part of which entails asking stupid questions to which the most likely answer is no. It paid off. Working with geologists at MIT for the past sixteen months, I discovered a new state of bliss, and this was even before the catalyst for my corny kelly green *Of quartz I love geology* t-shirt started to work there, namely—Everett Evans.

Hannah and I simultaneously whip out our phones so we can have our private conversation while my mother drives. Mom notices our phones come out, and she puts on the radio, tuned to the news.

"Mom, please," I say. "Can you turn it off?"

"When are you going to grow out of it?" she asks me.

"Never," I respond. "But if you really need to listen, for work, then go ahead," I offer.

My mom caves, as usual. She changes the station to classical.

As the Boston correspondent for an international news agency, she lives and breathes the news. I can't listen to a lot of news outlets. The state of the world disturbs me. I don't understand how some humans want to destroy or subjugate other humans. What disturbs me almost as much is the state of the news, which for the most part, only reports bad things, further perpetuating what is disturbing about the state of the world.

Now that Tchaikovsky's Waltz of the Flowers fills the car, I fire off the first text to Hannah.

Me: What're you doing? Don't you have cheer practice now?

Hannah: Not til 5. I'll grab a car service back here AFTER I see what a geek with just the right amount of cuteness looks like. AND I need to make sure you don't ditch the t-shirt

Me: Just don't giggle in front of him

Hannah: Like the silly school girls that we are?

Me: Ugh

Hannah: So?

Me: So what?

Hannah: What DOES make him more interesting than a pile of rocks…other than his cuteness?

Me: >40% of students at MIT were valedictorians in high school

Hannah: Was he?

Me: I haven't asked. I don't want him to know that I want to know. But there's >40% chance the answer is yes

Hannah: You first laid eyes on him 3 weeks ago?

Me: Yep

Hannah: That was just after Josh started reciting poetry to me

Me: He recites poetry to you?

Hannah: Yep

Me: Is that what flipped your relationship from buddies to…whatever it is now?

Hannah: Definitely a factor
Me: Hmmm…
Hannah: Are you OK with Josh and me, you know…with Josh being, my guy
Me: I guess so
Hannah: Are you jealous?
Me: No!!!!!
Hannah: So what's the GUESS SO about?
Me: Am I going to become a 3rd wheel?
Hannah: No! No! and No!
Me: Are you two going to become a couple and abandon me?
Hannah: Again, NO!
Me: OK it's just weird
Hannah: Yeah. It's weird. I just wonder…are you conjuring up this college guy, just because Josh is now my guy?
Me: I'm not conjuring! He actually exists
Hannah: I'll put it this way. Are you crushing on someone just so you have an object of interest, you know, because now I do?
Me: He's neither an object, nor a rock
Hannah: A few guys at school like you. Not that you'd notice. But, if you're looking for a guy, you don't have to look far
Me: I'm not looking for a guy. Just promise I won't be a 3rd wheel
Hannah: Promise

Thirty-eight minutes and a total of ninety-four texts following our departure from school, we take a left, leaving the Charles River behind us, and drive onto the MIT campus. My mother pulls up to the tallest building in Cambridge, the Green Building. It's hard to miss. A giant 1960s era rectangle composed of reinforced concrete with a limestone grey façade that almost matches the pallor of my skin.

"Enjoy girls!" my mother presses a button and the falcon wings rise to let the eyasses fly free.

"Thanks, Mrs. Allerton," Hannah hops out.

"Thanks, Mom," I say.

"Dad's picking you up at six," my mother confirms. Then she adds the one word that is most frequently directed at me, "Careful."

As the word lands in my mind, I look down at the t-shirt I'm wearing. Yes. I'm going to be careful and not be seen wearing this horrid thing. My mother's white cardigan is lying across the front passenger seat. I reach for it. She gives me the *go ahead, take it* look of approval. I'm pleased with myself as I put the cardigan on and button in up all the way to my neck.

Another "Careful," is the last word out of her mouth as her foot hits the accelerator.

It's always that word, *careful.* I figure I've heard it 152,525 times during the course of my life. I've lived 6,101 days, during which time, my mother has spoken about an average rate of 16,000 words per day, with an estimated twenty-five of those words being the word *careful* delivered daily to me. That kind of repetition must have some efficacy. I haven't accidentally cut myself or bled to death yet.

"Welcome," I invite Hannah onto the green lawn in front of the Green Building. She stops, looking up at La Grande Voile, a giant sculpture about forty feet high made of four sheets of metal coming together like sails. She places a hand over her brow, shading her eyes from the afternoon sun that's ready to disappear for the day.

"I'd like to climb that," she says.

"Yeah," I grab her by the arm and pull her along.

We enter the concrete rectangle and take the elevator up to the twelfth floor. As the elevator doors close behind us, I grin. Because, instead of making the standard move that everyone entering an elevator makes, Hannah does something different. She doesn't just walk into the elevator, turn around and face forward towards the doors. She does what I hoped she would. Her eyes are glued to the plaque on the elevator wall opposite the doors. The header, in the largest font, delivers the message—*Unleash your natural curiosity*. Beneath that is written: *Welcome to the Department of Earth, Atmospheric and Planetary Sciences (EAPS), the place at MIT where the turbulent oceans and atmosphere, the inaccessible depths of the inner Earth, distant planets, and the origins of life all come together under one intellectual roof.*

I track Hannah's eyes as they scan the last words on the plaque. I echo her silent reading aloud, "the origins of life all come together under one intellectual roof." I put my hand on her shoulder and turn her around to face me, "How's that for a pile of rocks?"

"Wow," she delivers that single word in an understated manner that is rare for Hannah. I have to grin again, because when she's understated, that's a sign she's really moved, touched deep. Maybe this understated way of hers is a by-product of all the enthusiastic jumping up and down she does during cheer squad, whether she cares about the play-by-play at each football game or not.

The elevator doors open. We walk the long hallway towards our destination—L12-H. It's a large laboratory between the other lab doors marked L12-G and L12-I. The H in L12-H is merely a label assigned in alphabetic order. A very logical choice for a department that prides itself on understanding our world through hard, quantitative science. For me, the H stands for home. While I'm here, that feeling of something is wrong, that feeling of not belonging, ceases. I can just be. I can just exist, without feeling like I need to do something to make something feel better.

Hannah grabs me by the bicep just as I've put my hand on the door labeled L12-H. She stops me momentarily and whispers, "I have fifteen minutes before I have to grab a car service back to school for cheer practice. And you will be taking that cardigan off before I leave." I roll my eyes and press the weight of my body against the door.

We enter. Everett and Professor Ojigwe are across the room at the mass spectrometer, a machine that looks like an extra-long version of the photocopiers at a print shop.

"Let's run three more samples through and see how the data compares," Professor Ojigwe says to Everett. The rich smoothness of Ojigwe's voice filtered through his Nigerian accent is what poured honey with a hint of cinnamon would sound like, if cinnamon and honey had a sound. Everett nods in agreement and they both look up, as Hannah and I approach them. Ojigwe takes a few steps in our direction.

"Hello, Alexis," he greets me. The professor reaches out to Hannah for a handshake. "And you must be

Hannah. Welcome to EAPS." Hannah and I look at each other for a moment and I know we have the same thought. How does he know her name and that she would be here?

"Your mother called a minute ago and told us to expect a guest today," Ojigwe explains. Of course. My parents are always in the loop on whatever I'm doing and they inform any other adult with authority over my life about these facts. Sometimes, I feel like my life is orchestrated. So be it, but I want to be the conductor.

"Of course," I say out loud, even though I meant to keep that comment inside my head.

Hannah shifts her gaze to Everett, who has not stepped forward, and is keeping his hands in his pockets.

"Everett, this is my friend, Hannah. She . . . just wanted to see the lab and learn more about what we do here," I say, wanting to sound as natural as possible. No hidden agenda here. Nope. Hannah is not here to weigh in on whether you are a cute geek or a hot geek, I telepathically inform him, very pleased that no one at MIT has invented a mind reading machine—yet.

"Hey," he gives Hannah a distant acknowledgement without really looking at her.

During the three weeks that I've seen him in and around the lab, he seems to be short on greetings and small talk. I don't mind that he skips the salutation with me. Instead, he makes eye contact with me that just seems more real than words. This gives me the time and space to gaze back at his navy blue eyes just a moment longer than would otherwise be appropriate.

"We're using this mass spectrometer to analyze meteorites. Would you like to see?" Everett asks Hannah, talking over the low hum of the working machine. I wonder if Hannah even heard his words. Her eyes are shooting like laser beams at his t-shirt which tells a bad joke on Everett's behalf. The words, *I tell bad chemistry jokes because all the good ones argon,* are written across his chest, with the element argon featured in a box including its elemental symbol and number—Ar and 18. I can see Hannah's wheels turning and I'm wondering if she remembers enough of the periodic table from chemistry class last year to appreciate the bad joke.

"The machine does use argon," Everett says, pointing to the Ar on his t-shirt. Hannah's caught. Everett knows she was trying to make sense of the t-shirt. "Argon, the noble gas, gives us data on the isotopic composition of meteorites." Everett shuffles his feet and only looks at Hannah for a second before focusing his gaze at the mass spectrometer again. And then, I realize which meteorites he's talking about.

"We got the delivery from ANSMET?!?!" my excitement jolts Hannah and I nudge her along towards the big machine which is still humming and hard at work.

Ojigwe informs our geology neophyte, Hannah, "ANSMET. The Antarctic Search for Meteorites. It's a program funded by the National Science Foundation that looks for meteorites in the Transantarctic Mountains. To date, they've found around 20,000 meteorites on the continent. In other, more inhabited parts of the globe, when the average person stumbles across a meteorite, or when meteorite hunters search for and find them, these people tend to keep or sell the space rocks."

"Who could blame a person for wanting to keep one?" I utter as I spy the wooden crate, which I think, I hope, must contain the samples.

"Perfectly understandable. But ANSMET sends them to labs like ours so we can analyze the space rocks and advance our knowledge of the universe," Ojigwe says.

My feet move in the direction of the crate housing the extra-terrestrial rocks. Everett notices my move and brings the crate over, meeting me halfway. He hands one small piece to Hannah and one to me. As he does this, I'm much too aware of the tips of his fingers that make contact with the skin of my open palm.

"Antarctica's vast, snow covered white surface makes it an ideal place to find meteorites," Ojigwe continues. Hannah analyzes the charcoal black rock in her hand.

"Are they all black like that?" Hannah asks.

"On the outside, yes they are typically black, dark brown or dark grey. Meteorites experience frictional heat when they come through the Earth's atmosphere. This heat melts the outside of the rock and creates what we call a fusion crust, giving it the dark color. When you cut through the rock, like we've done with this one," Ojigwe points to a meteorite cut in half, "then you see the rock is different on the inside, this one being grey. That's one of two big clues that it's an extraterrestrial rock."

"And the other clue? Martian fingerprints maybe?" Hannah asks, very sober and serious.

"We'll do a fingerprint analysis and see if you've just come up with a new method of identifying a meteorite," Ojigwe flashes a huge smile at her. "Actually, the other way to know the difference between a meteorite and a meteor-wrong is that meteorites have a lot of pure metal, specifically extraterrestrial nickel and iron that Earthly rocks do not."

"Meteor-wrong?" Hannah questions, as she carefully analyzes the one in her hand.

"Meteor-wrong. Slang for rocks that look like meteorites, but much to the dismay of people who find them, they aren't," I respond, squeezing the sample they have given me.

"So what's the mass spectrometer going to tell us about the meteorites again?" Hannah probes.

"It will tell us the isotopic composition of meteorites. By looking at isotopic ratios we know more about the meteorite's planetary origin and evolution," Everett answers.

Ojigwe confirms. "To take it back to your Martian fingerprint question Hannah, isotopic ratios are indeed a fingerprint record. They tell us things like, is the meteorite indeed from Mars? How old is it? How long was it in space? How long has it been on Earth?"

"So you sounded more informed than you really are with your Martian fingerprint question," I tell Hannah. "You were thinking of little green men touching the rocks, leaving impressions from their long twig-like fingers weren't you? Admit it."

"Guilty as charged," she admits as her phone lights up. "There's my ride. I need to get back to school. Dr. Ojigwe, Everett, thank you so much," she hands the meteorite back to Everett.

"Alexis, would you show me where the bathroom is please?" Hannah grabs my arm, signaling that answering no is not an option.

"Alexis, the sample?" Everett points to the meteorite in my hand. It's a rule that totally makes sense. No meteorites in the bathroom. Accidentally dropping the extraterrestrial rock into the toilet may feel worse than when I did the same with my phone. I hand it over to him.

"Would you like to see what's inside?" he offers.

"Yes! Yes. Can we?" I ask. He places my meteorite, well actually, the meteorite, onto the wire saw. I just feel like it's mine.

"We'll cut through it after you walk your friend out," he promises.

Hannah and I exit the lab. She firms her grip on my arm, as I lead her into the ladies room.

"Now. Well. I don't have a conclusion yet. Cute geek or hot geek. But, maybe there's a new category like sophisticated yet awkward geek. Or boyish savant. He does seem boyish and odd. Maybe he's shy. Did you notice he didn't make much eye contact with me?" Hannah asks.

"Actually, I did. And that's odd because he makes a lot of eye contact with me," I point out trying to hide a grin.

"Or, maybe geek is not the right word at all. I don't know. But I do know he's sort of into you, based on the way he looks at you. Maybe . . ." Her patter is interrupted by her phone signaling her again about her ride.

"Go. Go. I want to get back to work. We can speculate later," I push her towards the ladies room's exit door.

"As soon as you hand it over," she says pointing to my mother's cardigan which still protects me from displaying the goofy science t-shirt I'm wearing underneath. I brace my hands around the buttons at my neckline.

"Come on. Be fearless. Be brave!" she commands. She looks at me. Reassessing her strategy, she changes tack.

"Be . . . careless. He's going to be amused, or like it, or not like it, or not care. What's the big deal? At the end of the day you have a school girl crush on a guy who's too old for you, and you're going to be over it when you realize that," she says.

"Am I?" I question. Maybe I am. I do the mental math that I've been avoiding doing, despite my love for math. Everett most likely finished high school at eighteen, undergrad at twenty-two, and now he's probably twenty-three, or twenty-four. That's a seven to eight year age difference, while I'm still underage. Not good.

So, then, Hannah is right. It doesn't make a difference if he likes or dislikes my goofy science t-shirt. Even if the crush were reciprocal, and I'm thinking maybe twenty-something guys are beyond having crushes, even if he likes me back, this is a no-go. I guess he'd be creepy if he did like me, and I don't like creepy guys. So, that's it.

"Hand it over," Hannah points at the cardigan again. I hastily unbutton the cardigan-turned-security-blanket, peel it off my body, and hand it over. I'm annoyed. I'm also sad about the reality of the situation with Everett. The chronology of our Earth entry gap is indeed an insurmountable obstacle. Together, Hannah and I exit the ladies room.

"I expect to hear from you at 6:01 p.m. with results!" Hannah informs me as she hurries towards the elevator.

I turn towards L12-H, take a deep breath, hold my head high, and walk into the laboratory.

And—Everett is not there.

Dr. Ojigwe slides his laptop into its case, hangs his lab coat on its hook, and heads towards me at the door.

"I'll be out of town at a conference for the next four days. Everett is in charge while I'm away," Ojigwe informs me.

"Oh. OK," I say.

"He'll guide you on the research. But if there's an emergency, or any other issue, Dr. Hoffman or any one of the other grad students can serve as adult supervisory contact while I'm away," Ojigwe says, giving me a mischievous smile.

"What do you mean by adult supervisory contact?" I ask.

"Well, I can't just have two minors working in this lab, even if both of those minors have the intellectual capacity of adults," he hints.

"Are you saying . . ." I pause and look at the professor.

"I'm saying, young Everett ought to be in high school, but the public school system didn't know what to do with him. He has a brain the size of a planet. So, we have a sixteen-year-old grad student here at the university," Ojigwe winks.

I gasp. "Oh. Oh. Oh, my," I say, realizing Everett is a boyish savant, indeed!

That's how Hannah described him, as boyish. So, maybe his long lingering looks at me do mean something, something good. I wonder if Ojigwe has noticed some of those glances and is telling me Everett's age for a reason.

"But he doesn't like anyone here to know. He says he wants to fit in," Dr. Ojigwe puts a finger to his lips, giving me a conspiratorial look. "Don't tell him that I told you. See you when I return," he says as he walks out the door, leaving me alone in the lab.

Where is Everett? Do I tell him I know? My mind rushes through all the new possibilities. I make my way over to the wire saw where my meteorite sits, waiting to be cut. I cup it into my hands again. This rock is enough to take my mind off Everett Evans, for now.

I wonder what the meteor is composed of. What elements? How old is it? Where did it come from? How long did it travel in space before it reached Earth? I want answers.

I look at the saw. Ojigwe is headed to the airport. The professor knows that rule number one for me is not to touch that saw, or any other sharp object. My parents made sure he's well informed of my medical condition. Everett is not in the room and I don't know if he's been informed of the rules surrounding my existence. I assume they have more important things to focus on here at EAPS, like the origin of life as we know it.

Holding the meteorite, I feel what I believe is an adrenaline rush. I feel lightheaded, buoyant, and powerful all at the same time. This is a first. It feels just like what runners describe to be their adrenaline high when they push themselves to their limits. But the closest I've ever come to running is speed walking and better yet, skipping, not a terribly bad substitute in my opinion.

I place my space rock back onto the saw and turn the machine on. I've watched Ojigwe and grad students do this dozens of times. I know I shouldn't be doing this because I'm not allowed to, for good reasons. I should be careful. Careful. Careful.

But I have to see what's inside this rock and I have to see it now. My body moves despite the doubts in my mind.

I move the meteorite into the path of the wire blade. With my left hand on the rock and my right on the saw, I begin to cut. The buzzing pulse of the machine reverberates, stemming from my hands through my whole body. Even down to my toes, I can feel the vibrating force of the wire cut through the meteorite.

"Alexis . . ."

Startled by the voice, I look up. It's Everett.

He is staring at me in a very odd way. I split my attention between him and working on finishing the cut. Just a few more seconds and I should be done. I think he's staring at my kelly green *Of quartz I love geology* t-shirt.

Yes. Yes! That's what he's staring at, with this astonishing look of wonder on his face. Wow, I've really made an impact. Hannah knew what she was doing when she made me wear it.

"Do you like my t-shirt?" I ask, looking down at my t-shirt and then back up at him. I must sound ridiculous. But what else can I say?

I feel a little tickle on my right index finger. Maybe it's a reaction to the buzzing sensation of the saw.

"No," he responds to my question about the t-shirt.

Wow. That was blunt.

His eyes move just a bit lower, away from my t-shirt and towards my hand. "No. I mean Yes. I mean. Alexis. I think you may have cut yourself."

The wire saw has made its way fully through the meteorite. Half the rock is still in my left hand and the other rests on the saw's platform. I follow Everett's line of sight, which takes my gaze to my right index finger. The tip of my finger, where I felt the tickle, has a deep slice through it. Then, I see it. Is that my blood?

It's beautiful.

The first sight of my own blood.

Oozing out of my finger, it sparkles and shimmers under the fluorescent lights of the lab. Knowing I may never stop bleeding doesn't at all diminish the thrill. Entranced, I can't take my eyes off the flowing liquid.

As I witness the blood that gives me life, I feel a sensation of little snowflakes forming inside me and moving around my body.

I had been taught to fear this moment, to never allow it to happen. But my blood has invoked in me the greatest exhilaration I've ever felt.

I look up, remembering I'm not alone in the lab. He's staring at me. What is that look? Bewilderment? Yes. But there is something else.

"Alexis, you . . . your blood . . ." he points to the liquid dripping from my finger onto my t-shirt and the lab bench.

He's looking at me like he has not before. I like it.

3

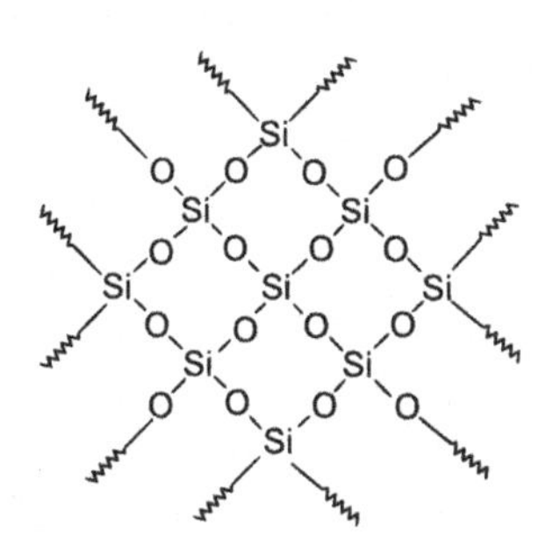

SORT OF DREAMY

"Alexis. What is that?" Everett asks. He's looking at my blood. It's a shiny, translucent, silvery white.

His eyes move up to meet my face.

"What are you?" he asks.

"I'm a hemophiliac," I respond automatically. The words flow out of my mouth without interference from my brain. A brain that now holds knowledge it was not privy to previously. A brain that now questions if I may have just stated an untruth.

Grabbing a test tube and towel, Everett rushes to my side. He puts the test tube under my finger to capture a sample of my dripping, shimmering blood. Then, he wraps the towel around my finger, applying pressure to the cut. I feel no pain. My eyes move to the meteorite I just cut. Or, maybe I should say it cut me. *My* meteorite. Split open, it now reveals its true content. Beneath its black fusion crust, it looks like white crystal.

Everett pulls back the towel, baring the tip of my index finger. No trace of a cut. It's smooth. It's healed. It's perfect.

Test tube in hand, he moves towards the mass spectrometer. He halts and turns around.

"Do you mind? Can we find out?" He holds the test tube out, asking my permission to investigate.

I shake my head no and say "Yes," addressing both of his questions in order. I give up the sample of my blood to science. I give it up to the machine that will tell us my isotopic composition. I look for other traces of my blood around me. The wire saw? The floor? Nope. The lab bench? There's a trace right there. I wipe it off the lab bench's surface with my index finger and rub it between my index finger and thumb. It feels smooth, firm, more like a solid, despite its liquid form. I look down at my t-shirt, remembering some had dripped onto the fabric. Where the drops had been, the fabric is now thicker, with a subtle glow. As I observe how my blood has turned the kelly green into a hue closer to that of an emerald, Everett comments.

"Nice t-shirt," he says. I believe he's sincere. I soak in the moment as my heart races, just a little. I stand as still as I can, a counterbalance to my heart's hyperactivity.

Everett has prepared my blood sample and is putting it into the mass spectrometer.

The machine starts to hum. My mind rushes. How did my sliced skin close up and heal? It's been about twenty-four hours since I had my last injection of blood clotting factor IX. The injections I have been receiving every forty-eight hours, for as far back as I can remember, are a precaution in case of an accident like this. Maybe the clotting factor IX worked really, really well. I'm excited to tell my parents. They don't have to worry! They worry so much about me all the time, but now they can know that the clotting factor really works.

The droplet of my blood I had wiped from the lab bench is now rolling around in my palm. Staring at it, I wonder, do I have some bizarrely rare form of hemophilia that creates blood which isn't red? But that makes no sense. Hemoglobin is always red as a result of iron bonding with oxygen. How can my blood not be red? Since platelets are colorless cell fragments, it would make sense that my blood would have platelets. The blood clotting factor IX injections induce platelet aggregation, causing the platelets to bind to and close up the injured area of a blood vessel. If I didn't have platelets, the blood clotting factor IX could not have worked. But my doctors said my body creates inhibitors that make the factor IX ineffective anyway. I stop my train of thought. This just doesn't add up.

This can't be real. I shake my head. Wake up. Wake up. It's a dream. I'm in a dream! I close my eyes thinking this will help and shake my head again. When I open my eyes, I'm still here in the lab. The mass spectrometer has just quieted. The results will be on the screen soon.

"Everett," I say. "Part of me doesn't believe what just happened."

"Yeah . . . It's weird," he agrees. While sounding understated, he opens and closes his eyes and shakes his head too. Maybe he's also questioning if this is a dream, and just acting chill so as not to alarm me.

"I want to use the scientific method and have a second data point, a second . . . experiment. Here," I show him my medical bracelet which has always been on my wrist. Two emergency contacts are written, one for Drs. Roman, Roman and Roman, and one for my parents. "In case what just happened was a fluke, or a temporary jump into an alternate timeline, or something like that, please call this number and don't let me die," I request as I pick up the sharpest cutting tool in the lab.

"Just . . . uh . . . don't try it on a major artery, just in case,." he suggests.

"Wasn't planning on it," I say. I cut into my left thumb. My blood oozes out. I grab a glass microscope slide and let my blood drip. Everett prepares a bandage and moves towards my thumb.

"Wait," I say. "Keep that handy. But, let's see what happens here." I put my thumb under the high powered microscope. Magnified at 1,000-X, the image on the computer screen connected to the microscope shows what's happening at the cellular level. I witness a silver blood vessel, the flesh of my thumb, and my skin heal. Layer by layer, the two sides of the cut merge without leaving a trace of what the cutting tool had done.

"Oh . . . my . . . god . . ." I say, watching this happen on the screen.

"Woah . . ." Everett adds. He looks at me in disbelief and looks back at the screen again.

I pull my thumb out from under the microscope and put the glass microscope slide under the microscope's lens. Everett increases the magnification level. On the computer screen emerges a picture of my blood. It has a very orderly, repeating pattern. It looks like lattice.

The mass spectrometer beeps, signaling it has assessed the composition of my blood. Everett looks at me. "You ready for this?" he asks.

I can't even answer. Entirely unintentionally, I let out a little nervous laugh. I didn't mean to do that. I probably sound like a silly little girl.

"I'll take that as a yes," he says and jumps over to the mass spec's screen.

He turns around to look at me, pushes his tortoise shell glasses up the bridge of his Grecian nose and tells me, "SiO_2". He adjusts his eyeglasses, as if to check if they are still working, and looks at the results written across the mass spec's screen again. "S . . . I . . . O_2?"

"Silicon dioxide?" I ask.

He shrugs his shoulders and nods his head in affirmation.

"Oxygen and silicon, the two most common elements in Earth's crust. Well, I'm nothing special then," I say with a bit of real relief.

"Common?" Everett lets out a half-gasp, half-laugh. "Yep, technically it is a fact that oxygen and silicon are the two most common elements in Earth's crust. But, SiO_2, structured in an orderly, continuous framework, in its tetrahedral form, as we just saw under the microscope, is quartz crystal. Liquid crystal blood. Sort of special," he concludes stepping closer to me.

I close my eyes and shake my head again.

"Wake up. Wake up," I whisper to myself. I am scared and excited at the same time. But the fear just pokes its head in for a split second and then retreats when it meets my excitement and curiosity. I think fear can't coexist with these other two states of being.

"Alexis, you're not dreaming. I am a witness to this and the microscope and mass spec are providing data," Everett says.

I open my eyes. Well. This is not exactly a nightmare. I did not bleed to death. I healed bizarrely fast. I'm making discoveries in the lab with Everett, who's my age! This is actually sort of dreamy.

"I need to go," I say, looking at the clock on the wall above the mass spec. My dad will be picking me up soon and I need to figure out how to tell my parents what I think is pretty good news, without freaking them out.

"Of course," Everett nods. "I can do parallel tests and observations on other mass specs and microscopes. You know, check for human and machine error, validate the results."

"Thanks. And, can we keep this between us for now?" I ask.

"Entirely," he confirms.

I bolt towards the door.

"Alexis," he stops me. I turn around.

"Can I . . . have your number?" he asks.

"Huh?" I'm a basket of emotions that can't make sense of this question.

"So I can text you the results from the other machines," he explains.

"Oh. Of course."

It's 5:42 p.m. and my father will be pulling up in front of the Green Building in eighteen minutes. I sit on the grass staring at the giant sculpture, La Grande Voile. My eyes scan the thick sheets of black metal, riveted together at their seams. It looks powerful and austere. It takes me to that feeling I sometimes get when I am at home. That feeling that something is wrong. It is the opposite of what I felt when I saw my blood. Maybe I can make some sense of this before my dad shows up. I take out my phone and call my sister.

"Amanda," I say.

"Hey. What's up?" she responds. I don't know how to answer her question. I'll just go with the facts.

"I got cut today, by accident," I say.

"Uh . . . huh. Yeah," Amanda says.

"I healed right away," I continue.

"Uh . . . huh, and . . ." Amanda prompts.

"I saw my blood for the first time . . . and . . . it's . . . maybe . . . I'm . . . different," I admit.

"Can you describe your blood?" Amanda asks.

"It's a shiny silvery-white liquid crystalline," I answer.

"Yeah," Amanda sighs.

"You knew?" I venture.

"Has dad pulled up yet?" Amanda asks.

"No," I answer. "But, you knew?"

"Do not say anything to him, alright? Don't say anything to Mom either. Especially, don't tell anything to Drs. Roman. Do you understand me? Alexis, promise me you won't say anything," she says in the most uncharacteristically serious voice I've ever heard come out of her.

"Is it something really bad? What's wrong with me?" I worry.

"Nothing is wrong with you. It's not bad," she assures. "I don't know everything. But I do suspect you aren't going to get the truth out of your doctors, and Mom and Dad trust them too much. They credit Drs. Roman for keeping you alive. Sit tight. I'll be there soon. Just act normal around them, like nothing has happened. Do you agree?"

"Yes. I agree," I say.

"Dad's not there yet?" she checks.

"No." I look at my watch. It's 5:54 p.m. "I've got a few more minutes."

"Alexis. Do something. Before he gets there, do something physical they would have told you not to do. What's the worst that can happen?"

"I might cut myself, see my beautiful blood again, and heal automatically," I say.

"Yeah. Not so horrible is it?" Amanda asks.

I put the phone down. Less than two hours ago, Hannah—who jumps, leaps, does cartwheels and is tossed into the sky doing her cheer routines—had looked at La Grande Voile and said, "I'd like to climb that." I decide, so would I.

I stand up, take several steps back, preparing myself to run. And I go. My legs start skipping instead of running. It's my body's natural go to. I don't remember ever actually having run. I skip fast. I skip faster. My last stride is more of a leap. My body feels oddly weightless as I gain a bounce that carries me up to a horizontal crossbar two stories up from the ground, about half the height of La Grande Voile. Gliding my hands along the sharp wing-like edges of the metal sheets that now flank me, I feel bird-like. It's exhilarating. The shape of the La Grande Voile gives me cover from the students walking past, as I crouch between the sheets of metal. From my perch I spot my father's grey Subaru driving along the Charles River on Memorial Drive. He'll be turning left towards me in a few minutes.

I look down at the ground. I jump. My feet land firmly on the Earth. I turn around to look back up at where I had just been, on top of that giant structure. My mind is clear. My body feels strong. Fear has no place in me at this moment.

Dad pulls up. I grab my backpack and make my way towards the Subaru. Act normal. Act normal, I tell myself, like nothing has happened. I hop into the front passenger seat and get busy buckling up, sifting through my backpack, all to avoid eye contact with him.

"Any new discoveries at the lab today?" he asks as he drives. I grab an apple from my backpack and take a huge bite, using the *don't speak with your mouth full* excuse to not talk to him.

"Alexis, any new discoveries at the lab today?" he repeats. That's a loaded question right now.

But it's the same question he asks whenever he picks me up from here.

"Forty-two," I blurt out after swallowing a bite of apple. It's the same answer I give him each time he asks the question.

"Still?" he asks.

"Yes, still." This is the best way to normalize things right now. I quote from one of our favorite books *The Hitchhiker's Guide to the Galaxy*. "Forty-two," I say "it is still the answer to the question of life, the universe, and everything."

Dad's phone rings. My mom's voice over the car speaker is nearly ecstatic. No, wait. It actually is ecstatic.

"Amanda's coming! She has a few days off from school and she's taking a red eye tonight!"

"Hey, hey. Alright!" my father is equally enthused that the distant daughter is coming in for a brief return. As they revel in their happiness, my phone signals. A text from an unfamiliar number. I read the message. It simply states: $Si0_2$ confirmed. I add the number to my contacts.

Everett: More research is required. You coming in tomorrow?

I start to type *Don't know. Gotta go.* I slow my fingers down and rethink this.

Me: Yes

I hit the send button on my response to Everett and shift gears to Hannah.

Me: Can I come over later?
Hannah: Of course. How'd it go with the t-shirt? Did he like it?
Me: Yes. Details later.

Mom is making veggie lasagna, my favorite. I sit at the kitchen table sipping the strawberry-banana-walnut smoothie Dad just made for me. My U.S. history book is open to a page that I'm only pretending to read. Amanda knew about my blood. What do my parents know? Why haven't they told me? Why am I being kept in the dark? Something is wrong. I make that feeling move away by focusing on my mother, as she places layers of wide lasagna noodles over each thicker layer of tomato sauce, cheese and vegetables. I used to love helping her build the lasagna when I was younger. Within this memory, a brief calm comes over me.

This is followed by a sensation I have not felt before. It feels like a buzz saw is making a horizontal slice across my skull about halfway between my ears and the top of my head. It's painful. But there is no buzz saw in the room. Visibly, everything seems normal in my kitchen. I can't stand the sensation of the top of my head being sliced off anymore.

Jumping out of my seat, I want to run upstairs and hide in my room. But my body wants a bigger exit, specifically the exit from this house. I text Hannah.

Me: Can I sleep over tonight?
Hannah: Sure
Me: Call me now and insist that I need to sleep over to help you study for the history test, otherwise you will fail.
Hannah: Why should I be the one who might fail? Why not say you might fail?
Me: Please! Help me!
Hannah: Fine!

My phone rings. I answer it acting like I didn't expect it.

"Oh, hi Hannah," I say. "What's up? Yeah, I think so. I'll put you on speaker."

"Hi Mrs. Allerton!" Hannah says over the speaker. "I was just asking Alexis if she can please sleep over tonight. We have this big U.S. history test tomorrow, and I really need her help, or, I might fail!"

"Really? You're a pretty smart cookie, Hannah. How can you almost fail at anything?" my mom questions.

"Ever since Alexis dispelled the myth that George Washington wore wooden teeth, well, now anything I read in a history book, I end up questioning. Did you know Washington's dentures were actually made of metal, cow teeth, human teeth and ivory? And so, as I question the veracity of history, I can't retain anything I'm reading for my test prep. Ultimately, it's Alexis's fault because she told me about the wooden teeth not being wooden, and so she would be a good friend to come over and help me jam this stuff into my brain." Hannah makes her case.

"She's right, Mom. May I?" I ask.

"I suppose. Go ahead. But when will you have the lasagna? Shall I bring it over to Hannah's when it's baked?" my mom offers.

"No. No. I'm sure Hannah's mom can feed us. We don't want to be rude, assuming they wouldn't feed me," I say.

"Totally," Hannah says. "You wouldn't want to be rude."

I'm in Hannah's room twenty minutes later.

I feel badly about lying to my parents. This is the first bald faced lie I have told them. Well, George Washington's

'I cannot tell a lie' cherry tree story was also a myth, so maybe I'm not in bad company. But I don't want to make a habit of this.

"What is going on?" Hannah demands. I decide that for now, I can tell Hannah at least part of the truth.

"I saw blood today, twice, and I didn't vomit either time," I state.

"Really? But you've never not vomited at the sight of blood before, have you?" she asks.

"Nope. So I wonder if it was just randomly the specific person's blood that didn't create the vomit reaction in me. Would you . . . would you mind, just maybe cutting your finger a little bit and showing me your blood? You know, so I can see how I react?" I ask while I pick up the little trash can in her room to serve as a receptacle for the strawberry-banana-walnut smoothie that's now in my stomach, just in case.

"But you vomited when you saw my blood just yesterday at the school blood drive," Hannah reminds me.

"Exactly," I say. "I'm controlling for a variable. Same person's blood. Different day." This is why I'm asking Hannah, in addition to the fact that this is such a bizarre request, one can only ask it of a best friend.

"OK. Here goes," Hannah says, pulling out nail clippers from her vanity drawer to do the deed.

A few drops of blood bead out from her finger. I feel nothing but normal. She applies pressure to the base of her digit, forcing more blood out. I am calm and neutral. I am not imagining a blood bath. Hannah runs her bloody finger on my hand. It's the first time I have had someone else's blood on me.

"It's just blood," I say. "How could I have had such a visceral, repulsive reaction to this before, just even yesterday?"

"What changed?" Hannah asks. "Whose blood did you see today?"

"I need to go back to MIT tonight. Cover for me," I say, instead of answering her question.

"What! Why?" She takes the liberty to unzip my zip-up wool sweater. "You're still wearing the t-shirt. It worked didn't it? You're not going there to see Everett at this hour! I won't allow it!"

"Just cover for me," I say zipping myself back up again. "I'll see you at school in the morning."

"Are you planning on spending the night there? Oh . . . are you exercising bad judgement? Don't do it!" she implores.

"No! It has nothing to do with a guy. It has everything to do with me. Just believe me," I tell her.

"Then what's going on?" she persists.

"I need to get away. Away from around here. Away from my parents. I need to figure some things out."

"And you're not even going to tell *me* what's up?" she pouts.

I want to tell Hannah. I want to tell someone, but I still partly feel like I'm in a dream. How can this be my reality? I don't know what I am or where I come from. My only instinct is to isolate myself right now.

"Soon. Not now," I hand her my phone. "Take this and keep it here. So my parents can't track me."

Hannah hesitates.

"Come on. Trust me. I'm not going to do something stupid," I reassure her.

"OK. OK," she tosses my phone on to her bed and pulls me into her little brother's room. Her eyes dart around his comfortably messy space. Hannah makes a beeline for the dresser on which his phone lays, half camouflaged by a pair of underwear, hopefully clean underwear.

"Hey what are you doing?" her brother challenges the invasion of his space.

"Noah, you're going to lend your phone to Alexis for a day," she informs him as she hands me the phone.

"Uhh . . . the undies were clean, right?" I ask. He shrugs his shoulders, in an *I don't know* kind of way.

"Am I? Really?" Noah asks Hannah. With a pivot he says to me, "Those undies were dirty, like from a few days ago. Take a sniff of the phone to confirm."

"Ewww . . ." is all I can mutter, moving the phone further away from my face.

"Noah! Just one day," Hannah insists.

"What's it worth to ya?" he asks.

"That mod you've been working on for weeks for your Kerbal Space Program game . . . I'm going to show you a shortcut to get it done . . . like tonight," Hannah says.

"Serious?" Noah asks, looking at his computer screen where he's clearly been working on coding the modification himself.

"Serious," Hannah responds. She is such a closer, always bartering her computer coding skills to get her way.

"Deal!" concludes Noah. He turns to me, "Oh. And. I was kidding about the underwear. They are fresh and clean. Really, just smell the phone to confirm."

"You're going to stay in touch with me on this," Hannah wraps both my hands around Noah's phone.

"You're not going to put the phone down or leave it anywhere. You're going to leave it on. Here's the charger too. And you're going to be in class tomorrow first period. Period!" Hannah rolls out the commands.

Several hours later, I'm lying under a lab bench in L-12H. It's not Noah's phone of questionable cleanliness that's wrapped up between my two palms. It's my meteorite, the one that led me to discover my own blood. Half the meteorite, actually. The other half remains by the wire saw. I have broken some rules to be at the lab and I have told some lies. Taking a cab to get here, I used my card key to gain access to the lab after hours, something I promised Dr. Ojigwe I would not do when he trusted me with the key. I lied to my parents, who think I'm still at Hannah's. These actions would not even have qualified as thoughts to me before. But I'm not living in before. I'm living in a completely different reality now, and the only place I want to be is near answers, in the lab where I made my own discovery.

I have spent the last several hours on the lab's computer doing online searches for phrases including—SiO_2 blood, liquid crystal blood, rare forms of hemophilia, hemophilia translucent blood, blood without hemoglobin, and many variations thereof. The search results produced hundreds of different tangents that, under normal circumstances, I would have happily pursued to satiate my curiosity. But today, my singular focus is to find out what I am. The great repository of knowledge known as the Internet does not have an answer for me.

This lab, this building, is the only place I want to be right now. Alone. I want to be alone and I want to know what I am. Two rolls of paper towels taped together serve as my pillow. My wool sweater keeps me warm enough. Here, in the place where—maybe—science can tell me what I am, I feel safety and comfort.

4

ZERO PERIOD PHYSICAL EDUCATION

Someone is shaking me awake. I'm trying to open my eyes, but can't. I'm returning from wherever dream world is. The voice I hear sounds like it's travelling through a tunnel to get to me.

"Wake up. Alexis. Wake up."

I recognize that voice. "Amanda?" I open my eyes. She's right in my face, nose to nose, eyes to eyes. She's intense.

"Come on," she nudges me up.

I look at my watch. It's 6:13 am.

"How did you find me?" I ask through my morning fog. "How did you get in here?"

"Hannah, and . . ." she puts some distance between her face and mine to reveal the person standing off in the corner of the lab, " . . . Everett."

"Ah . . ." is all I can mutter.

"Hannah grabbed Everett's number off your phone and he obliged with this," she explains as she flashes Everett's ID card which doubles as a lab key, before tossing it back to him. "Don't you guys keep a mat, or at least a sleeping bag in here?" she challenges Everett.

He catches the ID with one hand and opens the storage closet door beside him with the other. He points to the sleeping bag and pillow combo squeezed into the closet's top shelf. Everett cocks his head to the right a bit, pushes his glasses further up the bridge of his Grecian nose and gives me a subtle smirk.

"Next time you decide to crash here. Help yourself," he invites presenting the contents of the closet like a gameshow host would present a prize.

Apparently, these two college lab rats know something more about doing an all-nighter at the lab than I. Amanda grabs my elbow and coaxes me up and out from under the lab bench that had been my sleeping quarters.

"Come on. We're going outside for a little fresh air. Here. Clean it." She tosses a disinfectant wipe onto Noah's phone which lies on top of the lab bench. "Yeah. The undies were not clean," she clarifies. I start a text to Hannah with my disinfectant covered fingers.

"Skip it. She knows you're fine and that I've got you covered. Let's go." I follow Amanda towards L-12H's exit door. Everett follows us.

"Thanks for letting me in. But uh . . . we need some sister time. Understand?" Amanda tells Everett.

"Understood," he echoes. What does he understand? And can someone explain it to me? Amanda. She will. I hope.

"Be back soon," Amanda promises Everett as she points to her suitcase left behind in the lab, as we exit.

We walk out of the Green Building into the crisp, still semi-dark New England dawn. The sun is just rising over the Atlantic and about to make its appearance over the campus buildings to our left. I look at La Grande Voile, remembering what I did here a little more than twelve hours ago. I have the urge to do it again. But I'd rather keep hammering Amanda to tell me what she knows. The elevator ride down was too quick for me to get much out of her other than confirming that she knew I have liquid crystal blood.

"Come on!" Amanda breaks into an all-out sprint. My feet remain planted on the concrete pavement. In my head, I hear my mother's voice. "Careful!" I think about how devastated she would be if I got hurt and couldn't heal.

"Come on!" Amanda yells again as she gets farther away from me. "You want to know what I know? Catch me!" I lose sight of her. She's just taken a right at the Hayden Memorial Library and must be running parallel to Memorial Drive now.

I bolt.

My legs feel like springs.

The air rushing over my face and up my nostrils meets with words like *mustn't* and *careful* which have been on an infinite loop inside of my head. These words are accompanied by images of my mother's and father's anxious, worried faces in response to Drs. Roman citing horrid statistics about how I am more likely to die than the average person. The increasing force of air across my body knocks the words and images off their tracks and out of my mind.

I round the corner at the library to catch sight of Amanda for a few seconds before she hangs another right at Pierce Laboratory onto Massachusetts Avenue. I need to catch her. Amanda is not super-human. She's just in really good shape. I lift each leg higher and soak up more bounce with each contact with the ground. I will catch her.

I chase her along Mass Ave., gaining ground, until I grab her by the arm, right in front of the Alchemist, a large white metal sculpture. Witnessing her panting, I notice that I am not. My breathing would indicate that I'm in a resting position. Don't my cells need to oxygenate at the same rate as Amanda's?

"OK. You got me. You got me," she says through heavy inhales and exhales, and pulls her arm out of my firm grip. "Look at you. I've been waiting for this, to see what you can do." She tells me with a look I haven't seen on her before. What is that? Is it resentment? Admiration? A mix of both?

"Now, how about telling me what you know?" I demand.

She moves to the other side of the Alchemist from me. My favorite single piece of public art on campus is a two story high sculpture of a sitting person, with knees curled up at the chest. It is composed of numbers and mathematical symbols from Ω, to π, to ∞ in white painted stainless steel. Its center is empty, open and ready to accept the person who wishes to become a part of it.

"Jump!" Amanda points up to the Alchemist's head.

I step inside the sculpture and bounce vertically, rising two stories into the air, grabbing the inside of the Alchemist's head. My right hand grasps the zero and my left the #. I feel a bit like a monkey being asked to do tricks in exchange for a treat. I probably even look like a monkey hanging here.

"Back when we were little kids, like when you were three and I was about seven, I knew you were . . . different. No one told me that. I just kept seeing you in a different way. It was hard for me to believe that you were sick. Each time Mom and Dad told you to slow down, or be careful, or to not do this or that because you might get hurt, I would see you, in my mind, doing the opposite. I would see you powerful and happy," Amanda tells me. "And . . . in real life, together we proved it to each other. Do you remember? When no one else was around, when it was just you and me, I used to ask you to lift something heavy, or run really fast. I would ask you to do these things when we were in a safe space where you couldn't hurt yourself. Because at the time, I too believed you had hemophilia."

Hanging inside the Alchemist's head, looking straight ahead through the blank space where its face would otherwise be, I'm trying hard to remember the events Amanda is describing. I can't. I don't. Instead, my thoughts go to why the Alchemist is empty and has no face. I decide it's inviting me and anyone else who wants to use its numbers and symbols to create their own alchemy in the world.

I pull my legs up and swing them out from inside of the Alchemist's head, forward through the void that is its face. I feel like a gymnast swinging on the uneven bars, as my legs go up over the Alchemist's forehead, my hands let go of the zero and #, I flip and land my butt on top of the sculpture's head.

"Why don't I remember?" I ask.

"You were so young," Amanda responds.

"Did I do it? Did I lift heavy things and run really fast?" I ask Amanda, as she climbs up the back of the Alchemist, using the numbers and symbols like handholds and footholds on a climbing wall.

"Yes, for a while. But then, by the time you turned four, things changed. Drs. Roman kept dosing you with IV treatments for your alleged hemophilia. They scared Mom and Dad with horror tales of how you may get hurt and die. With each passing day that you didn't cut yourself and bleed to death, Mom and Dad became more grateful to Ira, Sam and Kan for keeping you alive and their trust in Drs. Roman increased."

"Why didn't you tell Mom and Dad about your . . . ideas about me and what I could do?" I ask.

"I tried. They wouldn't listen. They entertained my, what they called, active imagination and then went on to see what they wanted to see. They saw what they were told by adults. And, the more you heard *careful* and *don't*, I think you were sort of brainwashed, just like them. At that point, you refused to do the physical feats I asked you to do in private, so I couldn't prove anything that way," she says, climbing up and joining me at the top of the Alchemist's head. She gets right in my face again. Her two eyes beaming straight into mine, she tells me, "You believed them and you forgot who you are and what you're capable of."

"Who am I?" I ask.

"I don't totally know. But I think you do. I think you have the answers somewhere, you just have to discover them," she declares.

"Come on!" Amanda makes her way back down the Alchemist. Her feet hit the ground and she dashes off to the south, along Mass Ave. towards the Charles River.

I stand up on top of the Alchemist's head and let Amanda get a decent head start. The morning sun shines on me, from my face all the way down to my toes that rest on top of the sculpture. This feels really good. The beams of sunlight have not yet hit the ground where Amanda's feet just were. A few early bird students walking by spot me.

"Careful!" one hollers.

"Need a hand?" the other adds.

"Nope. Thanks. I'm fine," I say. I jump down and land like the rules of gravity have just been altered. Maybe the Alchemist helped. The look of bafflement on the students' faces is the last thing I see before dashing after Amanda. She's further down Mass Ave., already on the other side of Memorial Drive. I wait for the light to change before catching her in the middle of Harvard Bridge, over the Charles River.

"My blood. When I called you yesterday, you knew about my blood. How?" I ask.

"Yeah. Yeah I did," she says, adding nothing further to satiate my curiosity.

"And . . . ?" I prod.

Amanda looks down at the river below us. The Harvard and MIT crew teams are approaching the bridge. It looks like they're racing. Is it impromptu? It can't be an official race at this hour. This must be when they practice. The tip of MIT's boat is just inches ahead of Harvard's as they go under the bridge. When Amanda and I run across to the other side of the bridge and look down, we see Harvard has just edged ahead of MIT.

Amanda jumps over the bridge's railing and dives into the Charles River between the boats, startling both crew teams.

"What are you doing?" I yell at a submerged Amanda who can neither hear, nor respond to me.

She resurfaces near the stern of the MIT Engineers' boat. Amanda grabs the triangular tip of the back of the boat, right behind the coxswain, a petite woman commanding eight heavyweight rowers. The coxswain is facing forward and does not see Amanda behind her.

The rowers, who face the back of the boat, warn their coxswain with a holler, "Behind you!"

Amanda climbs up and sits on the triangular space on the stern behind the coxswain. Her weight has to be slowing the Engineers down, and the distraction of having someone climb onto the boat can't exactly help them either.

"Hey what are you doing?" the coxswain turns around and yells at Amanda. My sister totally ignores her, and hollers at me instead.

"You know how I've been spending summers away for the past four years?" she yells.

"Yeah," I yell back from atop the bridge, hoping Amanda can still hear me as the Engineers' boat gets further away from me with each rotation of their oars through the water.

"I go away, so I can see things more clearly, I saw . . ." Amanda continues but I can't hear her over the sound of oars rushing through water below and the roar of cars driving past me on the bridge.

The Engineers slip up on their rowing coordination and flow. The Harvard Crimsons increase their lead.

"Go. Go. Go! Ignore them!" the Engineers' coxswain commands. A few of the Crimsons bust out laughing.

I dive off of Harvard Bridge into the river, jumping away from everything I have known and moving towards my sister to find some truth.

My body seems to have a mind of its own now. It's swimming. I'm swimming. Still underwater. I've been underwater for a long time, I think. The icy-cold Charles gives my head a sensation close to brain freeze, typically courtesy of super cold ice cream. I have no memory of having swum before. It wasn't allowed.

I come up for air, despite feeling no need to. I'm about fifty feet ahead of the Engineers and forty feet in front of the Crimsons. I need to even out this unfair race. Diving back under water, I swim to the stern of the Crimsons' boat. I pull myself up onto the triangular space, behind the Harvard coxswain, which corresponds with where Amanda is on MIT's. Except, I don't sit like Amanda. I stand. Balance doesn't seem to be a challenge for me now.

"What the . . . ?" the Crimson coxswain yells at me. One of the Crimson guys looks at the *Of quartz I love geology* t-shirt that I'm still wearing from yesterday, now soaked and clingy on my body. He gives me an eye roll.

"How can you swim that fast?" one of the Engineers bellows over at me from his boat. Both sets of eight rowers, facing backwards, saw me jump off the bridge and swim underwater, surpassing their rowing pace, which reaches close to fifteen miles per hour. I don't know the answer to his question. I'm after a more pressing answer from Amanda.

"You were saying, you go away, so you can see things more clearly. What did you see?" I toss the question to Amanda from my boat to hers.

"I saw, in my mind, your blood," she looks around at our audience in the boats and then back to me again. I think she's trying to be discreet. "You know, like what you saw in real life. When I saw it in my mind, it was as obvious as the sky being blue and water being wet."

"Did you tell Mom and Dad?" I ask.

"No. They wouldn't believe me anyway. And, I don't trust them to keep it from Drs. Roman," she says. "I think Drs. Roman are lying and I think Mom and Dad are enabling them by not wanting to see something they don't want to see. You don't have hemophilia. Think about it."

I had searched online last night for hours. Medical databases. Peer reviewed journals. Nothing came up for a rare form of hemophilia where a person has crystal blood and that blood coagulates, thereby repairing and healing any wounds. That should not have been a surprise, but I searched hard and I hoped to find something. Because—the alternative is what Amanda just said, that I do not have hemophilia, ergo, I have been lied to by my doctors and parents. Being lied to by disingenuous pretend-friends, certain politicians, certain media outlets, or unethical salespersons, these are the usual suspects, but to be lied to by your parents and doctors—now, that takes it up a notch.

"Then, why the clotting factor IX injections every other day?" I ask Amanda.

"Exactly," she says. "This is why I made myself scarce during your treatments. I would go hide upstairs in my room. I couldn't stand being around it. I felt like, by witnessing them so-called treating you, that I was partaking in it. Maybe I should have tried to stop it. But avoiding looking at it was the only way I knew to deal with it."

I dive off the Crimsons' boat and swim to the stern of the Engineers' craft joining Amanda. I place my hands on the rear tip of the boat, my entire body, with the exception of my head and arms, is underwater.

"I'm sorry," Amanda says to me.

"Now I've got two of you weighting me down?" the MIT coxswain scolds us. "I'm about to shove you off," she motions towards us. "But I don't want you clocked in the head by an oar. Are you crazy?"

"I used to think so," Amanda says under her breath.

"I'll make up for it!" I holler to the coxswain as I kick my feet and propel the Engineers forward, giving the rowers a boost to even out the race.

"Alexis," Amanda gets closer to me and lowers her voice so that the crew teams don't hear this part. "During those years, from when you were about four until you turned ten, I wondered if I was the one who was crazy. The adult authority figures in the house acted so normal and rational, and all I had was what I saw in my mind and what I witnessed you do physically before you turned four. Do you see how I would think I might be looney?"

"Yeah. And you probably felt really alone with that. But so when I turned ten, that's when you started high school and that's when you started going away to camp for the summers right?" I say.

"That's what saved my sanity! When I went for the summers to Kazakhstan, Mom and Dad thought it was some kind of cultural exchange. Well, it sort of was, but sort of wasn't. I hung out with Bekzat and the Nomads and I learned."

"Bekzat and the Nomads? Sounds like some kind of music band," I say.

"With Bekzat and the Nomads, I learned how to access the information that I had been seeing in my mind before, the information about you. I learned to access it on demand, sort of like what we do with the Internet. Using something close to a scientific method, I was able to confirm info with the Nomads."

"Hey! Hey girl in the water!" The MIT coxswain looks down at me from her boat. "Keep pushing, we're almost at the finish line and we're almost ahead."

I obey. It's the least I can do for her and her teammates given how Amanda and I have meddled in their race.

"I learned that you are different and I learned Rule #1 of that difference, which is that you had to discover it for yourself," Amanda tells me.

I think about how I discovered my blood, by my own actions, in the lab. I think about how I wouldn't want that moment of discovery taken away from me by someone else telling me what's inside of me.

"There's a lot more I need to discover," I tell her. "And I'm totally prepared to do it. But . . . can you . . . will you help me? Does that fit within the parameters of Rule #1?" I ask.

"Yes. Because yes that does fit the parameters of Rule #1," Amanda says.

The MIT coxswain blows the whistle. The rowers stop rowing. I look around. There's a boat house on the bank of the river. The race is done. The Engineers beat the Crimsons. There's a relative silence while the rowers catch their breath. Amanda stands up on the stern of the boat, takes a good long look at the rowers.

"Thanks for the ride guys." And with that, she dives back into the river. We swim across to the river bank.

"How does it feel to move?" Amanda asks me.

"Beautiful," I respond.

Soaking wet, Amanda and I walk back into L-12H. Everett looks up from his computer. His expression communicates "What the heck happened to you?" in a way that is just one smidgen less obvious than the half dozen other people who have crossed our path since entering the Green Building.

"Morning laps in the pool?" Everett inquires.

"The Charles is so much more refreshing," Amanda responds. I don't even know what to say, so I just grab Amanda's suitcase, hoping to borrow something to wear to school today. From beneath the lab bench, Everett scoops up the taped together pair of paper towels that were my pillow last night and tosses them over to me.

"I'd offer you real towels, but we draw the line on our overnight accommodations here at a sleeping bag and pillow," he says.

"Thanks. Any new data?" I ask Everett, redirecting the conversation away from my river rat state, over to the mystery of my biological composition.

"Not yet," he responds.

"We just got some new equipment we're beta testing at New Mexico Tech. I can do some parallel research over there. You know, speed things up," Amanda says, egging Everett on. "Just need a sample," she walks towards the test tube containing some of my blood sample from yesterday. The liquid shines like silver. Amanda reaches for the tube, which rests in a test tube rack by Everett's laptop. In a knee-jerk reaction, Everett scoops up the entire rack and holds it up in the air out of Amanda's reach.

"I think MIT is the right place for this kind of research," he says.

"You don't own this R&D," Amanda responds. She lets loose her hyena laugh. It's the most annoying laugh in the world. The feral sound coming out of Amanda startles Everett. He takes a sudden, instinctive, self-protective step back, and nearly drops the test tube rack.

"Woah there. It's OK dude," Amanda says as she grabs me and pulls me towards the exit door. "You keep the sample. I've got the source."

5

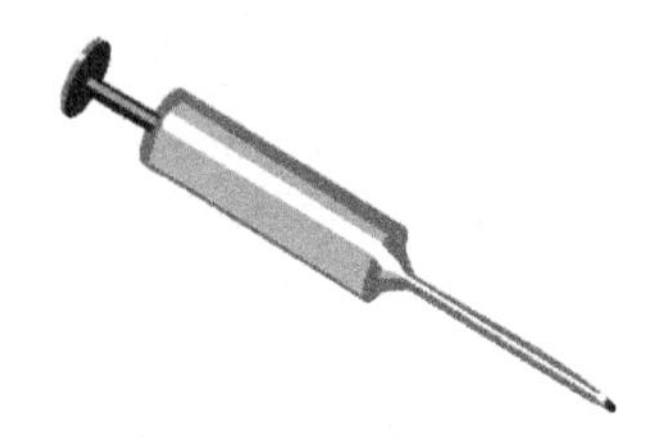

DRS. ROMAN RIDE THE ELEPHANT

Period One. Physics. I should be thinking about physics right now, but I'm not.

I try to push the image out of my mind. I don't like to picture Drs. Roman riding a creature as intelligent and sensitive as an elephant. I see Sam, Ira, and Kan, all seated in a row on the elephant's back, riding the large creature towards the front door of my house. Of course, an elephant would not fit through my front door, but this day dream is like anyone else's regular dream, it's not entirely logical or plausible. Drs. Roman are smiling at me and waving, looking like a circus act, as they enter my house. I snap myself out of it and return to the present moment.

Exactly two minutes ago, I hurried in through the high school's main entrance and just landed in my classroom seat a split second before the class bell rang. In the blue

Mustang convertible that she had rented at the airport, Amanda fought through the dense morning commute from Cambridge to get me to school on time, before she headed to the house at the corner of Sterling and Temple. The house we grew up in. I couldn't bear to be there yesterday. Basically, we've been living with an elephant in the room for sixteen years. That elephant is me. Me and my not-normalness is what everyone in that house, including me, has suspected deep down inside but refused to acknowledge to each other. Amanda has apparently known for some time about my crystalline blood. Years ago, Amanda tried to tell my parents that I'm different, but they looked the other way, attributing it to her active imagination. My parents still seem to be deluding themselves thinking I have hemophilia. Maybe it's this denial of truth that has made me feel so uncomfortable in that house. Like something is really, really wrong. Or maybe it's my affection for, and trust of, Drs. Roman, which is now morphing into confusion that is the problem. Or maybe it's simply that image of Sam, Ira, and Kan riding the elephant.

Hannah kicks my leg under the lab bench we share. She taps her elbow on mine. The signal. Drs. Roman and the elephant are wiped clean from my mind. I look over at Hannah's notebook. She's scribbled in questions to me like, *What happened last night? Why were you so freaked out? Why is Amanda back?* Her notes to me today are not about Josh, who still takes each opportunity to turn around and look at us from two rows ahead, but the normalcy of being in school and writing notes with Hannah is a special treat today, nonetheless. It strengthens my base in reality. I need this right now.

During the forty-five minute class, I spill the beans on the events of the past sixteen hours to Hannah via our physics notebooks. Through my bifurcated and sometimes trifurcated attention, I observe Mrs. Cromwell as she lectures. Writing on the white board with her left hand, she often rubs her growing pregnant belly with her right. I wish I could remember being in the womb. I wish I had memory dating back to the split of the DNA molecules from my mom and dad. Where did this crazy mutation happen? My crystalline blood must be the result of a mutation. This is the theory Hannah and I have come up with, effectively turning our physics class into chemistry this morning. I'm thinking the protein that cut the DNA that made me was on steroids on the day of my conception. Maybe more than one or two genes were altered. I wish we had the power to see ourselves being created.

Later that day, at the house, a monster breathing is what I hear. At least that's what it sounds like. It's the engine of the souped-up Cadillac pulling into the driveway. Drs. Roman are here. The presumed routine of necessity and comfort with which I have met my hematologists' arrival to my house one out of every two days at approximately 6:30 p.m. is transformed today. The visit's necessity is changed in my mind by knowledge that there is more truth to be found, by me, to replace the story that has been fed to me. Comfort is changed to courage fueled by rage. It's a cool rage that I control. It propels me forward. I imagine hearing my internal engine growling back, louder than Drs. Roman's Cadillac.

Amanda looks out my bedroom window. It's 6:28 p.m.

"They're approaching the door. OK. We're going to do this just as we planned," she says.

"Just as we planned," I confirm.

Stealing the so-called treatment, the clotting factor IX, is the plan.

Amanda and I worked through the possibilities this afternoon when she met me at school. Instead of walking the perimeter of Woodlawn Cemetery towards home, we went into the cemetery and sat down by a gravestone. On their way home, other kids gave us our space, assuming we were paying our respects to the dead. We focused instead on the substance that was allegedly keeping me alive, clotting factor IX.

Since I clearly don't have hemophilia, I have no need for clotting factor IX. So then, what have Drs. Roman been injecting me with? How does it react with my internal chemistry? Why have Drs. Roman been dosing me with it?

Sitting on the grassy surface of the Earth, above bodies that are six feet under, my sister and I put our heads together. We concluded Sam, Ira, and Kan must know I don't have normal blood, that I'm some kind of mutant. If they didn't already know this, they would certainly have figured it out over the course of over 2,000 IV treatments they have given me to date. Each time they poked my blood vessel to deliver the alleged clotting factor IX, there was a small chance of seeing just a little blood ooze out of my blood vessel, into the IV.

Staring into the vein-like patterns on the marble gravestone across from me, I realized that I could have caught a glimpse of my blood this way too, and known the truth a lot sooner than yesterday. Instead, I allowed my mother to turn my face away from the injection site and look instead into her eyes. Comfort. Security. Comfort and security over truth. The fact that I had opportunities to observe the truth, and didn't, ignites an unwelcome but all too familiar feeling of shame, a brand of shame that I've felt in that house, without knowing its source.

In the graveyard, I told Amanda the various theories I came up with during Language Arts, when I should have been fully focused on our class discussion of *Fahrenheit 451*. Maybe, I told her, I really have been receiving clotting factor IX injections and they have had no impact on me because I don't have hemophilia, or it is merely a placebo, something that also would have no physical impact on me, and either way Drs. Roman have been using such unnecessary so-called treatments in order to be a constant presence in my life. But why would they want to be a constant presence in my life? Or, maybe the substance they have been shooting into me has morphed my blood into the crystalline liquid that it is today and I am the subject of Drs. Roman's bizarre lab experiment.

Amanda dismissed these theories and told me she's 99.99 percent sure I was born with crystal blood. She suspects Drs. Roman's injections are something else. Something that reacts with the unique chemistry of my blood to mess me up. She also confessed that she has, on more than one occasion, tried to sneak a sample of the treatment from Drs. Roman's black doctor's bag, to analyze it. But she failed to even get close to it. So we made a plan. Instead of stealth mode, we decided to go for overt capture of the clotting factor IX vial. After gaining possession of it, our plan is to take it to the lab for analysis.

Amanda and I take a deep breath and walk downstairs. It's 6:33 p.m.

Drs. Roman are ready for me. Mom is at the dining room table and Dad is in the kitchen. Taking my seated position at my regular chair by the dining room table, my eyes study the elements laid out on the table's polished walnut surface. In front of the black doctor's bag lie the red rubber tourniquet, the needle, the cotton swab, the small bottle of alcohol disinfectant, and the vial labeled clotting factor IX. They are so perfectly presented.

Mute Sam nods at me, then turns to nod at Amanda. She's standing in the doorway between the dining room and kitchen.

"Hello, Amanda. What brings you today?" asks Kan. Her eyes gaze at Amanda's mouth, ready to read my sister's lips.

Amanda doesn't answer the question immediately. Silence hangs in the room. Is this the kind of silence that deaf Kan lives in every day?

"Let me tell you," Amanda says, over-articulating the words and the motions her mouth makes to express them. Abruptly, Amanda turns around. Kan loses sight of Amanda's lips. Kan shoots a glare at my sister's backside which is covered nearly down to the waist by her thick caramel colored hair. I examine Kan more closely because that glaring person is a side of Kan I have not seen before. When Kan sees me looking at her, she immediately changes her expression. If my parents and I weren't here right now, I wonder if Kan would unleash the expression of hatred that I notice, hidden, just beneath the surface of her skin.

Amanda, with her back still to Kan, gesticulates like she's talking. But she's not. She's just annoying Kan, toying with her. One hand in the air pointing, the other pushing her hair back, Amanda cocks her head to one side and shuffles her feet, pretending to deliver a monolog. Normally, mocking a deaf person like this, or any other person, would not be acceptable. But, as I've recently discovered, there is nothing normal going on here.

Amanda's earlier "Let me tell you," words, plus her shuffling, alert blind Ira to her location. He turns his body to look in her direction. I think he's looking directly at her, but I can't know for sure. His eyes are always hidden behind his dark tinted black sunglasses.

"Amanda surprised us with a quick visit from school," Mom answers Kan's question on her daughter's behalf, trying to smooth over the awkwardness on steroids that is now in the room.

Ira finds the table with his hands stretched unnaturally in front of him. He moves his body between Amanda and the part of the table where the clotting factor IX vial rests.

Kan picks up the red rubber tourniquet and gives it a gentle swing, creating in me the feeling that she might want to tie it tightly around Amanda's neck today instead of my arm. Staring at me with her pale blue eyes, she proceeds to fasten the tourniquet around my right arm, as usual. Ira repositions himself closer to me and glides his fingers over my forearm. Per standard protocol, he feels around for a good blood vessel candidate that Sam can poke into, all while blocking Amanda's line of sight from the vial that we need to get our hands on. Kan picks up the cotton swab from the table and wets it with alcohol. Sam's hands move towards the vial labeled clotting factor IX.

This is our trigger.

Dashing in between Sam and the table, Amanda grabs the vial and makes a move for the door. I bounce out of my chair and follow in her direction.

"Amanda. Dear Amanda, your sister needs that medicine. Come. Bring it back here," Ira says in a calm, almost hypnotic voice.

"Girls, what are you doing?" my mother asks, with a curious look on her face. Dad steps into the dining room and stands next to her. They are always a unified front.

Kan and Sam both take slow steady steps towards me and Amanda.

"Alina, please instruct your lovely daughters to step back over here so we can finish Alexis's treatment. Amanda, you wouldn't want your sister to not be well, now would you?" Ira continues his hypnotic drone.

A part of me, that part of me that is a young child, wants to believe him. That part of me wants to retreat back into the routine of unquestioning comfort, that feeling of being wholly taken care of by these adults. But another part of me that is now stronger, the part of me that chooses courage over comfort, speaks.

"Mom. Dad. I am well. I am more than well!" I blurt out. "I don't need this!" I put my hand over Amanda's hand, which holds the vial, and together we raise the container labeled clotting factor IX into the air.

Mute Sam's eyes and face are now raging. He opens his mouth. It's the first time I've ever seen his lips part. Every tiny muscular movement on his face, his throat and lips tell my mind that he's screaming, screaming a guttural primal scream, but I hear nothing. Not even a breath.

He lunges for Amanda, grabs her by the shoulders, separates my hand from hers, and throws her to the floor. The thud of her body hitting the floor is only slightly softened by the layer of Persian rug between the hardwood flooring and her body. Sam lands on top of her. The vial remains in Amanda's firm grip.

My mother jumps out of her chair. "Amanda!" she screeches.

"Hey! Hey what the heck!" I hear my father roar like I never have before.

Kan moves towards Amanda. Before she can get there, I thrust my elbow, with my newfound strength, into Kan's mid-section. She hinges over, groaning in pain.

Dad lunges towards Sam, commanding, "Get off her!" Sam ignores him.

Dad grabs Sam and tries to pull him off Amanda. Ira jumps in, followed by Mom.

The melee is a cocktail of grunts, punches, kicks and screams.

I swiftly get myself to Amanda's hand. My palm meets hers. She releases her grip, giving me the vial. I stand up, ready to run with it.

Sharp nails tear into the back of my right arm just above my elbow, where the tourniquet maintains its tight grip on my blood flow. I look down at my arm to see Kan's black lacquered nails lead her fingers into the tight space between my skin and the rubber of the tourniquet. She twists the red rubber hose to tighten it further. Once, twice, three times, until my arm goes numb below the elbow. Involuntarily, my hand opens and the vial leaves my grasp.

Kan grabs it with her free hand.

Amanda's foot emerges from the melee on the floor to kick the vial out of Kan's palm. It falls to the floor, where the hardwood meets the Persian rug. The top of the glass vial breaks on the wood. A few drops of the content in question drip onto the carpet. I lunge for the vial. So does Sam.

Both our hands are on it. Both our hands are cut by its jagged edges.

Sam's very red hemoglobin-rich blood mixes with my crystalline, translucent blood to create a marbleized pattern of pinks, reds and smoky whites. Maybe he's as stunned by its beauty as I am. We both freeze, staring at the pattern as it moves and morphs.

"Alexis!" My mother gasps, ripping my focus away from staring at my blood. "Oh my god! You've cut yourself! Dale quick!"

She looks down at my hand bleeding my own special version of blood. She looks up at my face. "What is that?" She shakes her head.

I maintain my grip on the broken factor IX bottle which Sam tries to wrestle away from me. I move myself up, so my mother can see exactly what is flowing from my cut hand.

"That's not blood. What is that? Dale! Is she OK?" she asks my father.

Dad's got Ira on the floor in some kind of bizarre vice grip. Never seen mild mannered Dad like this before. He looks at my hand.

I'm focused on interpreting the shock on my parents' faces. It's now evident to me that they have not seen my blood before. They don't know that I am not normal.

Taking advantage of the moment, Kan grabs the vial. Her eyes dart around the room. Kan opens her mouth and pours the remainder of the vial's contents down her throat. The image of the grin across her face could be the meme for the cat that ate the canary. She hurls the empty vial across the room. It shatters into tiny little pieces.

"You beast!" Amanda screams at Kan, pounding her feet on the floor, fists tightening.

"What have you been pumping into me?" I ask looking at Kan, Ira, and Sam.

Kan wipes her mouth with the back of her hand, grin still broad across her face. Sam grabs some cotton balls off the table and firmly presses them on his cut.

"Mom, Dad," I say holding up my hand to show it has fully healed already. "I do not have hemophilia. Look at how fast I heal." I take a step closer to them, my hand held out. "Amanda tried to tell you when I was little. Why didn't you listen? How could you not know? Why are these doctors here? And what have they been pumping into me?"

Dead silence.

My parents look dumbfounded.

Dad gets really sad. His vice grip on Ira softens.

Ira strains. He groans. He pulls himself out of my Dad's grip. Lunging up off the floor, he flings his dark glasses off. They go flying across the room. I see his eyeballs for the first time. They are simply white. All sclera. No iris. No pupil. White never looked so wicked. I feel like he's staring at me. Looking right through me. Is that even possible?

"My dear. They have lied to you about far more important matters than the color of your blood. Theirs runs red. Yours runs crystal clear. Do you really think they are your biological parents?" he asks, his voice now pitched to intimidate.

Waves of hot and cold electrical shocks run through my body. It feels as though the electricity is using my arteries, veins, arterioles, venules, and capillaries like copper wires of varying diameters to reach every point in my body.

I know I've heard a truth. But I don't want to know. I don't want to know this. Not this.

Altering his voice to sound like a parent reading the last words of a fairy tale, like he's reading the words *happily ever after*, the sweet sincerity with which Ira delivers his conclusion immerses me in a state of horror.

"You do not belong to them and they do not belong to you."

6

AFTER THE HALF-LIFE

I scream.
I scream.
And I scream again.

I look at each one of them. Each of them with whom I had shared a blood bond, or believed I did, in my prior existence. The existence before ten seconds ago when blind Ira opened my eyes.

Mom.

Dad.

Sister.

No, no and no. They are Alina Allerton, Dale Allerton and Amanda Allerton. But who am I?

The silence in the room seems to hold every particle, each atom still. I feel I am the only one moving, thinking, feeling. The two triads, Allerton and Roman are in a freeze frame.

I gaze across each of their faces.

My eyes come to rest on Amanda.

"You. You!" I point at the one person who has been my center of truth. Why do I feel more betrayed by Amanda than every one of the others in the room combined at this moment? "You didn't tell me this. You hid this. So I'm adopted? Is that it? How did I get here? Did Drs. Roman morph into wicked storks, steal me from my real family and deliver me to your doorstep?"

"Alexis. I couldn't tell you. It was up to Mom and Dad to do that. Telling you that part. It, it, it just wasn't my place," her soft whisper can only be heard in the absence of any other sound or motion in the room. The breath which carries Amanda's words to my ears is the only movement in our shared space.

"I trusted you," I whisper back.

BAM!

I spin around to see the front door thrust open. Josh's huge stature fills the doorframe.

"Alexis! You OK? We heard screaming." Josh glares at Sam, Ira, and Kan, adding, "My mom just called the police."

I look at Josh, who stands solid in the doorway and I think, nobody's getting past him.

The three white coat-clad doctors move at the same instant. Like three cut up parts of the same slithering worm, with fluid synchronistic motions, they gather their medical supplies and move towards the door.

I blast past them, putting my hands on Josh's chest. He feels like rock covered in a layer of warm muscle.

"I have to go. I have to go. Keep them away from me? Just until I get far enough away?"

Josh nods and steps aside, letting me out of the house of lies. Like an unmovable stone pillar, he blocks everyone else at the door.

I stand behind him for a moment, and peak my head out around his shoulder to look at Dale and Alina.

"You aren't my parents. You're liars!" I yell. Then, I bolt.

Drs. Roman's Cadillac is right here in the driveway. Any more alleged clotting factor IX vials in there? I stride over to the white truck. The door handles won't open. Locked. I peer in through the windows, but can't see past the dark tinted glass. My anger moves my body to the back of the truck. For the first time, I know what it is to be the angry beast. I am exactly that in this moment. I feel no need to change from this state.

TWACK!

I pound my fist down on the hardtop that covers the truck's cargo bed, just over the lock. The cover pops open. Looking for medical supplies, I come up empty. Clean. Nothing. Almost nothing, except for a neatly folded towel. Mine now. I grab it and wrap it around my fist. Walking the perimeter of the truck, I smash each window as I go. I kick at the Dr. R^3 logo on the passenger door. It now looks like the truck has collided with another moving vehicle. Opening the passenger door, I reach into the truck. My eyes scan as my towel covered hand feels around for vials among the shattered pieces of window glass that now cover the seat. Nothing.

Looking up to the front door of the house, I see Josh holding them all back. Holding them inside the house and away from me. But one gets out. Actually, he lets one out. It's Amanda.

I need to get out of here. Before I do, I move to open the glove compartment. It's locked. With one punch I smash it open. In a small, rectangular black leather binder are the Cadillac's registration and insurance documents. I grab the binder and bolt out of the car, dashing for the fence that separates my yard from Josh's. Amanda's right behind me.

She's saying something but I can't hear it. Sirens blaring from the police cruiser approaching us drown out her voice. The cops pull up to the gate. I see my parents trying to squeeze past Josh. His 200 pound, 6'4"frame continues to very effectively block the door. Red and blue spinning lights emitted from the cruiser's roof create a kaleidoscopic effect on the moving picture of mayhem. Chaos.

Instead of feeling wrong, it feels better than the previously visible quiet normalcy, under which my feelings of *something is wrong* used to live. I exhale.

I bound over the six foot high black wrought iron fence into Josh's yard, where I can avoid the cops and let them focus on Sam, Ira, and Kan. I look back to see Amanda climbing a tree that might help her get over the fence. Can I believe her anymore? Maybe I don't need to. I glide my hands across the smooth black leather binder from the doctors' truck.

The sound of chains gliding over wheels, I hear the front gate open, allowing the police car into the driveway. Amanda, straddled on a tree branch high off the ground, puts the gate remote back into her pocket. She let the police in. I run across Josh's yard, and four additional adjacent yards. Then I spring across the street towards Hannah's.

"Alexis ends the era of an evil administrator armed with an enigmatic elixir. Eagerly, Alexis eternally eliminates an element encircling her entrails. An element enabling Alexis's existential enigma is eviscerated. Emancipated, Alexis expects to encounter her axiom," Josh's goofy voice emanates from the phone's speaker. Hannah and Josh are doing all they can to help me feel better. Arriving at Hannah's a few short minutes after I fled the scene at my house, I simply told her the truth, starting with, "I feel bad."

Josh's silly alliterative poetry is supposed to make me feel good. I'm surprised it almost works. This is the so-called poetry that flipped Josh and Hannah's relationship from buddies to budding romance.

"Roman reduced to rubble after the rumble . . ." Josh's next round of alliteration is cut off by Amanda's repeated calls to Hannah's phone. I left my phone at home. I don't want the leash.

"Hang on sweets," Hannah says. "I'll be right back to you." Hannah swipes from Josh over to Amanda.

"Update," Amanda reports. "The first cops to arrive on the scene took Drs. Roman. Seeing those three handcuffed and taken away . . . that was just so satisfying. Just seemed right. Oh, and, they had to carry Kan out. She was passed out cold. A second cruiser showed up, to question Mom and Dad."

Kan, Sam, and Ira in a cop car. Yes that does seem right. But not my parents. No, I mean Dale and Alina, Are they arrested too? I can't stand them right now. I don't want to be anywhere near them. A part of me hates them. I know that for sure. The rest of my awareness of them is in tattered fragments, strewn across the different zones of emotion and thought inside of me. The fragments landed after the tornado of truth erupted today.

"And, Alina and Dale?" I ask. I really don't want to talk to Amanda right now, but I have to know. I don't want to see them in a cop car.

"I think I was able to tell a good story to the cops, so that Mom and Dad did not get arrested and social services won't show up, we hope," Amanda explains. "They are pretty shocked and devastated. Alexis, would you look out the window please?"

I walk over to the window and see Amanda pacing back and forth across Hannah's lawn. Hannah is as surprised to see Amanda out there as I am.

"Hey, Amanda. You can pace all night. My parents agreed that Alexis needs her space. We're not letting you in," Hannah taps the hang up button on her phone.

"OK babe. Continue," Hannah says after switching back over to Josh.

"Suspect sister surrounds the circumference so—" Again Josh is cut off.

"Josh, how about a sweet bedtime story instead?" Hannah whispers into the phone. She places it by me on the bed and seats herself at her desk.

Josh starts, "Once upon a time, Alexis adventured and attained an uncanny understanding . . ."

Taking in Josh's words, I lay my head on Hannah's pillow. Dragon, Hannah's ginger cat, does a soft pounce onto my chest and starts to purr and rub his head against my face. Past Dragon's head, I see Hannah across the room at her desk, the black leather binder from the Cadillac beside her. She is furiously keying away at her computer. The sound of her finger pads across the keys serves as the percussion rhythm section to Josh's goofy brand of poetry. It lulls me to sleep.

I am awakened by a soft buzzing sound. I know this sound, this vibration, is coming not from outside of me. It's originating inside my eardrum in response to something within. I keep my eyes tightly shut, because I'm scared. In the space in front of my face, I feel a small equilateral triangle form and hover. The three lines forming the triangle feel like bars of cool mist against my face. The buzzing sound gets louder. The vibration gets more intense.

My eyes pop open and I bolt up into a seated position. I see a triangle with a silvery shine floating in front of my face. I look around and see that I am still in Hannah's room, in normal space and reality. The triangle moves with my face as I turn my head. Two of the triangle's vertices are lined up by each of my eyes. The third is aligned with my forehead.

Suddenly, three beams of white light burst out from each of my eyes and my forehead. They point at, and merge with, each vertex of the triangle. The beams of white light come together in the center of the triangular plane and break out into the spectrum of the rainbow. These rainbow colors start to take shape.

In the dark room, I listen and I watch, as the triangle becomes a screen. The buzzing sound that had awoken me is gone. I view an incredibly high-resolution moving image on the surface of the triangle. Chills and heat take turns going up and down my spine. I have never felt more calm and more alert at the same time.

On the triangular screen, I see myself, like I would in a dream, in what looks like a crystal cave. Enormous crystals, the size of pillars, opaque milky white in some parts and transparent in others, fill the space. They jut out of the walls, the floor, and down from the roof of the cave. I'm sitting by a pool of water in the center of a chamber. I look around. It's strange. I am watching myself on this flat two-dimensional screen, yet at the same time, I'm in the moving image, in the three-dimensional reality. Is it a hologram? No. It's more real than I would imagine a hologram to be. This feels more solid, more alive.

A person in an orange hazmat suit approaches me from the passageway to my left, which looks like it leads to an adjoining chamber of the cave. A beam of light from the headlamp on the person's helmet moves from left to right, and up and down, as the person aims their head in different directions, scanning for something. I don't understand why the person needs the light. The space is perfectly illuminated. I look around again to confirm. But there's no sunlight. Before the person in orange entered, there was no artificial light either. I look closer. The crystals are emitting a soft glow. In fact, it looks just like moonlight.

The headlamp is pointing straight at me now. Hazmat suit walks towards me, taking off what looks like a respirator mask that was covering the person's mouth. Hazmat kneels down, and gets closer to my face. I recognize all too well the person looking at me through the suit's clear face shield.

"Naica," Hazmat says.

"What?" I question. "What is Naica?"

"You need to come to Naica, with me," Hazmat clarifies, a bit. So Naica is not a what. It's a where.

"Huh? Wha . . . What?" Hannah's voice, coming from a different place, startles me. I close my eyes, shake my head and reopen my eyes. The screen is gone. I can't feel the triangle anymore. I'm in Hannah's room, sitting up at a sharp 90° angle on her bed, just where I started before I got lost in the screen's crystal cave.

"Is it morning?" Hannah's groggy voice matches her current state, as she lifts her head off her desk. Still wearing her clothes from yesterday, her right hand is on the black leather binder from Drs. Roman's car. Hannah gets up and walks to the window, opening the blinds, she invites in rays of sunlight.

I jump off the bed and look out the window. Amanda!

Is she still pacing? No. I don't see her. I run across Hannah's room, down the stairs, out the front door, and nearly trip over the tent—that apparently popped up overnight—in the front yard.

"My mom respected your wishes to not let Amanda in," Noah's voice calls out from inside the house. "But we never said anything about not making her comfortable."

"Great. Thanks Captain Underpants," I say.

I unzip the tent door and hop inside. Amanda is enveloped inside the sleeping bag, like a caterpillar in her cocoon.

"Naica! Where is Naica and why do I need to go there with you?" I demand.

Her head pops out of the sleeping bag. "Naica is a mine, a cave in Mexico. And I don't know why you need to go there with me. I'm scheduled to go there tomorrow for my astrobiology research for school. What's this all about?" she questions as she unzips herself out of her cocoon.

"I saw something this morning, right as I woke up. It was like a little triangular movie screen playing in front of my face. And I was in a crystal cave. And you were in a bizarre orange colored hazmat suit. And you told me I had to go to Naica with you."

"OH! Oh! Oh my! My GOD!" Amanda jumps up and down, her raised arms and head hitting the low ceiling of the tent. The tent shakes like we're having an earthquake.

"What?" I plead.

"Drs. Roman couldn't dose you last night. Whatever that substance is, that the doctors religiously injected into you every two days, must have worn off, or mostly worn off. So maybe the half-life of the drug, the substance, is something like fifty or sixty hours. Oh! That's a big clue!"

Amanda grabs my hands in hers. "This morning, you accessed information you wouldn't have, you couldn't have, before. You know something that wasn't available to you before." She gets right into my face. "Welcome to your life after the half-life."

Amanda rips into her extra-loud, ninety decibel hyena laugh. I do indeed know something, but so does everyone else in the neighborhood. And that is, we're all awake now.

7

KNOW, NO & GO

"Alexis, get in!" Amanda is hollering at me from the school's car pick-up lane.

The honking horn of her electric blue convertible Mustang rental calls out to me. Obnoxious.

"I'm not letting her take you home! You're staying with me," Hannah says, confirming our after-school plan. Our, after-last-night's-high-drama-rumble-with-the-three-headed-doctor-cops-showing-up-at-my-house, plan.

"Alexis!" Taking advantage of the standstill at the pick-up lane, now more of a parking lot really, Amanda stands on top of her seat, arms waving in the air and yells my name out again, and again. Thanks for the embarrassment. Word got out about the scene at my house last night. So, during the school day I've tried my hardest to keep a low profile and not respond to curious and concerned looks. Amanda isn't helping.

"This way," I grab Hannah by the arm and tug her away from the pick-up lane. We cut across the campus' grassy field where Amanda can't drive after us, and we run to the street on the southeast side of the school.

A streak of electric blue cuts across our path. It's her again. Amanda jumps out of the convertible without opening her door. Show off, I think. And then, I take that thought back. I would have thought she was a show off and I would have felt a tinge of jealousy, back when I was prohibited from being physical. Yeah, now that I can, I would hop out of the topless car, over its closed doors too.

We march towards each other, fists clenched, heads angled forward. She's reaching for her hip. I feel like I'm entering a duel in a cowboy western, so I instinctively also reach for my hip, for what reason? I have no idea. I'm just mirroring my big sister.

Amanda whips out a piece of paper from her back pocket and points it in my direction.

"You," she points at me. "Are coming with me."

"Whatcha got there?" Hannah questions Amanda while trying to step between us. "An arrest warrant? A subpoena?"

I have nothing in my back pocket to whip out, so I point my index finger towards Amanda, using it as an object of aggression. "I have not forgiven you for not being my sister!"

"Oh, that sounds weird," Hannah says to me. "Like, it's not her fault you're not biological sisters." Hannah's right. I recalibrate. Deploying my other index finger, I'm now dual handed in this duel.

"I have not forgiven you for lying to me about not being my biological sister!" I blurt out.

"That makes a bit more sense, but only a bit," Hannah confirms.

Amanda takes three wide strides in my direction and holds the paper up in front of my fingers of aggression, which are now pointing directly at a print out of an airline ticket with my name on it.

"I'm not going anywhere with you," I tell her. "And . . . paper?" I ask.

"I don't know if you have a phone, or whose it is, or what it smells like these days so, yeah, paper," Amanda retorts.

Then, I look closer at the ticket.

"Chihuahua, Mexico?" I ask. The only image that comes to mind is a cute dog with a Mexican accent.

"About two hours by car to the Naica mines. The Cave of the Crystals," Amanda reveals.

"Oh . . ." I say.

"Oh . . ." Hannah echoes. Her mind is probably racing back to Period One, when our physics notebooks got partially filled with my revealing to her the very non-physical screen upon which I saw myself in a crystal cave. Naica.

"Oh . . . coming?" Amanda asks. She points to two suitcases in her backseat. One of them, mine. I think this over. Well, to enter the Cave of Crystals, I will indeed have to go with her.

Taking a few quick steps and a hop, I jump over the Mustang's closed front passenger door and land in the seat. Yep, that felt good. Amanda does the same on the driver's side.

"Wait! Wait!" Hannah pleads by the car. "Before you go. Can I? Can I just see it?"

I know exactly what *it* she's talking about. I look around in the car for a sharp object. Hannah pulls a metal nail file with a sharp pointy edge out of her backpack's front right pocket. I poke the point into my index finger. My blood oozes out.

"There," I look at Hannah for her reaction.

"Wow . . . Umm . . . here," Hannah stares in wonder at it and pulls out a hand mirror from her backpack's same personal care pocket. She places it under my finger.

I let my blood drip onto the mirror, creating a little pool of liquid. Beams of light that originated in the center of our solar system ninety-three million miles away, bounce off the mirror's dry surface. But the sunlight's effect as it returns from the mirror and through the thin layer of clear viscous liquid that is my blood is different. Little sparkles of light, like tiny, tiny stars float up above the mirror towards our faces.

Hannah cups the mirror carefully in her palms. Staring at it, she moves away from the Mustang, taking tiny backwards steps. "I'll take this with me. I'll hide it in my desk at home." She looks up at me with a grin, "I think I'm on the verge of cracking something wide open on Drs. Roman. That vehicle registration you swiped from their car was a key. Oh! And," she takes out Noah's phone from her backpack and tosses it to me. "Take it."

"Ummm . . . Thanks?" I sign off with Hannah looking at a boy's phone, which may once again be contaminated by dirty boy underwear.

Within seconds, my thick black mane is blowing in the wind as Amanda drives us out of Wellesley and east towards Logan International Airport. Her caramel colored curls wave behind her like a flag. Sometimes the ends of our long strands mingle together to create a chocolate-caramel swirl, through an elemental mixture of mostly nitrogen and oxygen that blows by us at fifty-five miles per hour.

"So. Are they OK with us, with me, going to Mexico? They. Alina and Dale," I ask. I can't call them my parents. Amanda gives me a quick glance but doesn't answer.

"Not that I care, really. But are they OK? With the police? Are they in trouble?" I continue.

"Their heads are spinning. They don't know what to make of your blood. I told them not to say anything to anyone until we return," she tells me.

"That sounds familiar," I roll my eyes.

"This morning, they wanted to take you to a different doctor, for a second opinion on your condition," Amanda says.

"Wouldn't that actually be a fourth opinion?" I ask.

"I know, right? I told them you didn't want anything more to do with doctors for now," she says.

"That does sound about right," I respond.

"Yeah. I knew you'd think that. I know what's best for you. For now, think of me as your legal guardian," Amanda delivers that last sentence like she's declaring ownership of me. I don't like it.

"I don't need a guardian. I'm on my own," I declare.

"You're only sixteen!" she reminds me.

"I officially proclaim myself emancipated. So, nobody owns me," I announce.

"Congratulations," she belts out over the increasingly loud

traffic surrounding us on the Massachusetts Turnpike as we enter the Williams Tunnel under Boston Harbor.

"Who are my biological parents?" I can hear my voice echo back at me from the tunnel walls, over the sound bed of wheels turning on pavement and combustion engines combusting.

"I don't know," Amanda responds.

"When did I become an Allerton?" I ask.

"You were three. I was seven. Mom had severe preeclampsia with me, so they decided not to risk another pregnancy. Me ravaging Mom's body was the reason they adopted you. Mea culpa," Amanda says.

"Gee. Thanks," I say, not knowing if I am sincere or sarcastic. I can't decipher my own emotions right now.

"Mom and Dad told me we were going to Kazakhstan, and that there, we would find you, and that you would be my sister. They did plan to tell you that you were adopted, you know," Amanda reveals.

"They did?" I seek confirmation.

"Yes. But you were only three, so they wanted to give it a few more years, maybe wait until you were about five when you could more fully understand," Amanda says.

"But they didn't," I state.

"They didn't. I think it had to do with two factors. One, I overheard Drs. Roman telling them you weren't ready to know and that they should wait, wait, and wait. Two, the other factor, I think the more important one, was that I think they themselves wanted to forget you were adopted. They wanted to believe you were their flesh and blood because you were so different from day one, and they could see that. I think they were trying to convince themselves that you were an average child, normal, nothing unusual.

Hiding the truth of your adoption was their way of coping with having a child who felt so different from themselves," Amanda explains. "Those were their reasons, I believe. As for me, I was just a kid too, and I went along with what they asked of me, to keep the fact that you were adopted a secret."

"Will you forgive me for not telling you?" she adds.

I'm not prepared to answer. I realize I'm a little too numb, a little too overwhelmed with all that's happened in the past forty-eight hours to give an honest yes or no.

Amanda continues, "I am not your sister by random chance of nature, the genetic roulette wheel of being born to the same parents. I am your sister by my own choice, at this very moment. Otherwise, I wouldn't be here with you now. I could have, from the time you were brought home, treated you like a house mate instead of a sister. I made a different choice."

I remain silent.

"Well. Whatever," Amanda shrugs. "What we can do now, is do our best to get to the truth."

"It looked like this." I show Amanda an image of a triangle. We're sitting in the airport, waiting to board our flight to Mexico, and I've been explaining to Amanda how I saw her in a hazmat suit in the crystal cave. On my phone, well, from Noah's potentially smelly phone, I searched online for: impossible triangle.

"So, you really felt like you were there? Like in real life, not just seeing it on this hovering triangular 2D screen?" she asks.

"Presumably 2D," I say. "I actually didn't touch it. It just looked like a flat surface, but at the same time, I was experiencing myself inside of it."

Amanda traces her index finger around the impossible triangle on the phone's screen. At each vertex, the two merging bars appear to be both on top of, and beneath, the other. It sort of looks like a triangular Mobius strip.

"It's an impossible triangle," I say. "Also called a Penrose triangle. It's an optical illusion. It can be depicted in perspective drawing and art, but can't exist as a solid three-dimensional object, that is, unless . . ."

". . . unless, we are outside the bounds of three-dimensional Euclidean space," Amanda completes my thought. "It's a paradox," she says. "An impossible triangle is a paradox in which a 2D drawn object appears 3D, but cannot actually exist in 3D. So, let me get this straight, you are seeing whatever you're seeing in 2D, but you are actually experiencing it in 3D."

"Yes," I confirm.

"Bizarre," she says.

"Yeah, you know, it sort of feels like virtual reality. Like, when Noah lets me use his VR headset. That's the closest analogy I can give you. Wearing the VR headset, you see this stuff on what is clearly a 2D screen, but you move around in it, like it's all there in real life all around you."

"So, in this Impossible Triangle world of yours, did I look the same?" Amanda asks, tossing her hair back and touching her face.

"Are you being vain?" I ask. "Are you asking me if you looked good?"

"Well, yes," she admits.

"I don't know! You were all covered up in an orange hazmat suit. I recognized you because of your intense stare into me when you said the word Naica," I say.

"They say the camera adds ten pounds, so I'm just wondering what an Impossible Triangle does to one's shape," Amanda says.

"Next time I see the Impossible Triangle, if there is a next time, I'll make sure to let you know how you look," I tell her.

"Passengers seated in rows fifteen through thirty are now invited to board," the polite voice, which sounds a touch too automatic, calls us forward. Amanda and I make our way to the jetway. We continue working through the events of the past few days.

"Kan was passed out cold by the time the police arrested her?" I confirm with Amanda.

"That couldn't have been more than twenty minutes tops after she drank your so-called clotting factor IX," Amanda estimates.

"Part of the dose spilled onto the carpet, so she took in less than I do, less than I did, every forty-eight hours. But it never knocked me out," I observe.

"She's got hemoglobin and standard red blood . . . as far as we know. The mystery substance they've been injecting into you has to be interacting differently in your body. There's just no way it wouldn't, given your unique biological makeup. True, you never passed out. But it has probably dulled you. Dulled your strength. Dulled your senses. Hasn't it? I mean, the whole hovering triangle as a screen thing? Come on! That only happened after you missed your regular injection," she prods.

"The Impossible Triangle thing happened like, sixty hours or so following the last treatment," I calculate. "That's why you estimated the half-life at fifty to sixty hours this morning right?"

"Right, that's when the stuff would have lost half its pharmacologic activity. But you've still got half of its potency circulating in you." She says this as I'm thinking the same exact thought. That thought is followed by this thought—I want to take a shower. An internal shower, to scrub my cells, blood vessels, and organs, to get that stuff out of my system, forever. I don't want to wait for more iterations of fifty to sixty hours for it to halve its pharmacologic activity until its impact on me becomes infinitesimally small.

"Now that I know, I wish I could magically, retroactively say NO to each dose I've taken in," I tell Amanda.

"Imagine what you might be able to do once it's all cleared out of your system. Once you're totally clean!" Her excitement grabs hold of her volume and raises her voice one notch too high for what is supposed to be a confidential conversation inside the aluminum tube as our eyes scan for seats 17 A and 17 C. I can only assume the grey haired couple behind us has concluded I am a drug addict.

"Google it. Pharmaceuticals with a half-life of fifty to sixty hours," Amanda tasks me.

"You think they used a prescription drug?" I express my doubt.

"Maybe. Easy access and ample supply for doctors," she says as she slides into the window seat, 17 A. I take the aisle, 17 C. I look at the empty seat between us.

"Did you think I wouldn't want to sit next to you?" I ask.

"More like, I don't know if I'd trust you not to strangle me if, when, I fall asleep," she responds sarcastically. "You know, for not being your real sister."

No comment. I take her directive and start googling about drugs and their half-lives. First hit, the very authoritative Wikipedia, presents me with a list of common prescription medications and their biological half-lives.

"Check it out," I show Amanda the screen. On this chart alone, there are five of them in the fifty to sixty hour half-life zone. Methadone. Buprenorphine. Clonazepam. Diazepam. Flurazepam. Amanda's eyes scan the list.

"And this is far from a comprehensive list. It's going to be hard to narrow down to the target. If we could have just gotten a bit of a sample last night!" she laments.

"Oompa loompa doopadie doo, I've got another puzzle for you," the song sounding out from my phone startles Amanda. Actually, it's Noah's phone, which displays Hannah's name on its screen. Does she set that song up as her personal ringtone on everyone's phone?

"She's an oompa loompa fan," I explain, as I swipe the screen.

"What?" Amanda questions.

"Oompa, loompa, you know, from Charlie in the Chocolate Factory," I enlighten her. Amanda rolls her eyes.

"Benzos!" Hannah's voice tells me over the phone.

"Benzos?" I have no idea what that is.

"Yes. Benzos . . ." are the next words I hear from Hannah, before we are rudely interrupted and I can't hear what I really, really want to hear, because—

"Welcome. This is your captain speaking."

Really? Now the captain speaks? Shut up captain!

"Hannah. Hold on. Hold on," I tell her.

"Please take your seats and fasten your seatbelts. We're just waiting on a few passengers to board, and we should be on our way to Houston in a few minutes. Passengers with connecting flights to points within the U.S. or Mexico and other international destinations may check with our flight attendants regarding connecting gate information. We'll be on our way shortly."

"Now! Tell me quickly before he tells me to shut off my electronic device," I say.

Amanda pulls the phone closer to her, so she can hear without putting Hannah on speaker. We're each leaning into the empty seat between us, listening for Hannah's next word. Our butts solidly in our respective seats, I imagine that our heads merging at the phone look something like the top of a wishbone.

"Benzodiazepines. It's a class of psychoactive drugs. More specifically, you've been on flurazepam, a long-acting and rapid-onset version. It's a sedative, a hypnotic agent. Usually prescribed for insomnia. Side effects include impairing your memory, judgement and muscle coordination. It's a muscle relaxant, reducing physical strength by making it harder for muscles to contract. Half-life of forty-seven to one hundred hours. And get this, one side effect, for some people is blue skin. And you've always described your skin as a lovely shade of concrete grey. Nope. It's blue!" Hannah pauses to breathe, then starts back up again at the speed of a fast-talking side-effects reader from a pharmaceutical ad. "Recommended for short term use only. Almost always administered orally. Drs. Roman had to get specially made, extra potent liquid doses for IV administration from a compounding pharmacy. High doses can lead to amnesia and dissociation, as well as detachment from surroundings on a physical and emotional level. A meta-analysis of more than a dozen studies shows long term use can decrease IQ," Hannah pauses to breathe again. "You're welcome."

I feel a tap on my shoulder.

"17 B. I believe that's my seat," he says. I look up.

"Everett? Everett!" I say. Oops. I realize I need to tone it down. I give him a casual, "Oh. Hi."

Hannah heard me. "Everett!" she says, loud enough that I'm pretty sure he heard that, since the phone was not glued to my ear, but hovering somewhere between my head and Amanda's. Gotta fix that. I tightly apply the phone to my ear, and my ear only, as I stand up to let Everett into his seat.

I look at Amanda and silently mouth my words to her while Everett still has his back to me, "What in the world is he doing here?"

"The pilot was ready to take off without you," Amanda says to Everett, totally ignoring my question.

Hmmm, she's not surprised he's here.

"Preparing for takeoff. Please turn off all electronic devices," the pilot instructs. I turn my attention back to Hannah before they try to confiscate my phone.

"How did you find out? The flurazepam and all that stuff?" I whisper into the phone.

"White hat bug bounty baby!" Hannah says. "If I can hunt down software bugs for a financial bounty, why not do it for my best friend?"

I see sharp pointy black fingernails tapping on the seat in front me. My heart races and I feel like I've jumped out of my seat, yet I know I haven't. My eyes slowly follow the black fingernails up the hand, elbow, upper arm and all the way north to the neck and face of the flight attendant. The flight attendant. Not Kan. Wow. I wonder if I've got some kind of PTSD after last night. All I could see in those few seconds were Kan's black pointy fingernails coming at me.

"Miss, please put the phone away," the flight attendant kindly requests.

"Thanks, Hannah. Bye." With Everett sitting so close to me now, I realize that given the whirlwind of events in the past few days, I had not told Hannah the news yet. I think she'll be happy for me. As I put the phone away in my backpack, I send her a quick text.

Me: Everett is 16!

Before I can receive a response, I put the phone on airplane mode.

I feel the airplane's wheels pick up ground speed beneath me. The very tight seating arrangement in the aluminum tube means my shoulder, down to my elbow, is in full contact with Everett's. I feel something in my stomach. Maybe it's the flurazepam wearing off. Maybe it's what they call butterflies, which I haven't felt before. I look at him. Hannah's words at the MIT bathroom ring in my ears again--boyish savant. Why didn't I notice that he really doesn't look like a grad student? Why has he not told me he's my peer? Well, my peer in age at least. Ojigwe had said Everett doesn't want people at the university to know. But we're not at the university anymore. Will Everett mention his true age, I wonder. I'm tempted to ask him if he needed a permission slip from his mommy and daddy to get on this flight, but it turns out because I'm over 15, even I didn't need my parents' or the airline's approval to buy the ticket and board the flight.

But then, I think, maybe I'm not important to Everett. Maybe he's not interested in me in that kind of way, so why would his age be relevant? Yeah, that must be it. So if he's not interested in me, then why is he here?

"Why are you going with us to Naica?" I ask.

"Astrobiology," he answers. "The focus of my graduate work is astrobiology. I want to know the origin and evolution of life on the planet and the universe. I believe clues, information, lie in unexplored parts of Earth as well as in the meteorites that land on Earth."

He takes a quartz crystal geode out of his backpack. Cupping the rocky exterior of the half-sphere in his hand, he faces its crystal lined cavity towards me.

"Can you imagine being inside of this?" he asks me with a certain intensity I haven't quite seen in him before. "Crystal. Perfectly ordered molecular structure. Symmetry. Harmony."

I had to think about giving him an honest answer about my ability to imagine myself inside a crystal geode. I didn't have to imagine hard, since just last night I saw myself in a round crystal structure, a crystal cave.

Everett puts the quartz crystal into my palm and takes his eyeglasses off with a smooth semi-circular gliding motion. OK. So, that move is so Superman. I get to see his bare Clark Kent face for the first time, his navy colored eyes unmasked. My gaze naturally goes down to his chest to look for the big red-on-yellow S. Nope. Just another goofy science t-shirt. This time its message is—*You Matter until you multiply yourself times the speed of light squared then You Energy.*

Holding his glasses between me and the crystal in my hand, he explains, "My glasses. These lenses. The molecular structure is chaos. No order. No symmetry. Chaos is great raw material for creation, but the crystalline form indicates order. The atoms are lined up, orderly, where they belong. It's a more evolved state."

Amanda interrupts, "If the great force of creation on Earth were to be personified, then he, or she, would have been seriously OCD when inventing crystals."

Everett slides his glasses back on, gives Amanda a nod of approval, and questions me again. "So, can you?"

"Can I what?" I ask.

"Can you imagine being inside of that?" he points at the crystal quartz geode that's still in my hand.

"Yes. I suppose I have already imagined it." That's the closest thing to the truth I could say, without getting into the whole bit—*I watched myself inside of a crystal cave on a high-res 2D triangular screen that hovered in front of my face and I experienced it simultaneously as a 3D reality.*

"I imagined it too. But thanks to Amanda, and you, I have the chance to go beyond imagining and actually go into the giant crystal caves at Naica," he says, pushing his glasses up the bridge of his nose. The plane tips upwards and I hear the wheels retracting. I only have one thing left to say.

"Alright then. Let's go."

8

INNER SPACE

Bump, bounce, and repeat. This off roading motion rocks the four-wheel drive tan colored Jeep that Amanda rented at the Chihuahua airport about three hours ago. After more than two hours of smooth, paved roads, Amanda decides we should approach the Naica mine from behind, off the paved roads in town that lead to the mine's main entrance. I am thinking she chose the color of the Jeep so we can have some degree of camouflage against the arid mountain landscape. I don't think we're successfully hiding from, or fooling, anyone. The population of about 5,000 Naicans is here in the valley below us, as are the miners who work daily to excavate lead, zinc and silver. I had some time on the plane's wi-fi to investigate the Naica mine. It was the economics of modern mining that led to the discovery of what is now officially called the Cave of the Crystals, one of several caves full of beautiful and rare crystal formations discovered at Naica mountain by miners.

"Why are we going this way? We're not sneaking in are we?" I ask. My recently heightened awareness of truth and lies nags at me. I wonder if we're breaking any rules.

Amanda guns the accelerator as the Jeep aims straight up the steep mountain incline. It looks like a 45° angle. We're picking up momentum.

"Uhh . . . Don't you want to do some switchbacks?" I ask.

"Nope. In the absence of rutted tracks, it's straight up. Head on is the best way to take on a mountain, and many other things. Doing switchbacks, we're more likely to side slip and lose control. Hold on!" she advises.

I imagine this is what a roller coaster's ascent feels like, though due to my alleged prior delicate state, I was not allowed to get anywhere near an amusement park. For about five seconds, I descend into resentment about all the "don'ts" that have been imposed upon me—by the parents. Until—

"Wooaahhh!!!" Everett, Amanda, and I break into simultaneous exclamations, as one major bump puts all three of us into a state of what feels like anti-gravity. The amusing look of Amanda's long locks and Everett's thick brown waves hovering five inches over their respective heads for a split second invites me to forget about what I missed out on in the past. Here is my real and now amusement park.

Through a plume of sandy desert dust, Amanda successfully drives us over the crest of the mountain, and manages to put on the breaks at the narrow plateau that becomes our parking spot. She jumps out of the Jeep and motions for me and Everett to do the same. We're coughing to clear our throats of the waft of dust that entered our mouths during the *Wooaahhh*.

"Witness that," she points down to answer my prior question. "That is why we came this way."

A steaming white water river gushes out from a hole at the bottom of the mountain upon which we stand. I can feel the steam rising up to my face, up my nostrils.

"The largest quartz crystals known to humans grew under this land over hundreds of thousands of years in this mineral-rich water. Only when the mining company started pumping out the water for mining purposes did they discover the great crystal caves," Amanda says. "They have to keep pumping the water out, or the crystals will be submerged again. Which would be great so the crystals can keep growing, but . . ."

"Then we wouldn't be able to go in there and explore," Everett completes her sentence.

"136°F water being pumped out at 1 million gallons per hour," Amanda adds.

To me, the white water looks inviting. It's the same shade of pure white, and to my eyes, has the same degree of softness as the tall puffy cumulonimbus clouds against the blue sky above us.

"It's beautiful. Not that I've ever white water rafted, but a part of me just wants to jump in there and have it take me where it will." Oops. I said that out loud. My internal dialog went external, sort of without my permission.

"At 136°F, thirty seconds in there, and you'd get seriously burned. The Charles River this is not," Amanda warns. "I'm just showing it to you, so you can see how hot and dangerous it is inside." She points at both me and Everett. "Now this is for both of you. When we get in there, listen carefully to the group leaders, follow instructions exactly, and don't wander off."

"Don't wander off? Are we on a kindergarten field trip? Why are you . . ." I'm cut off before I can complete my statement.

Amanda. Like a NASCAR driver, cuts me off, and then speeds up her words per minute as though she's slamming her foot on the accelerator that controls her mouth. "One person, a mine worker who went in on his own to satiate his curiosity, passed out from the heat and was later found dead. On a prior scientific expedition, a researcher almost died when his respirator malfunctioned."

"OK. OK. We got it," I tell Amanda, hoping to calm her. "With your warnings of doom and gloom, you just sound like Drs. Roman."

Amanda gets closer to me and privately whispers in the same demanding patter, "If you start feeling some super-human strength or ability coming on, keep a lid on it."

Stepping back away from me, and with her volume louder, for Everett's benefit, she warns me, "If those scientists see your blood . . ."

"Yeah. You don't want to become the subject of their experiments," Everett says.

"No. No, I don't. I would rather be the researcher than the researched. I'm figuring this one out by myself. I don't need scientists telling me what I am," I say. But, it was only two days ago that I only felt safe in the lab, where perhaps science could offer me answers. I look at Amanda and Everett. "Well, maybe I'll accept a little help from the scientists in present company," I add.

Was that almost the beginning of a smug smile emerging from Everett's face? I think so.

Amanda continues her 150 mph speed-talk "Good. Then be careful! There will be cameras on each person's suit, in addition to camera fixtures inside the cave. They'll be tracking you from the staging area outside of the Cave of Crystals. Just be normal."

I nod in understanding and agreement.

"Now. One more thing. Again, for both of you. Due to the dangerous conditions in there, I had to do some tricky convincing, negotiating, and fudging, on short notice yesterday, to get you two in on this expedition," Amanda explains.

"Convincing? I'd call it a very fair and even trade. I—well, Alexis and I—on behalf of Dr. Ojigwe come here with Dr. Collins and her New Mexico Tech team, in exchange for you and Dr. Collins coming to Antarctica with MIT next summer. What's the problem?" Everett challenges.

"Problem is that the Cave of Crystals is potentially a much more dangerous location than Antarctica, and, she's a minor," Amanda points at me, highlighting what she assumes is the chronologic Earth-entry gap between me and Everett. Right, of course she assumes he's over eighteen. I need to fill her in. Amanda continues, "Alexis is non-essential to our research and she's being put in a dangerous situation."

"Non-essential?" I bark.

"If you think she's non-essential, then why is she here?" Everett asks.

I shoot him a nasty glare. I think he caught that. Wow. That was my first time being a little nasty and angry with him. That didn't feel entirely bad or unnatural.

"No offence, Alexis. I'm not the one who said you're non-essential," he says to me with a smirk and turns back to Amanda. "Why is she coming?"

"Because. Because. She just is that's all," is Amanda's non-answer to Everett.

I want to know the answer as well. But I'm not clear on it myself. All Amanda told me, while at the airport waiting for our flight, is that because I saw that vision of me and her in the crystal cave, that there must be something in that cave for me to discover, for me personally, not for Amanda's research. And therefore, that meant I had to go. Who am I to argue? Count me in. I get to be in a large structure which is potentially the solid form of my liquid crystal blood.

"Why is Everett here?" I ask Amanda before I out him as being under the age of eighteen. Not that I don't want Everett along, but since he's challenging my presence here; I have to challenge his. "Is he here just so you can go to Antarctica?"

"Antarctica is an unexpected bonus. But, no. That's not the reason. Everett is the only scientist, other than me, who knows about your blood. So, he could be helpful to us. We need to double check and validate whatever discoveries we make, while keeping things really quiet," Amanda explains. Then, she gives him a longer sizing-up kind of glance and adds, "He seems trustworthy and smart."

"Dr. Ojigwe says he has a brain the size of a planet," I add.

"He said that?" Everett asks. He's either blushing, or the Mexican sun has already given him a light sunburn, or both.

"Today. Right now. About the crystal caves of Naica, all you both need to know is this," Amanda says. "We're not mentioning anything about Alexis being a high school student. All I've told Dr. Collins is that you are both research assistants, so she's just assumed you are both college aged or more. Don't dispel her assumptions."

"Got it," Everett confirms.

"What if Dr. Collins knew there were minors on this expedition?" I ask Amanda staring at Everett. He bends down to re-tie a shoelace, taking his face out of my line of sight.

"Only miners, spelled with an e, are allowed down there, not minors, with an o. So, said minor, with an o," Amanda points at me, "could be staying right here at the surface, doing nothing, while the rest of us explore planet Earth. Don't tell Dr. Collins!"

"You want me to lie?" I ask. I have a newfound hatred for lies thanks to Drs. Roman, my parents' gullibility, and Amanda's non-bio-sister cover up. "Like, what if Dr. Collins asks me point blank how old I am? You don't have to be eighteen to be in college. Maybe I'm some kind of genius who just skipped high school and went to college at the age of like ten or something." I stare at Everett as he stands back up after playing with his shoelaces. He looks in every direction but mine.

"You flatter yourself," Amanda insults.

"No, I don't," I retort defensively.

"Careful. Self-flattery is directly correlated with a declining IQ," she warns.

Everett coughs violently. Wait. Is he coughing? Or is he laughing at me and hiding it behind the cough? I glare at him again.

"Are you laughing at the notion that one could be a child genius?" I ask.

Everett shakes his head no. He points to his throat.

"Coughing," he says with what sounds like a faux rough voice. "That dust I inhaled when we crested the mountain top, still clogging up my airways. Not laughing. Anyone of us could be a child genius."

I want to say something right now about him being sixteen, but I also don't want Amanda to abort the mission into the crystal cave because she has two minors on her hands, not one.

"99.99%, Dr. Collins is not going to ask you your age," Amanda says. "She'll assume you are the norm. The norm is the norm for a reason and generally, people assume everything around them is normal." Amanda is exceeding the speed limit of speech again. "That's how people miss and overlook the bizarre, wacky and miraculous things that go on everyday under their very noses. So, I'm not asking you to lie. Not exactly. Just don't volunteer some information that you have. Unless, of course, you just want to skip the caving and go back home right now."

"I am going into that cave," I declare. It's not even a question in my mind. This is an absolute.

"Of course you are going into the cave. I see. Now you are willing to not disclose some important info about yourself. It's not exactly lying. Maybe now you understand and see things in a different way. So, you are also now going to forgive me for not disclosing to you that you were adopted," Amanda jabs.

"Huh?" Everett asks, not following where Amanda is going with this.

I am silent.

"You are forgiving me, right?" Amanda asks.

"I'm trying," I say. This is the most honest answer I can offer.

I roll my eyes and turn my face away from her. This motion lands my line of sight on a cement block off in the distance, near the base of the adjacent hill.

"What's that?" I ask.

"Is that the Robin Hole?" Everett questions Amanda.

"Yep," she nods. "That's what they call it. A 2,000 foot deep shaft drilled by the miners to ventilate the mines. Scientists thought it might lead to a currently inaccessible extension of the crystal caves, or maybe even a different cave system. A skilled mountain climber repelled down to explore, strapped in by ropes and cables, but it just didn't lead to much. The pictures they were able to capture show small crystals that they describe as looking like cauliflower," she looks up. "A mini, more solid, version of the clouds above us."

"Are we going to enter that way as well? Into the cave?" I ask.

"No. I told you. They didn't find much there. That's not our purpose here today," Amanda clarifies. "We're going to demo . . ."

"Spacesuits!" Everett interrupts. Wow. He sounds like a little kid. "We're demoing spacesuits today. The only thing that would make this better is if it were the Z series.

"Let me guess. Are you a more of a Z-1 Buzz Lightyear kind of guy, or a Z-2 Tron kind of person?" Amanda queries.

"I'd take either one, really." No clarity on preference of spacesuit flavor from Everett today.

"It doesn't matter. It's not the Z-series anyway," Amanda disappoints.

My eyes are still affixed on the cement block across the valley.

"I'll be back, like, in a minute," I say, realizing that by the time the word minute left my mouth, I was probably too far away for them to hear it. I'm about halfway to the Robin Hole. I can feel the desert dust on my lips and on my eye lashes. I squint to keep the dust out. Then, I arrive.

The Robin Hole has a square cinder block perimeter wall about four feet high, maybe ten feet long on each side. An iron lid caps it off. It's locked. Very locked. Four iron cross bars are fastened across the lid. Each is bound by chain and lock. I put my hands on one of the locks. Hmmm, can I? Maybe I can. I squeeze and twist it. Nope. I haven't broken it. But I have successfully bent it.

The sound interrupts me. It's like chimes ringing in the valley but it's not. I can see Amanda on the adjacent hill with her fingers to her mouth. Her whistle amps up into an echo, giving it multiple lives before it quiets down. I'm back at her side before that happens.

"Thanks for returning Tasmanian Devil," she says, shooing the sand and dust from her face.

"What, was that? How did you move that fast?" an astonished Everett looks at me. I can't tell if his lips are trying to move into a smile or if they are merely working at keeping dust out of his mouth.

"That is crystal blood activated by her knowledge that she actually has crystal blood," Amanda answers on my behalf, because I just don't know what to say. "Knowledge being the catalyst, the turn on switch."

We're so excited to use outer space technology today to explore inner space," Raul says as he hops out of the van. The low rocky ceiling in this part of the cave network could easily make one feel claustrophobic. It's the antithesis of outer space.

"The suits you sent are in the tent, ready for the demo," Raul adds, looking at the two-person NASA contingent of the group that will explore the Cave of Crystals today. Dr. Robert Krist, Director of Exoplanet Research at NASA and Dr. Emma Wang, Director of NASA's NExSS coalition, the Nexus for Exoplanet System Science. These two are here looking inward to Earth, to discover the truth about what might be out there, in distant space. Raul, that is Dr. Raul Cabrera, is with the local group tasked with preserving, protecting, and exploring the caves at Naica. He and his team are the gatekeepers here and I think he's excited to demo some new toys today. I'm not sure if the new gear makes us guinea pigs, but even if we are, sign me up.

People are sweating. We're not even exerting ourselves yet, just sitting still in the van. All are sweating profusely already, except for me, and I'm hoping nobody notices. I scan their faces thinking they may just be more concerned with staying and appearing calm and cool in this heat, than paying any attention to me. We left the Earth's surface twenty minutes ago. Since then, we have been passengers in a van, driven down a winding mine shaft to this location, the entrance to the Cave of Crystals, 1,000 feet underground.

Raul directs us out of the van and points to a tent a few hundred feet further into the narrowing mine shaft. It's just bizarre seeing a tent, inside of a cave. There's something Russian nesting doll about it.

"This is our staging area. Please proceed towards the tent. It's a comfortable 78°F in there," Raul directs.

Just past the tent, I see the sealed gateway, which must be the entrance into the crystal cave. Despite the barrier of this huge, heavy looking door, the heat from the crystal cave is permeating into the staging area.

One by one, we hop out of the van. I go first. Everett's glasses are fogging up, so he raises them off his face to see the surface beneath him more clearly. Next is the two-person NASA team, followed by Amanda and her professor, Dr. Elizabeth Collins, an astrobiologist at New Mexico Tech and leader of this expedition.

A bead of sweat drops from Amanda's nose and lands on her chest, as she takes the big step down out of the van. She wipes her brow. I elbow her and subtly point to my nose and brow. Dry!

Creating some distance between us and the rest of the group, I hang back near the van and wait for Raul and the scientists to make their way towards the haven of the air conditioned tent.

With both her hands, Amanda wipes the perspiration from her neck and then proceeds to glide her wet hands over my face. Eewww.

Is that supposed to fool anyone? Won't anyone even notice that I'm not really sweating? Or that I'm actually sporting someone else's hot cave dew on my skin?

Everett takes a few steps back towards us and acknowledges with a nod. He acknowledges the fact. The fact that my biochemistry is different and we don't want anyone here to know that. He takes Amanda's cue and with both of his big hands, wipes the sweat off his face. He gently places a sweaty hand on my cheek. Is it eewww or is it aahhh? I'm not sure. I'm confused about my own reaction. Noticing that my t-shirt is totally dry, whereas his and Amanda's display the standard signs of perspiration, he moves his other hand towards my t-shirt. But then he stops. What a gentleman, I think. I hold my hand up to his for a slow high-five glide. Then, I pat my own t-shirt with the bit of liquid that transferred from his hand to mine.

"Your skin. It looks different. Like, a healthier shade of you," he says to me.

"Maybe it's because I'm shellacked in both of your sweat," I offer, my eyes darting, Everett to Amanda, and back to Everett again.

"Maybe it's because you're happy to be closer to the huge solid version of your blood. You know, a happy glow," Everett suggests.

"More like you're nearing the next half-life mark of flurazepam," Amanda blurts out. After observing me more closely she adds, "Actually, your skin looks as beautiful as it did when you were like three, when I first saw you." She turns to face Everett. "We'll explain later," she says in response to his curious, questioning look.

"Ikal!" Raul hollers in our direction. I look behind us.

How long has this person been standing there? It's like he appeared out of nowhere. I'm guessing he's in his thirties, handsome in a very native Central American kind of way. This—Ikal walks around us and makes his way towards the tent entrance. We follow him and catch up with the group waiting for us by the tent.

"My colleague, Ikal, will direct you inside of the tent," says Raul. He looks to the NASA team, "In addition to your space gear, Ikal set up the suits we used last time, as a basis for comparison."

Ikal holds the tent door open for us explorers as we stream into the cooler inner space. He does a top-to-bottom visual inspection of each person who walks through the tent door. I feel like he's lingered a little extra on me, but maybe that's because I may have lingered a little extra on him after we noticed him lurking behind us back near the van.

"Welcome. Make yourselves comfortable. Ah . . . the magic of evaporative cooling," Ikal says with impeccable English, through his Mexican accent. Everyone takes a seat, relaxes, letting their skin and clothing dry off.

As the other humans here take a moment to enjoy the relief of this process, my eyes scan the tableau of tech equipment set up along the tent wall to the far right. Four workstations with multiple screens connected to each computer are lined up next to monitors that look like they might belong in a hospital. I don't recognize the other equipment along this wall but want to know more about what each knob and gauge on the mystery tech boxes will tell us about the crystal cave.

When my gaze travels back to the front of the tent room, I see Ikal is looking at my t-shirt. His eyes scan each person in the room and return back to me. I can see he recognizes the pattern of sweat on my clothing is different from everyone else here. The wet marks are simply my handprints, not big round blotches under the arms, around the neck, and around the chest. Not too smart on my part, really. That's why he looked at me a little extra long as I walked into the tent. Hmmm. He's perceptive.

He steps forward and engages his audience.

"When we get in there, it's going to be nearly 100 percent humidity at 120°F, with some parts of the cave reaching 140°F. Evaporative cooling will be nearly impossible. Your sweat won't be able to change from its liquid state into vapor in order to cool you off. There is so much water content in the air that it makes it very hard for the sweat to evaporate. Without the right gear, you will suffer from heat stroke and your body will begin to cook itself," Ikal says as he steps closer to me, Amanda, and Everett. "Rare? Medium rare? Well done? All depends on how long you are in there before Raul or I have to go in and pull you out," he goes on with a touch of arrogance. "I don't see any concern in the faces of our young scientists?"

"I believe they are well prepped and well researched," Dr. Collins assures Ikal. She stands up and paces in front of the group. Her body language tells Ikal to step aside. "But, thank you for the informative talk, which bordered on hazing. The scare tactics aren't necessary with these folks. Dr. Ojigwe's assessment is that Everett and Alexis are two of the most promising young researchers he's worked with lately."

Did I just hear that correctly? Most promising young researchers? As it pertains to me, did Ojigwe really mean it? Or, did I just benefit from being grouped with Everett, who seems to have the glow, the aura of scientific excellence, armed with a brain the size of a planet.

"Alexis, if you are like your sister, then I have full confidence that you three will be safe and productive during our time here. I look for every opportunity I can to work with my sister. How many years are between you two?" Dr. Collins's question drops like a brick on my head.

"Nine months," Amanda jumps in before I can say anything. "We're Irish twins. We're from Boston. So. Yeah. With people of Irish ancestry being the single largest ethnic group in Boston, the city has the highest percentage of Irish twins in America." Amanda lays out her ludicrous lies in a patter so fast, I only hope these people didn't totally catch the made up Irish twins stats and offensive slang that she slung around to deflect Dr. Collins's question.

"Are you two half-sisters or full?" Ikal's whisper emerges from the space between me and Amanda. The lurker has reappeared behind us.

"Ikal, if you would please come up here and help with the demonstrations?" Dr. Collins saves us from having to address his question. She turns to the two NASA people, Dr. Robert Krist and Dr. Emma Wang. "Robert, Emma, let's do a little before and after. I'll take the before. You take the after." The NASAns nod.

Robert darts behind a room divider screen stationed by the tent wall to our left. It's made of aged, distressed wood and features hand painted religious folk art in bright oranges, reds and yellows. A strange juxtaposition to the bank of 21st century equipment on the opposing wall of the tent. Our Lady of Guadalupe's icon, the local version of the Virgin Mary, covers the middle panel of the room divider. Her head and shoulders are draped in a blue robe and an oval of golden light surrounds her. I remember learning about Catholic accounts of the Virgin Mary appearing on four separate occasions, about 500 years ago, to a Juan Diego, who subsequently became the first indigenous Catholic saint in the western hemisphere. Apparently, the Virgin asked Saint Juan Diego to have a church built in her honor in what is now Mexico City. Mary almost looks like an apparition on the room divider down here.

A plonking sound jars me. Robert's belt buckle, hanging from his cast off pants,, hits the Virgin Mary on her head. Apparently, he's changing his clothes back there. Next, his t-shirt lands on top of the pants. Raul looks bothered. He walks over to the room divider and moves Robert's clothes off the Virgin's head and over to the right-hand panel. Mary can look down upon us again.

"Before," Dr. Collins says to draw our attention back to her. Standing beside her is Ikal, who apparently will serve as our model. He puts on a miner's helmet and headlamp. He zips on a vest and some kind of over-pants. Both have rows and rows of slot-like pockets sewn all over them.

"This is where the ice packs would go in. About thirty to forty pounds worth," Ikal explains as he puts his fingers in some of the slots on the vest and pants. Dr. Collins hands him items which he puts on one by one, a clear plastic mask across his eyes, boots, and gloves. Then, she hands him a bright orange suit. He steps into it. After he's zipped up, Dr. Collins puts a backpack on him that looks heavy, based on the way she is maneuvering it. She pulls a respirator mask from the side of the backpack and places it over Ikal's mouth.

"And, voila!" Dr. Collins presents the before. Orange hazmat suit. It's the exact suit and equipment Amanda was wearing in the vision I saw of her before I had ever heard of Naica. Our Lady of Guadalupe is staring at me from the changing screen panel. I wonder, was Amanda an apparition in orange?

"We used ice to keep us cool, a respirator to protect our throats and lungs from burning, and this mask to protect our eyes from boiling," Ikal explains.

"Up to eighty minutes is the maximum time we had in there." Dr. Collins points towards the crystal cave entrance.

"This will change everything," Robert announces as he bounds out from behind the protection of the Virgin's screen. One look at him and my eyes dart down towards the floor, just like the Virgin Mary's. I am uncomfortable. He looks like a ballet dancer in a white, skin-tight, spandex bodysuit. It just feels like this should be a private moment for him, but he's not acting that way.

"It's a liquid cooling garment, or LCG," explains Emma from NASA, answering the question, *What the heck is that?* which has been running around in my head. "It's worn under spacesuits. The network of thin flexible tubes in direct contact with the astronaut's skin, or in this case, with your skin . . ." She points at us.

Oh, I'm an astronaut now. Cool.

Then her finger points to Robert's LCG. " . . . carries cool water, which warms as it continues to cool the body. For our purpose today, the warm water will filter through a Portable Life Support System, or PLSS where it will travel through a refrigeration system, cool back down to about 60°F and travel back over the body again."

"The PLSS," Robert shows us a large metal backpack. It looks like a higher tech version of the one Ikal is wearing on the back of his orange suit. "Off planet, the PLSS gives our astronauts freedom of movement and independence from the spacecraft. It provides oxygen, cooling through the LCG, a communications headset, and biometrics."

Everett shuffles. He pulls out his phone and texts Amanda and me. Wow, there's wi-fi down here. I feel like I'm in school and my instinct is to not look at my phone. But I do.

Everett: Biometrics? How's that with Alexis?
Me: No problem
Amanda: Already checked it out
Me: I'm normal, according to electronic devices...at least

"Deep inside the planet, as we are here," Robert continues, "the PLSS will enable you to ditch the ice packs. We've customized the ones you'll use down here with a mini portable A/C unit that will take care of the cooling, significantly extending your exploration time in this cave network."

"And this is the exterior suit you will wear, over the LCG, and in conjunction with the PLSS. This is your version of an EMU, extravehicular mobility unit," Emma says, her voice coming at us from a speaker on one of the computers to our right.

Wow! When did she put that on? She does a runway walk for us, showing off the indigo blue fitted spacesuit. She does the runway thing way too well. I suspect Emma is a model-turned-NASA-scientist. Robert is still standing there, like a male mannequin. Because his LCG looks like a full body leotard, all I can picture is the two of them pirouetting together.

Emma's blue spacesuit looks like it's straight out of 2001: A Space Odyssey.

"The Starliner spacesuit!" Everett breaks his silence. He's been focused like a laser beam on every word spoken, every action made by the team here. He's been calm and still, taking in the download, but now he's ready to jump out of his seat.

"Form fitting, flexible, light, simple, with fewer parts to malfunction," Robert explains. I'm thinking form fitting was his favorite attribute on the list.

"The helmet and visor are attached to the suit," Emma says, from inside the suit, which covers her entire body. Her voice comes at us again from the computer's speaker, which is hooked up to the communications system. The boots look more like high top sneakers and the spacesuit itself is less Michelin Man, and more one-piece ski suit. "This suit is designed to be worn on the Starliner, to take our colleagues back and forth to the International Space Station."

"Yes." Dr. Collins affirms and steps in with a touch of excitement in her usually serene tone, "Our goal today is to be able to stay in the cave for up to three hours, instead of the eighty minute limit set by the equipment we used last time. With these spacesuits, we can have up to eight hours in there, but we are testing them today, so we won't push anywhere near that limit. With the full three hours, we can reach previously unexplored regions of the cave and look for lifeforms . . ." My mind goes to images of little hobbit-like creatures, but then I snap back into reality with

Dr. Collins's next two words, " . . . bacteria, microorganisms."

Of course. This is science. Last time they were down here, they found forty-three ancient pollen grains that were preserved in two different crystals. Mineralogists who studied the grains believe underground streams carried them from what must have been a forested climate on the surface above this cave hundreds of thousands of years ago. These grains and other substances found down here were previously unknown to science.

No hobbits. No Jurassic Park. Just science. Yes. Just what was previously unknown to science.

9

HOLY CRYSTAL CAVE, SUPERMAN

"Holy crystal cave, Superman!" says Everett looking up at the sky. Well, looking up at where the sky would normally be. It's huge! Cathedral-like ceilings over a length and width the size of a football field get my mind onto the mental math of the estimated volume of this cavern. Maybe it's close to the height of the Sistine Chapel. No, less than that. I think it's more like two stories high. And I don't think Michelangelo could improve upon this. No offense to the eternal soul of Michelangelo, but nature does not need humans. The opposite is not true. I won't let my art history teacher hear that thought. I estimate this giant womb of a space has a gross volume of about one and a half million cubic feet.

We've descended fifty feet since the entrance into the crystal cave to get to this central vantage point. Enormous crystals, the size of tree trunks jut out in every direction from the walls, floor, and ceiling. Those that point straight up look like the Washington Monument, like obelisks made of ice. This is real. But it feels beyond real. Like, I'm in some kind of reality where not only does Superman exist, he comes here, here to his Fortress of Solitude.

"Don't you mean Batman?" I ask Everett. "Like, *holy crystal cave, Batman*? Are you getting your superhero references mixed up Robin?"

"No. No I'm not. I do mean Superman," then he steps closer to me and through his space helmet looks right into my eyes. "Maybe, I mean Supergirl."

Amanda changes the subject, real fast. "That part," she points back towards the cave entrance from which we came, "is actually called the forest." We are all on one communication system. Six of us in spacesuits are in the crystal cave, supported by Raul and Ikal back in the tent. Every word that any one of the eight of us utters is heard by all. I think Amanda doesn't want to out me and my superpowers just yet.

"The forest. I can see why it's called that," I reply. I love walking through the forests in Massachusetts. Mohawk Trail was my favorite. This is the same thing. Just switch out the tall pine trees for giant crystals.

"The longest crystal we've measured is just over thirty-seven feet and we estimate it weighs about fifty tons," Raul chimes in with commentary from the tent. They've got cameras positioned throughout the cave, plus one on each of our helmets, so they can see each person's point of view. I wonder if this makes them feel omnipresent. Raul and Ikal are giving us a guided audio tour like we're in a museum. They told us their main reason for staying behind was to closely monitor our biometrics. And of course, Ikal had to remind us that they are like lifeguards who will jump in to save us when needed. Yes. He used the word when, not if.

"And over there," Amanda points in the direction opposite the cave entrance, "That's where we'll be climbing into the other chamber, I believe. Is that right, Dr. Collins?" She points more specifically now to a very long crystal that looks like a downed tree trunk. It might be about four feet in diameter. The crystal member starts at the bottom surface of the cave and reaches up towards a landing that leads to an opening shaped like a gothic arch.

"Yes," the professor responds. "We need to get into that part of the cave again."

"That's about a twenty-five foot diagonal incline," adds Ikal through the communication system. "Hold on tight to that slippery surface," he adds with a touch of menace in his voice, a voice that sounds way too intimate through my earpiece.

This sort of makes him super-lurker-on-steroids. Breathing a little too heavily into his mic, and thereby into my ear, he adds, "We call it our very own Slip N' Slide." It feels like he's inside the suit with me. I get chills down my spine. We actually had a Slip N' Slide when I was younger, one of those classic summery toys. I was not allowed to use it, lest I cut myself and bleed to death, or so they told me.

"That twenty-five foot incline is exactly what the suction cups are for," Robert offers his first few words since entering the cave. I was wondering why he had suction cups hanging from his spacesuit. For people who live and breathe for extra-planetary science, the NASA duo seem to be the most speechless and awestruck by inner Earth. Robert has been busy focusing his Raman spectrometer at sections of crystal where they suspect life may reside. Not the hobbits of my imagination of course, but tiny microbes, pollen, viruses, or bacteria. Unlike the huge spectrometer in our MIT lab, this one is a small portable version. The way Robert is handling it, one could mistake it for a groovy 1960s era sci-fi movie ray gun. He aims it directly at the crystal that lies across my path and looks like a horizontal I-beam. I need to step over it. I would have rather jumped, but we were cautioned, *no jumping or running allowed!* They didn't include skipping in that list. I'm tempted.

"Any signs of life yet?" I ask him.

"Nope. Maybe they're finding more on Mars," he responds.

Maybe. They did send one of those little Raman ray guns up with a Mars Rover mission.

We slowly make our way towards the grand crystal Slip N' Slide. And I do mean slowly. We were forewarned about the dangers of going too fast through the crystal jungle gym. As we near our destination, there are more crystals jutting out all around. We duck here, climb there. Not exactly a straight path. When my mind goes to the fact that some of the most interesting microbes and pollen found in the last expedition at Naica were up in that second chamber of the crystal cave, then my feet just move faster. It's not premeditated. My feet just respond to the thought, to the call of curiosity. I want to get in there. I'm surprised when I sense everyone else is picking up the pace too. We might be more of a herd than I thought.

"Slow down," commands Raul. "The gypsum is relatively soft. The pillars could break if you put too much pressure on them. Watch out especially for the younger, smaller crystals. The edges are quite sharp."

"Slow down everyone," Dr. Collins confirms that we are supposed to obey Raul.

"Ah . . . mazing . . ." utters Emma. She puts her gloved hand on one of the crystals protruding into her path. " . . . these were once hydrothermal fluids emanating from the magma chambers beneath the cave's floor. Started as fluid and then solidified, like water into ice."

"What's messing with my mind," says Everett. "This looks exactly like ice. I feel like I'm in the Erebus ice caves of Antarctica again. The visual cues say ice. But knowing that if I take this suit off, I'll cook from the heat, it's a mind trip."

"Those magma chambers, they are actually about one and a half miles under the cave floor," Raul clarifies Emma's earlier statement. "The heat comes up through fault lines. We estimate about half million years ago, what is now this open cavern was full of mineral rich water. Calcium and sulfate molecules deposited along the limestone walls. Then, when the magma below cooled down, the water in here also cooled to about 136°F. At that temperature, the calcium and sulfate molecules, with the water, formed into selenite crystals."

$CaSO_42H_2O$. I see the chemical structure in my mind. I spin it left and right, forwards and backwards. Each calcium atom, surrounded by several oxygen atoms, are then in turn attached to sulfur and hydrogen atoms. The 3D image rotates in my head. Atoms line up in the most orderly fashion, no room for chaos here. Repeating, over and over, building upon one another, like bricks forming a formidable wall, the crystal grows.

We reach the base of the Slip N' Slide. I look up at the landing and look past the gothic arch, into the upper chamber. I can see the inside of the chamber. I wonder if I could see it better without my headlamp. Stepping back from the group a bit, hoping no one will notice, especially the two back in the tent, I pretend I'm adjusting my headlamp. Instead, I turn it off. I look up at the upper cave's entrance again and focus my vision further, deeper into the space. The crystals glow like moonlight, just like they did when I saw Amanda in my vision early that morning back home in Wellesley, just a few days ago. The artificial light of the headlamps and the floodlights that Raul and Ikal set up in here obscure the actual softer, more organic glow that I can see without the aid of the LEDs, especially the one on my head which is specifically supposed to help me. Now that I've gotten a real look, LED free, I turn my headlamp back on, conforming with the rest of the group.

Robert grabs the suction cups he'd mentioned earlier and positions himself to go up first.

"Did you use ropes, anything like that last time?" asks Robert.

"No. We just sort of shimmied up like monkeys, in slow motion. It worked, but at the pace of a tortoise. Let's see if these do better for us," Dr. Collins says.

"You have two hours, twenty-one minutes before you need to be back here in the tent," announces Ikal.

Robert reaches up with his right hand and slaps one suction cup onto the Slip N' Slide, and then with his left hand, he slaps on the other. His boots appear to have a decent grip on the crystal member. He releases the left suction cup, moves it about three feet up the length of the crystal and slaps it on again, moving his body north.

"Moving right along. Wow. It works," Dr. Collins comments.

So, I'm thinking, but I just don't want to say it out loud, out of respect. It took a NASA rocket scientist to figure this one out—suction cups.

"Almost there," chimes Raul.

I see Robert pulling on one of the suction cups. He pulls again and again.

"It's stuck," he grunts. He pulls harder and the suction cup suddenly comes loose. Robert loses his balance. As his body weight shifts, Robert's right hand and leg lose contact with the crystal.

A collection of soft gasps echo-whisper through the communications headset. It happens in unison. It's hard to hear who has gasped and who has not.

"Whoaaa!" Robert exclaims. His other foot loses contact with the crystal too, and now he's hanging from just one hand gripping the suction cup. Legs dangling high above the cave floor, he looks like a blue LEGO minifigure clutching on for dear life.

Everett moves to the base of the crystal, ready to shimmy up like a monkey without the aid of the suction cups. "Need a hand?" Everett offers Robert.

"Don't do that, Everett," Raul commands. "Robert, you aren't that far off the ground. Look down and pick a good landing spot." Robert obeys. "Do you ride a motorcycle Robert?" asks Raul.

"Yes," Robert responds. " . . . and . . . I now know where you're going with this."

"Exactly. You go where you look. Focus like a Raman spectrometer laser beam on your preferred landing spot, and let go," Raul instructs.

Robert lands with a thud. The sound, "Oauuuhh" escapes from his mouth. "Well, the padding on the Starliner suit helped . . . a little, very little."

Emma's next to him now, helping him up.

"You have a tear," Emma points to the back of Robert's thigh. We all look down at where he landed. There's a shred of blue spacesuit clinging to a small protrusion. Emma crouches down for a closer look.

"One of the small, sharp baby crystals you warned us about Raul," says Emma, looking up at where Robert was dangling a minute ago. "It would not have been visible from up there."

"Either I've just started peeing 60°F urine, or the baby crystal sunk its teeth into one of the LCG tubes returning from my PLSS," Robert reports as he stands up.

"Assuming the latter is the case, I think you need to head out of here—Now," Dr. Collins tells him.

"Make your way back immediately please," Raul adds. Robert obeys.

Dr. Collins is already climbing up the crystal member towards the landing, the old fashioned way, simply using hands and feet.

Amanda shrugs her shoulders, "Who needs another suction cup malfunction?" She follows Dr. Collins up the pillar. Emma motions her hand, suggesting I ought to go next.

Two days ago, I leapt onto La Grande Voile. I leapt onto the Alchemist. I would really like to do the same here on the Slip N' Slide. But, *keep a lid on* it Amanda had said, and so I shall. I mimic the motions and pace set by Dr. Collins and Amanda. Emma is next behind me.

Sure footed, Dr. Collins reaches the top. She steps forward a few paces and bends down so her head doesn't hit the top of the entry into the cavern that is our destination. The opening must be about five feet high at the peak of the gothic arch. At its bottom, sharp jagged crystals jut out, seemingly warning, *DO NOT ENTER.*

On my way up, I grab the suction cup left behind by Robert near the top of the Slip N' Slide and take it further up with me. With two more steady motions, I reach the top.

"Mind tossing that down to me?" Everett asks, looking up at me. He's got the other suction cup, which Robert had left where he fell.

"Really?" I ask.

"I can't pass up this Batman and Robin scaling a wall with suction cups fantasy," he says to me.

"OK. Have your fantasy," I respond, tossing it down to him.

Emma and Amanda disappear into the cavern past the gothic entry. I want to do the same, but right now, I can't take my eyes off Everett. This person in the blue spacesuit, who looks like he ought to be on the Discovery One with his buddy HAL, is instead pretending he's Batman climbing up a downed crystal pillar with suction cups. Batman is a stretch. He might be more of a Robin. I feel a glove on my foot.

"Made it up here faster than you I believe. I'm faster than you," he says looking at me through his helmet. He knows I can't say a thing to negate his claim right now. Our communal conversation technology restricts me. Annoyed,

I pivot on the heel of my space boot like it's my favorite pair of pumps and vector into the destination of the cavern. I hear the thud of two suction cups dropping to the surface at the bottom of the gothic arch and he's right behind me.

It's a much smaller cavern in here. The three of them, Amanda, Emma and Dr. Collins are crowding around one spot on the wall. I almost expect them to step away to reveal prehistoric cave paintings from the Paleolithic era depicting bison, panthers and bears. Not so. As I step up to join them, I see Emma is pointing the spectrometer at the wall.

"Right there," she says. "Looks like an air pocket. And my spec is saying it's got the signature of organic life."

Dr. Collins pulls out a small, shiny core drill, a hollow steel tube that will capture a cylindrical sample. "Tube?" she requests.

Amanda has a test tube, a bit wider in diameter than the core drill, ready to receive the sample. The soft sound of buzzing heard through my spacesuit and the chips of crystal that look like tiny little flecks of stardust indicate the drilling has begun. Dr. Collins moves with caution and care like she's a neurologist drilling into a person's skull. Slow, steady, gentle, and it's done. Dr. Collins points her drill into the test tube in Amanda's hand. She makes the drill spin in the opposite direction and the core sample slides into the test tube. The test tube is sealed, and they all look pleased, at least as far as I can tell through their helmets.

"That's one down. Two to go," Dr. Collins says.

They look around for their next two samples.

"Where does that lead?" I ask, pointing to an opening not much wider than a ten inch crack in the wall. It's shaped like a lightning bolt stretching from the floor to the ceiling of this upper cavern.

Raul responds from the tent-turned control tower, "You're not the first to ask that. Unless we break that narrow opening wider, we won't know. And we won't break it open. We are balancing preservation with exploration."

I step closer. The crack is just wide enough for me to put my helmets' bulbous face guard, the widest part of the helmet, into the crack. There's something in there that's not white selenite. It's red. Maybe it is red selenite, but they haven't mentioned seeing any selenite in these caves that is anything other than clear or white. It looks like it is moving. I really, really need to get in there. The need feels like an imperative that doesn't require logic or reason to justify it.

"Raul and Ikal, did you just see what I saw in there?" I ask. I know they are spying on me through my helmet mounted camera, so I may as well pump them for info.

"See what?" asks Raul. Maybe he didn't have his eyes on my monitor. He is scanning, I'm going to guess, a dozen cameras between the ones we're wearing in our suits and the ones they have mounted in the main cavern. But I don't see any mounted cameras in the chamber we are in now. That means Raul and Ikal are restricted to seeing the sum total of what Dr. Collins, Emma, Everett, Amanda, and I each see individually. They are a little less omnipresent now, and I feel a little less restricted.

"All we saw was darkness," says Ikal. "And what did you see?"

"Try adjusting your headlamp so we can pick up more with the camera and look again," Raul advises.

I follow his instructions. Taking off my headlamp, I use my arm like a boom, extending it farther than my helmeted head would manage without the rest of my body. I light up the interior of the space beyond the lightning bolt shaped crack.

"How's that?" I ask.

"Red . . ." Ikal says, confirming they can see exactly what I do.

"Does it look like it's moving to you?" I fire away my next question.

"Hmm . . . that could be just the reflection from the head lamp," says Raul. For a quick second, I shine the lamp in the opposite direction, cutting off visibility of the red stuff for the viewers up in the tent. I take a look with my bare eyes, LED-free. I see what they don't. Yes. It's moving alright.

"Do you see better in the dark?" Ikal taunts.

"Nope. It's just, my wrist got sore," I fib, and think, I don't want to make a habit of this fibbing thing. I point the light back to where my camera is facing, through the crack. It's a passageway and that red-whatever-it-is, is beckoning me like the yellow brick road.

I can feel a team huddling behind me. I turn around. Four blue suits in a semi-circle stare at me.

"Well, move out of the way already!" Amanda is the only one close enough to me, in relationship, not current physical placement, to actually say what all four are thinking. I move.

Ranging from Everett on top, on his tippy toes, down to Emma who takes a knee, with Amanda and Dr. Collins in between, they all peek into the crack. Four heads stacked on top of one another. To whatever red moving thing is in there, they probably look like a space age totem pole.

"It could be a stream. Clear water running over red selenite, making it look like it's moving." Dr. Collins offers her hypothesis.

"It looks like a snake," says Emma. I see the other three helmets looking down to Emma at the bottom of the totem pole and I imagine they have curious expressions on their faces. "I'm not putting that forth as my hypothesis. I'm just describing it." Emma explains herself.

"How about the end of a dragon's tail?" Everett offers. "That's just a description for our notes of course. Also not a hypothesis."

"Maybe nothing is moving at all other than shadows and light," Amanda suggests.

"Or, it could be organic life that is actually still alive," I boldly put forth my hypothesis. "May I have the Raman?" I ask Emma. The totem pole dismantles and they all step aside, maybe because they know I could be right? I can't be sure. A part of me hopes that after the next half-life cycle of flurazepam, I will have the power to read minds.

"You know how to use it?" Emma asks, moving the Raman spectrometer further away from me.

"Yes. And I promise not to drop it." I grab, even though she's not motioning to give. Now I'm a ray gun girl. I aim at the red slithering thing in question. The spectrometer lights up.

"Score!" Emma says.

"It's organic. It could be a large, well for here, a relatively large swath of bacteria. Having access to that, could inform a lot," Dr. Collins says. "Raul?"

"We'd have to put in a request for permission to open up that wall and that's not going to happen within the minutes you have left down there," responds Raul. "It's a long term project."

Long term project? I don't like the sound of that.

"You have thirty minutes before you need to come back down that Slip N' Slide," Ikal warns.

"Raul, let's work on that request later. Now, in here we need two more samples," Dr. Collins orders. Dr. Collins and Emma return to the spot where they were about to start drilling before I got curious about the next beyond. Turning her head to the three of us, "Amanda, Everett, and Alexis, would you please do a visual inspection for the potential third sample?" Dr. Collins requests. Being far more professional college researchers than I, Everett and Amanda jump to it. They are carefully scanning the cave walls. I hear the sound of soft buzzing again, as the professor and Emma, hyper focused, are extracting their second sample. I look around. Confirmed, there are no other mounted cameras on the walls. All four blue spacesuits have their backs to me—I do it.

Detaching the PLSS's connection to my LCG, I quickly slide the PLSS off my back and gently set it down. I could just as easily have been setting down my backpack at school. My body has made that motion thousands of times in a classroom.

The LCG is disabled. No more 60°F water to cool me down. I make minimal movements so as not to alert the guys up in the tent. They can see everything I see through my helmet camera. They will find out what I'm doing, and if I'm careful, they will only find out once I've done it, not before. I turn sideways, and thanks to how streamlined the

Starliner spacesuit is, I squeeze through the ten inch wide crack in the wall.

And—I am on the other side of the lightning bolt.

"Alexis! No! Dr. Collins!" Raul's voice is way too alarming and loud inside my helmet. I hear the chorus from the four that I left behind shouting at me in unison.

"Alexis!"

"What are you doing?"

"Get back here!"

"Please return immediately, per our training and protocol."

Yeah. So, we know Dr. Collins was the last one who spoke, with respect and authority, of course.

"Dr. Collins, I will be really quick and I will be fine. I apologize in advance," I say and I move. I move fast through what I quickly discover is a narrowing passageway.

"You are ordered to return right now!" Raul roars. "You are putting yourself and everyone else down there in danger."

I gaze down to see that what had looked like a red mystery substance from a distance, now, close up does indeed appear to be red selenite. What is moving is water, clear water, just like Dr. Collins thought. The stream is getting wider, covering more of the surface beneath me. It feels like I'm running really fast, but it's hard to tell. I can't use the environment to orient my location like I did up on the surface when I ran to the Robin Hole. And I don't know my newly discovered physical abilities well enough yet to tell the difference between what's just average old fast, and really, really fast.

I stop for a moment and look down. The stream is now as wide as the narrowing passageway, which I can just barely get through without having to turn into profile. I hear Raul and Ikal whispering but can't make out what they are saying. They must be covering their mics.

"Raul, Ikal, what are you seeing on her camera? How are her vitals?" Dr. Collins asks, sounding both highly agitated and concerned.

"Assuming the suit's biometrics are still working correctly, her vitals are completely normal," Raul says.

"Of course the suit and its biometric detectors are working correctly," insists Robert who is apparently up in the tent with Raul and Ikal now.

"From what we're seeing on screen, she's moving so fast, she would perspire even if she weren't in 140°F," Raul points out.

"So it's actually not possible for your vitals to be unchanged. Isn't that right, Alexis?" Ikal asks. I consider giving them a red herring, pointing them back to the suit not working, but then they might really get crazy thinking I'm in worse trouble.

"I'm an athlete. Due to all my rigorous training, my body isn't straining." There I go, fibbing again.

"Alexis, why don't you use those athletic abilities of yours to get back here? Like, fast!" Amanda yells at me. Amanda and I had agreed that we'd probably find something important down here, a clue that might explain me. But it certainly wasn't in the plan for me to break off from the group like this. I think she may be really mad at me.

I'm still running, following the red selenite path. Now the passageway starts to widen. The stream's current accelerates.

Wow.

What is that?

I put the brakes on my space boots.

It's a large pool of water. As I step closer to it, the water starts to spin. The spinning accelerates and it becomes a whirlpool. One more step for a closer look, and it spins even faster.

"Look at that!" Robert exclaims.

"What is it?" Dr. Collins demands.

"It's a giant red whirlpool," I respond in a deadpan voice that hides my surprise.

I look down. I'm standing right on the edge of the whirlpool, along the narrow rock circumference within this cylindrical cavern. I press my back up to the cave wall. Good thing I ditched the PLSS because there isn't room for it here between my back and the wall. This has been fun. But now I'm getting nervous.

My eyes circle around the whirlpool that keeps accelerating. It's almost hypnotic. I feel like it's sucking me in, but at the same time, I know I haven't moved an inch. My back is still glued to the cave wall. I feel nauseous.

"Now her vitals are moving," Raul says.

"Alexis, listen. We can see you don't have much room in there. Just back up. Back up into the passageway and return to your group," Ikal says calmly in rescue mode. It's oddly comforting to me.

"Alexis, please listen to them," Amanda pleads.

"OK. OK. I'm backing up," I agree. I need to get the heck out of here. I'm getting really dizzy, like the whirlpool is sucking my brains out. I take two steps back.

Then it happens.

It's like the last time, at Hannah's house. It starts with a buzzing sound, but here, the buzzing mixes with the sound of the whirlpool's rushing, swirling water. Last time, I had my eyes closed. This time, I'm seeing it happen. The Impossible Triangle hovers in front of me, just outside my space helmet. Three beams of light, one from each of my eyes and another from my forehead shoot out of me, straight through the helmet, lining up with the vertices of the triangle. The white lights merge in the center of the triangular plane and split into a spectrum of colors that create an image. Can they see this up at the tent? I'm not exactly keeping a lid on it here.

"Pulse is highly irregular now," Raul softly states, probably trying to inform others while not alarming me.

On the screen, I see myself climbing through a narrow cylindrical tunnel. My body is stretched out, with each of my four limbs pointing four different directions. My legs are pressed to the sides of the cylinder. My arms are similarly so, but there's some kind of extension on my hands. They look like hand stilts, made of blue painted wood. The blue is the same shade as my spacesuit, so the hand stilts look like a natural extension of my arms. My hands only make contact with the walls via the black rubber stoppers at the end of the stilts.

I'm a blue spacesuit version of Leonardo da Vinci's Vitruvian Man. Actually, I am Vitruvian Woman. Using the force of my muscles to keep moving, I remove one limb off the tunnel wall, move it forward, and press it back to the wall before lifting another limb.

I can't tell which way is up or down. Which way would gravity pull me if I let go? I'm just moving, moving towards the light at the end of the tunnel. I move faster and faster until I reach the tunnel's end. I must be going up, because I grab onto a cement surface and pull my body up against the force of gravity. I leap out of the tunnel. But there's nothing to land on, or to grab onto. I'm floating in space in a state of anti-gravity. My blue spacesuit may be more than a fashion statement at this moment. I look down to the tunnel from which I just emerged. I scream. But I can't hear my own yelp. It's silent.

Below me I see Ikal's giant face. His mouth, with square shaped lips made of cement walls, is wide open. His mouth is the tunnel from which I emerged.

Anti-gravity becomes gravity again. I fall past the cement wall lips, into his mouth, down the cylindrical tunnel. Or is it his throat? I look back up from where I came. His mouth closes when a metal door slams shut. It's like the metal doors to a storm cellar. I hear the pull of heavy chains over the doors and a padlock clicking.

"No!!!!!"

I close my eyes, shake my head.

"No! No! No!"

Opening my eyes again, I'm relieved the Impossible Triangle is gone. Raul, Ikal, and Robert are silent. They must not have seen the Impossible Triangle. I'm glad my personal screening of the horror flick is over. I'm relieved to be on the edge of a whirlpool, with my back against the wall, 1,000 feet underground instead of where I just was in that vision.

I run back towards the lightning bolt crack, much faster than I ran towards what ended up being a giant red whirlpool. I run, hoping to rejoin my group. I run, hoping that the safe, normal reality beyond the lightning bolt crack still exists. The reality where giant crystal forests deep beneath the surface beckon humans to be as awe inspiring as Earth.

10

TEQUILA WITH A SIDE OF ICE

The stench of too much alcohol is offset by the sweet-savory smell and sizzle of chili peppers and corn on the open grill. Smoke from the BBQ mingles with smoke from cigarettes in the hands of miners who have come up, after their work day down below.

At the local post-work hang out in the mining town of Naica, the bartender refills Amanda's glass with 100 Años brand tequila, a blue topped bottle featuring an agave plant on the label. This is her third refill as we play musical chairs around the bar. I go sit next to her, with Everett following. She gets up and moves away again.

"I'm sorry!" I plead as she puts distance between us.

The bartender looks at Everett's glass and mine, each of which remains full with the original pour. Water glasses, that apparently double as shot glasses in this place, are way too large for a drink so strong, in my opinion. My hands wrap around the thick glass, as I look down into the gold liquid. It's so calm and stable, unlike the red whirlpool that wanted to suck me in four short hours ago.

Everett and I move again towards Amanda's new position at the bar, seating ourselves to flank my very angry sister.

"What the hell were you thinking?" Amanda asks for the twentieth time. Is she really hoping for a different answer? I repeat what I've said each of the prior nineteen times.

"Curiosity. I just couldn't help myself."

"Curiosity killed the cat," she says with a look and voice that says she's curiosity and I'm the cat. "What happened to your impulse control?"

I shrug my shoulders.

"She is still an adolescent, so scientifically speaking, her prefrontal cortex isn't fully . . ." Everett explains. I cut him off.

"And just how developed is your prefrontal cortex?" I prod Everett. He doesn't volunteer an answer.

"OK, Professor Everett. Don't lecture. I'm not buying it," Amanda looks at me. "You've gone from Miss Obedience a few days ago, before, you know, before, to Miss Curiosity today."

She slams her empty glass onto the distressed wood of the bar, further distressing the horizontal surface. The bartender, who is tending to miners at the other end of the bar, turns in response to the sound of an empty glass. He makes his way back over to us. Before he can fill Amanda's glass again, I try my classroom Spanish with the bartender. I need to slow Amanda down.

"¿Puedo tomar un vaso de agua para ella, por favor? " When he nods, giving me a *I'll-go-along-with-it* kind of look, one of the long curls of thick black hair piled on top his head drops down across his very green eyes. He pulls out another one of these shot-water glasses, fills it with H_20 for my sister, and takes away her empty tequila glass.

"Curiosity can't kill me now, can it?" I ask. "Curiosity is the only way I'm going to figure out what I am."

"There is a lot we can learn in the lab that doesn't involve a 140°F atmosphere and being sucked into the center of the Earth through a whirlpool," Everett adds calmly and matter-of-factly. I wish some of his calm would rub off onto Amanda.

"Tomorrow, at the lab they're going to be running tests on the three samples they got from the upper chamber. I don't even know how I'm going to face Dr. Collins. She's really mad. I've never seen that woman mad. And now, she's mad," Amanda's words trail off into sadness.

I feel really terrible. I hope I haven't jeopardized Amanda's position as research assistant to Dr. Collins. But I think I may have.

After we emerged from the crystal cave, in the air-conditioned tent still 1,000 feet below, the first order of business was to confirm everyone was safe and healthy, especially me. Once that was established, Raul banned me from ever being permitted below ground in Naica again and Dr. Collins turned ice cold on Amanda.

"Well, you did take the calculated risk," Everett points out to Amanda.

"I did. Now I'm paying the price with no reward. I took her down there because I thought she would learn something, discover something, see something that would explain . . . explain . . ." Amanda can't say it.

I finish her sentence for her, " . . . what on Earth I am?"

"Yes. Yes, that's right," she confirms. "But how could you come up with nothing? And I may get kicked out of school for this."

"You could come to MIT," Everett offers, as though he were an admissions officer.

"I don't want to go to MIT. I chose New Mexico Tech and that's where I want to continue to be!" Amanda declares.

I didn't tell Amanda and Everett about what I experienced in the Impossible Triangle. I don't even know what it means. What am I going to say? I crawled up Ikal's throat which looked like a tunnel and fell out of his mouth?

"Oompa loompa doopadie doo, I've got another puzzle for you." The song sings out from my vest pocket. Noah's phone, my phone for now, tells me it's Hannah calling. This might be a welcome break from the situation at hand.

"Hello," I answer.

"Alexis! I need to give you some info. Are you in a good place to talk?" Hannah asks.

"Umm . . . you decide," I say, putting her on video chat and holding the phone up to scan the Mexican miner's bar.

"Not exactly Taco Bell is it?" she asks.

"Nope. We've gone a lot more authentic than Taco Bell today," I respond while continuing Hannah's visual tour of the bar.

"There! Looks like a quiet corner at the booth over there. Can you go there so I can download you?"

I'm there and seated in a split second. Within an audible radius of my booth, there's a miner sitting at a table with a woman. They are so into each other, that they won't be looking at me I think. The miner scooches his chair closer to the woman's. My eyes go to the legs of the wooden chair, which are painted blue, Starliner spacesuit blue, and fitted with black rubber tips where the leg makes contact with the red Mexican tile floor. Hmmm.

Hannah starts.

"That black leather binder from Drs. Roman's Cadillac, it led to some interesting info, which, I think only I could unlock," Hannah says, her pride shining through the digital connection.

"I'm sure," I say sincerely, fluffing her pride a bit more.

"Sam, Ira, and Kan. Your so-called doctors, did you know they're not American?" Hannah asks.

"No. They sound American. No accent. At least Ira and Kan do. As for Sam, he's mute, so I wouldn't know," I respond.

"They are Kazakh nationals who came to the U.S., when you were around three years old," Hannah continues.

"Kazakhstan. Where my mom's family is from. Where I just learned I'm adopted from," I let Hannah in on my newly discovered secret.

"You're adopted . . ." Hannah mutters, trying to hide a shade of shock that overcomes her face.

"They entered the U.S. the same time Alexis did?" Amanda cuts into our conversation.

"Who are these people?" I ask Amanda. "Were they involved in the adoption?"

"No. Not that I know of at least. They didn't show up in our lives until after we brought you to the U.S.," Amanda says.

"Are you sure?" I question.

"I was seven years old. I remember," she assures me.

Amanda moves my full glass of 100 Años closer to me. "Here. Just pretend to drink. Blend in," she commands.

Nope. I'm still not taking a sip. It smells awful. I catch Everett pouring some of his tequila out into a potted succulent as he makes his way over to our corner booth. I wonder if this will kill the plant, or make it happy, or both. I also wonder if he, like me, is a sixteen year old who doesn't care to experiment with alcohol.

I'm now flanked by Amanda and Everett who slide into the booth on each side of me, with Hannah on video chat taking center stage on the table.

Looking at Everett's glass of tequila, which is now only half full, I ask. "So, did you drink a lot during your college frat party days? You know, going out to bars, showing your ID, that kind of thing?"

He lifts his drinking glass to his mouth, but doesn't take a sip. Instead, he uses his lips to respond to my question. "No. Instead of frat parties and bars, I used my time to accelerate my learning, so I can potentially be one of the younger PhD candidates at the university."

"Oh, really?" I ask.

"Really," he says. I want to ask him just how young. But then, Hannah reminds us she's with us, in a digital kind of way.

"Um . . . ahh . . . you're adopted?" Hannah interrupts my side conversation with Everett. She still has a shade of shock on her face, which I assume is a reaction to the adoption talk. She probably thinks I feel terrible and I don't want her to feel terrible because she thinks I do. I offer an observation to get us both back on track to the trio in question.

"I am soooo lucky to have you helping me with this Hannah. It's OK. You are helping, and it's OK. What else did you find out about them?" This gets Hannah out of sad mode and back into action mode.

"I can't track them back any further than their arrival in the U.S., under the names Ira Roman, Kan Roman, and Sam Roman," Hannah says. "Despite their thriving house calls medical practice, they are not licensed to practice medicine in the U.S. They are frauds."

"I knew there was something wrong with them from the first time I laid eyes on those three. Mom and Dad didn't listen. They just didn't listen to me," Amanda says. "From under which rock did Sam, Ira, and Kan crawl and what do they want from my sister?" Amanda takes another swig of her drink.

"I'll get to the bottom of it all," Hannah reassures.

"But for now, here's your big choice to make, Alexis," Hannah pauses, leaning into her phone, so we see nothing but her pretty petite face looking very serious, framed within the phone's screen, on top of our Mexican table.

"Do you want them deported?" Hannah asks.

"Do I want who deported?" I ask, not sure if I'm following her.

"Drs. Roman, Roman, and Roman. Do you want them deported? I discovered that they have long, long, long overstayed their travel visas and have been in the U.S. illegally for like, thirteen years!" Hannah pulls back away from her phone. She reclines in her chair, petting her cat Dragon, who is comfortably curled up on Hannah's lap. "One phone call, one online anonymous tip, from you to ICE, and it's done!" she laughs a menacing laugh.

"You're kidding, right?" I ask. Visions of a horrible Immigration and Customs Enforcement raid, tearing a young family apart come to my mind.

"Who's kidding?" Hannah demands, sticking her face close into the phone again. She's a talking rectangle. "This isn't some innocent family seeking a life free of war, or political persecution, or something. These people have been drugging you since you were three years old!"

"Are they still being held at Norfolk County Correctional?" Amanda asks.

"Yep. One phone call, Alexis. Just one tip that they can quickly verify, and ICE will pick them up from the local police," Hannah sits away from the phone again, petting her cat, with a deep-thought look on her face.

"So, these criminals were the people who were hurting you? And you can have them potentially taken out of the U.S. before, or just as, you return to the U.S.?" Everett asks.

"Yep!" Amanda answers on my behalf.

"What's there to think about?" Everett asks me.

"What's there to think about?" Amanda echoes.

I shrug my shoulders and give Hannah a nod, signaling my agreement.

"Done! I'm texting you a link right now," Hannah says. "It will open up to the anonymous tip form. I've filled out everything about the Romans for you. You don't need to fill out the part that asks for your info. Just leave it blank. It's fine. ICE will still accept it. And they will act on it, we hope."

"It's an anonymous tip form, but they ask for info on the person submitting?" Everett questions.

"Yes," Hannah confirms.

"Because . . . ?" Everett questions again.

". . . because it's the government? I don't know." Hannah is getting a little annoyed with Mr. Logic.

"I've set this up on a temporary virtual private network so they can't track the IP address it's coming from. Just review, answer their—*Are you a human visitor?*—question and hit submit."

The ding alerts me to the arrival of Hannah's text. I open the link. Wow. That's a lot of info about Sam, Ira, and Kan, and their suspected violations.

"And . . . how did you get this much data on these Drs. Roman, Roman and Roman?" Everett asks Hannah.

"Alexis, I permit you to clue him in," Hannah permits.

"White hat bug bounty?" I ask, confirming. She nods in affirmation.

"I'm signing off now. Physics test tomorrow. A test you will miss, Alexis," Hannah informs me.

"It's OK," I respond. The importance of my academic performance has taken a back seat, something I thought would never happen.

I pull the phone closer to me and review the Homeland Security Investigations form again. I answer the simple math question at the bottom of the form, which is supposed to prove I am a human. OK. Maybe I'm a different breed of human but I can still do math. I place my right index finger, the same one that I accidently cut in the lab just three days ago, on the submit button. I press. My part is done. It's in ICE's hands now.

A different breed of human, I think again. That's a possibility. Maybe that's what I am. Why not? I think of canines and the vast differences in breeds amongst just domesticated dogs. Yes. I'm just a different breed. Maybe

I'm a greyhound, and Everett's a great dane, and Amanda a saluki, and Hannah a poodle. But then again, humans have basically genetically engineered domestic dog breeds.

Well, then, who engineered me? My mind is about to drift further from this mining bar in Naica to explore the possibilities, but then, Everett jumps in with a question.

"White hat bug bounty. So she's that good?" Everett asks, pulling me back to my current reality.

"Yep," I respond.

"She's a haaaaackeeer . . ." Amanda sings out the last word.

"I think she can hack into almost anything, but only wants to do it for good," I feel the need to clarify, so Everett doesn't get the impression my best friend is a criminal.

"I'd consider hacking into Drs. Roman's private info, in order to protect you, in the *for good* category . . . I guess?" Amanda taunts. "But only if I temporarily ignore the bad thing you did—potentially getting me fired as Dr. Collins's research assistant."

"Thanks," flows from my lips to Amanda's ears. "Hannah nailed a bug for Facebook but said identifying two vulnerabilities on the U.S. Department of Defense's network was more fun and paid better," I inform Everett.

Amanda kicks me under the table. I look at her. Then Everett does the same.

"What?" I snap. Everett nods his head towards the seat across the table, which had been empty the last time I looked at it. Woah—it's Ikal. How does he keep showing up without detection? Looking at his face, my mind races back to what I experienced in the Impossible Triangle when I was in the far reaches of the crystal caves, by the red whirlpool. I was falling out of Ikal's mouth in a gravity free environment and then I fell back into it again. The sharp chills going up and down my spine resume.

"Surprised to see me?" he asks. The way he's looking at me, I honestly don't know if he's asking me about seeing him here, in the bar, or seeing him in my weird Impossible Triangle. I'm searching for an answer. It's silent at the table. Neither Amanda nor Everett offers a response. As I stare at Ikal, wondering what to say, his lips morph into square cement walls. It makes his otherwise handsome face look monstrous. These are the cement wall lips I saw on his face in the Impossible Triangle. I close my eyes and shake my head, quickly. When I open my eyes, his face looks normal again. He raises an eyebrow and looks at me in a way that says, *Well?* It's a binary question. Am I surprised to see him or not. I toss a mental coin. It lands on no.

"No." I say.

Ikal moves his hand from his pocket to the table. There's a clank sound.

It's the sound of a small hard object hitting the wooden surface of the table. Moving his hand away, he reveals it.

"Surprised to see this?" he asks, his eyes darting between my face and the red crystal he placed on the table. I don't have to ponder my response, or flip a mental coin on this one.

The word, "Yes," just jumps out of my mouth.

He makes a motion with his hand that just placed the rock on the table. The motion is a *give me* signal.

My hand goes into my pocket. I retrieve it and place it on the table, next to his. They are about the same size, shape, and shine. How did Ikal get a sample?

"Dragon's tail!" Everett jumps forward and grabs the one I just put down on the table. Dragon's tail, that's the funny way he had described what he saw as a shimmering red band of something that led from the lightning shaped crack in the crystal cave, all the way to the red whirlpool that only I was able to explore.

"Red selenite?" Everett proposes.

"That's certainly what it looks like. I wasn't aware that there was red selenite here at Naica," Amanda looks up to Ikal. "Is there?"

"Apparently so," he responds. "For those who can venture deep enough to find it."

Amanda's two accusatory index fingers come out, pointing each at me and at Ikal. She interrogates us, as though her hands were locked and loaded. She looks to me first, left barrel pointed.

"You took a sample, and didn't tell us? You didn't tell Dr. Collins! At least we could have offered her the potential of some new findings, as a reward for the risk of your ventures through the lightning crack. How did you sneak that out? When were you going to tell us? Would you even have told us, if this guy hadn't popped up out of nowhere again?" She turns to Ikal, with her right barrel.

"And you! We know how she got the sample. And how did you?" Amanda demands.

Everett is inspecting my selenite in his hand, now with a magnifying glass. Ikal picks up his red selenite.

"This," Ikal tosses the red crystal up and catches it in his palm repeatedly as he speaks. "This has been in my family for generations, in fact for thousands and thousands of years. My ancestors, the people who were here before the European explorers came, we were keepers of these, what you call samples," he says.

"I don't suppose your ancestors did any lab work on these?" Everett asks. "Because, there's something more here than just red selenite. It's hard to tell with a standard magnifying glass. That Raman spec would have been useful right now."

"Hmmm . . . what would you do without technology Everett? Nothing. You could do nothing," Ikal says in a voice that's more intimidating than I've heard from him.

"If I didn't have technology, I would invent it," Everett responds, totally unfazed.

"Without technology, you would know nothing," Ikal repeats like he's spitting on Everett's face, without the spit though.

"Technology lets us prove things to each other, instead of just saying *trust me.* So, Ikal, can we trust you?" Everett stares down Ikal, who turns away and shifts his gaze to me.

"Tell me, Alexis. Are you Native American?" Ikal asks.

"Quite the opposite," I respond. "Almost literally, the opposite. Like, the other side of the globe opposite. I'm from Central Asia," I reveal. With my right hand, I gather my long, straight black hair, and drape it in front of my shoulder. "But I was cast as Pocahontas in my elementary school's stage production of the Disney classic."

"Am I supposed to be impressed?" Ikal asks, disappointment on his face.

"I'm sort of impressed," Everett offers, smiling at me. OK. That's sweet. I can't help but smile back at him. I'm kicked under the table by Amanda again. What, was I being too high-school girlish with Everett? She nudges me, signaling to look back at Ikal.

"Why?" Amanda questions Ikal. "Why were your people the keepers of this red selenite?"

Ikal nods towards Everett. "Looks like he's going to get you some answers, technically speaking, once you return to your labs in the U.S. Especially now that you know of this thing's existence." Ikal rolls the red crystal around in his large palm. He moves his intense gaze to me, "But, Alexis, you weren't going to share it with them were you? You were going to keep that all to yourself. Why?"

I don't know the answer to this. Yes, I grabbed a sample. I broke off a small piece of red selenite that was jutting out of a wall behind me, when I was standing on the edge of the red whirlpool. I did this carefully, out of view of my helmet cam. I hid the sample well, first inside the glove of my Starliner spacesuit. Then, when we got out of the crystal cave and into the tent to get changed out of our spacesuits and LCGs, back into our jeans and t-shirts, I snuck it into my mouth. I knew my desire to hide that rock would force me to literally keep my mouth shut, as I got scolded by the team for not following protocol and *endangering my life and the lives of others.* I think they just wanted to make me feel more guilty than I was already feeling. All I knew was that I had to have that sample. It called out to me. Other than keeping it on my person at every moment since I acquired it, I really didn't have a plan for it.

I look at the two red rocks, held by the two men, Everett and Ikal. It hits me.

"There's life in it," I whisper. That's all I know, and I don't know how I know.

Ikal's face lights up. His lips part wide, showing off his very white, toothy grin.

"May I?" he asks me, pointing at my glass still full of 100 Años.

I move my glass in his direction. Ikal picks it up, moves it towards his face. He tilts his head up and back, and pours the tequila down his throat. I see his lips turn into a square made of cement again, like I had seen in the Impossible Triangle. At this moment, I am living the memory. I'm half here and half there. There, in my blue Starliner spacesuit, being pulled back down by gravity past Ikal's cement lips and down into his throat. As I start my fall down the tunnel again, I look back up to the cement wall opening. Metal doors slam shut. Once again, I hear the pull of heavy chains and a padlock locking and I'm locked in the tunnel that is Ikal's throat.

With the sound of a clunk I'm pulled back into this moment in the bar when Ikal slams the empty tequila glass onto the table.

A moment of silence. Then come a clink.

The sound of a set of large rusty keys falling from Ikal's hand into the empty tequila glass. My eyes move from the keys in the glass up to Ikal's face, which looks totally normal again. Raul may have banned me from ever going underground in Naica again, but Ikal has just offered me the keys to the kingdom.

"The Robin Hole," I say.

He nods approvingly.

The Impossible Triangle was showing me that Ikal would lead me to the Robin Hole. There is something there for me.

"Good girl," he says.

I grab the keys. They're in my palm now. Ikal grabs my hand, pries my palm open and takes the keys back. He wags a finger at me. With his very real fleshy lips he informs me.

"I am your escort on this escapade."

11

DOWN THE ROBIN HOLE

Heavy metal doors behind thick chains, secured by padlocks stand between me and the 2,000 foot descent back into the Naica cave network. The doors are an industrial, heavy-duty version of a storm cellar entrance back at home. Ikal's flashlight is attached to his cargo pants. He said we are minimizing the chance of being detected out here by keeping the artificial light off and benefitting from the moonlight. I agree. The full moon provides ample light for us to see the cement walls that mark the entrance to the Robin Hole. Earth's natural satellite seems to provide more light tonight in Naica than I remember it offering back home in Massachusetts.

Down here, at the bottom of the desert valley, a crazy wind is blowing. My black hair, a few shades darker than the dark of the moon lit desert night, is whipping around my face and I forgot my hair elastic.

"Here," Amanda hands me hers. "You'll need it more than I will." Now her caramel curls are swirling around her face.

"It probably won't be windy down there," I say, declining her offer.

"Yeah, but do you really want your hair hanging like a mop around your face for 2,000 feet on your way down?" big sis asks. She's right. I grab the hair elastic and strap my straight thick strands back into a ponytail.

"Are your hair needs taken care of, Everett?" Ikal asks Everett, dripping with something like sarcasm, but I can't quite place it. Maybe it's the local version of mock and irony.

"Oh yes. Quite. And yours?" Everett responds, playing Ikal's game.

OK. I'll join in. "Mine too. Quite, quite."

I tap my pocket to confirm I've got my test tube with me. A hair tie and a test tube is all I need for a science expedition.

I look at Ikal, flicking my ponytail back with one hand and opening my other hand towards him. "Keys?"

Ikal reaches into his back pocket and pulls out one singular key. It's shiny and looks new. It's entirely unlike the rusty keys on the clunky old keychain he had tossed into the tequila glass back in the bar less than an hour ago. He tosses the lone shiny key to me.

I catch.

I feel the cut. It's not a hurt. It's a sensation.

I feel myself bleed.

I open my palm.

Ikal steps forward to see it. A broad smile and look of approval light up his face.

In my palm is the shiny key, which I now notice has a razor sharp edge. It's partially covered in my crystal blood. Amanda and Everett simultaneously step up closer and flank me.

"What are you doing?" Amanda barks at Ikal.

"You cut her on purpose," Everett doesn't quite accuse but more condemns, as he takes a step towards Ikal. It's the first sign of anger I've seen in him. That's intense. Controlled. Everett pauses. I can see him almost pulling the anger back into himself. He takes another step forward, minus the anger, towards Ikal and resumes. "You knew."

"How did you know?" Amanda demands of Ikal.

Ikal slowly moves towards me and gently places his large palm under my bleeding hand.

"I didn't know for sure. I suspected. I had to have proof, before I let you in, before we send you down there," Ikal whispers.

I repeat Amanda's question, suspecting Ikal will respond to me. "How did you know?" I ask, matching his whisper. He doesn't respond.

Now comes my offering. I tilt my hand a bit, letting one drop of my blood fall into his palm. It beads up like a diamond droplet on his cocoa colored skin.

"Creation and evolution. Evolution of the human species," now he's talking. "This has been in the legends, the legends of the ancients. The ancients and the planet have been waiting." Ikal darts his eyes between the drop of blood in his palm and my face. "Humans came to be and have survived on this planet only because they evolved.

You ask me, how did I know? About you? And what you are? I know that you are the next wave of evolution."

"Evolution, like Darwinian evolution? Natural selection? In other words, I'm still a mutant?" I gasp. I grew up thinking I was a mutant because of the F9 genes on my X chromosomes which caused my alleged hemophilia. But—I'm still a mutant! Why am I disappointed? I feel like I'm back where I started. I'm different totally due to a random roll of the genetic dice, again?

"Maybe you've hit the mother lode of mutations," Amanda speculates.

"The crystal blood," Ikal watches my drop of blood roll around in his palm. He holds it up to the moon, which lights up the sparkles in the translucent liquid. "The ancients didn't know exactly how it would change the human. My great grandmother told me and only me. She was the only knowledge keeper on this continent then. Following her death, now I am the only one here. The legend has been passed down, as far as we can trace back, 40,000 years. She told me that during my lifetime, one would come. One person with the crystal blood would cross my path, here, in and around these caves. I am placed here for a reason. When I saw your biometrics in the crystal cave, I knew. It's you."

"This is getting a little too legendary for me. Can we get back on the mutation and evolution track?" Everett requests.

Amanda jumps in, mimicking what was Ikal's all-too-serious voice, lowering her pitch to match his baritone with, "When I saw your biometrics in the crystal cave, I knew. It's you." With that out of the way, she returns to her own speaking voice, "She's so important to you, but you basically tossed a razor blade into her hand."

I hold up the key, pointing to the blade along its side. I also hold up my hand that had caught the key, showing Ikal where the cut used to be.

"Good thing I heal quickly. What if you had been wrong?" I challenge him.

"I wasn't wrong," Ikal says.

Legends, evolution, creation, I toss it all out of my mind and get myself closer to the padlock. I don't want to hear a story. I want proof.

Hopping up on top of the four foot tall cement wall, I land on the metal doors. Oops. That was loud. The sound of my pounce on metal reverberates through the valley. Kneeling down to grab the padlock that secures together two ends of a heavy chain, I insert the shiny razor-key into the hole. It doesn't go in. A closer look, and it's obvious. The key's pattern doesn't even visually match the lock's.

I stand. Towering over Ikal from above, I demand, "Where's the real key, Ikal?"

He tosses up the rusty old keychain that he taunted me with at the bar earlier this evening, "It's the one with the cross shaped ward on the bit."

I kneel back down to the padlock and grab it. I try it. The key goes in, but it won't turn. I try again to turn it. Nothing. The wind intensifies, kicking up sand which gets into my eyes. Wiping the sand from my eyelashes, I look at the keys, the padlock and Ikal. I pull the key back out and hold it up.

"Ikal, where's the real key?" I demand.

"That's the one! Just turn it harder," he says.

I look at him. My throat starts to tighten. It comes with a feeling of anxiety, a feeling like I can't breathe, like someone else, not me, has control over my next inhale and exhale. I know this feeling. It's what I felt when Drs. Roman would lie directly to my face about needing the clotting factor IX injections.

"You're lying!" I say through a muted scream.

Everett climbs up next to me, motioning for the key. I toss it to him. He inserts it. The lock won't turn. Everett eyes the other keys, studying their patterns in relation to the lock. "This whole thing has been a sham." He jumps down off the metal doors, landing in front of Ikal. Everett grabs Ikal's collar. "You didn't have the key to begin with. You're a con. This whole story, the legends of 40,000 years, it's all a con."

"The only thing I've conned you about is, in fact, the key. And she doesn't need it," Ikal says removing Everett's hands from his shirt and straightening out his collar.

I feel an expansion in my throat. I feel like my throat is wider than my head, nearly out to my shoulders. I put my hands on my neck. Physically, nothing has changed. But it feels lite and open, with a warm tingling sensation, like how sunlight feels on skin on a warm day. My entire body relaxes. I feel like I can breathe a thousand breaths in a moment. It is the opposite of what I felt earlier when I knew he lied.

I crouch down, putting one of my hands on the body of the padlock and the other on its shackle. When I tried this earlier today, before we went into the crystal cave, I was able to bend, but not break the lock. Now. I bend it further, breaking it. It opens. No key. Done. Ikal was right.

"Alexis . . ." Amanda says. She just witnessed this, while the men were still staring each other down.

Releasing both ends of chain from the shackles of the lock, I toss one end of the chain to the ground. The rest of it follows with a clank, clank, clank, as each link hits the edge where metal door meets cement wall, until the chain, in its entirety, drops to the sandy desert ground with a thud.

I repeat this three more times, removing all four chains.

The industrial storm cellar doors are ready for me. I lift one door open and then the other. They creak.

I hop down from the cement wall and into the square area within its boundary. My feet are on the narrow dirt surface that surrounds the Robin Hole. Amanda, still on the outside of the cement wall, leans forward and looks down.

"It's like a wishing well! No. No. It's like a black hole. And you're standing on the event horizon!" she observes.

It looks black to me too, with the exception of some faint light at the very, very, very end of the 2,000 feet. That must be crystal down there because it's the only thing that glows for me.

Ikal comes up beside me, aims his flashlight down and turns it on. It looks like the inside of a cement tunnel, maybe eight feet in diameter. Ikal moves the light around so we can see the Robin Hole's walls from different angles. Yep, looks like the same tunnel I was climbing through in the Impossible Triangle when I was back at the red whirlpool.

"Ikal, where's the gear?" Everett asks. "I thought you said it would be just under the metal doors, between the cement walls and the hole."

"What gear?" Ikal feigns ignorance and fools no one.

"What? Was I in a parallel universe?" Everett snaps. "The mountaineering gear that you said would be here, so Alexis can get down there. You know, ropes, wires, pulleys, some kind of gear here to support her." Oh, there's that anger again. Angry Everett, didn't think I'd like that, but I sort of do. "Didn't we say she would go down the same way the researchers did last time?"

"She doesn't need it," Ikal says. Amanda grabs Ikal's flashlight and inspects the Robin Hole more closely.

"2,000 feet. That's like more than the height of One World Trade Center. This is stupid. We can't do this," Amanda declares pulling out of the plan we hatched while walking from the bar to here.

"WE aren't doing this. I am! We all agreed," I tell her.

"Maybe I had too much to drink. Maybe I'm sobering up. How could we have agreed to this?" Amanda shakes her head.

"The cave that is her destination is only 1,500 feet down, not 2,000," Ikal says dismissive of Amanda's concern.

"Yeah. But that doesn't change the fact that she would still fall 2,000 feet!" Amanda retorts.

"Why did they call it the Robin Hole and not the Rabbit Hole?" I ask, admitting, "I sort of feel like Alice in Wonderland right now."

But, unlike Alice, I jump in like Spiderman. Minus the webs.

"No!" and "Don't!" Amanda and Everett simultaneously shout.

Each of my four limbs spread out and make contact with the cylindrical tunnel wall of the Robin Hole. This is how I hold myself up. Instead of webs coming out of my wrists, I have hand stilts that extend my reach the eight foot diameter of the hole.

While still in the bar, I had recognized something quite familiar in the Starliner blue colored wooden chairs. The legs of the chairs looked just like the hand stilts, made of blue painted wood, that I had in my hands in the Impossible Triangle while in the crystal cave. Ikal talked to the bar owner and got him to contribute one chair for our cause. I broke off the bottom part of the chair's legs and voila! In the Robin Hole, I'm eight feet in diameter. While we were walking out to the Robin Hole, Amanda and Everett had questioned why I had two L shaped chair leg parts with me. I told the curious duo the blue wooden parts might come in handy. Indeed, they did.

Stretching out, my hands and feet hold me firm about ten feet down from the top. I am now Vitruvian Woman—for real—not just on the screen of my Impossible Triangle.

"See you at the top, ASAP!" I announce as I move myself down the cement tunnel in something like a four legged run, keeping at least two limbs firmly on the tunnel's wall. I accelerate as my focus sharpens on the luminescence at the bottom of the tunnel. I look back up and down again. I'm about halfway to my destination.

My mind jumps to the recent memory of how my throat felt constricted upon hearing Ikal's lie about the key. Memory after memory of what I now know to be lies in my life runs through my mind like panels in a graphic novel. With the view of each panel, I feel my throat constrict right now, in this moment, in the living memory. The panels of Drs. Roman and my parents imploring me to be careful because of my hemophilia are interspersed with some surprises. There's one where in a silly childhood disagreement, Amanda, in a moment of anger, tells me she wishes I were not her sister. I had believed her at the time. But, my throat, oh my throat restricting is now welcome! I realize now it was a lie. There's the one from this summer when I asked Hannah if she was developing a crush on Josh and she denied it. My throat tightens with pain. She must have been lying, to herself first and foremost.

Images of moments of my life that were flooded by lies recede. My throat relaxes. A different kind of panel appears. It's Alina and Dale. They tell me they love me. My throat expands in lightness and tingles. Truth. I realize my four-legged run has slowed to a turtle's pace. I stop. I rest within this truth. Alina and Dale weren't lying about that part. A tear drops from my eye. It descends. I hear it land with a soft plop.

Accelerating, I chase the tear down towards my destination. Still on all fours, I feel like an animal. I feel like a nocturnal hunter. My hearing is heightened. Maybe it's just the cylindrical tunnel, but I sense I can measure the distance to the bottom through echolocation, just from the sound of the plop from my tear. I stop moving. I need to confirm.

"Well, here I am, deepest wishing well in the world," I hear my words come back at me in two waves. The first bounces off a surface maybe fifty feet away, and the second from about 500 feet. The closer one is my destination, the cave entrance according to Ikal. It's a landing along one side of the Robin Hole.

Aiming for the landing, I let go. Retracting my limbs from the cement wall, I point my feet down. Just for fun, I do a few aerial somersaults on my way down.

Whoosh, whoosh, whoosh, and I land at the cave entrance.

Under my feet, the surface is covered in crystal. I take a few steps into the cavern. The space is small, hardly a chamber. I see a passageway that I need to explore. Before I move on, I pull out the red laser pointer Ikal had given me during our walk from the bar to the top of the Robin Hole. Pointing it up, I press the button. The laser beam shoots up. My neck angles back at nearly 90° and I focus on the red point, as far as I can see. The red beam reaches up into the night sky. I move about a foot to my right. And wow! There's the full moon. It's literally the light at the end of the tunnel. If I went no further into the cave, my four-legged animalistic 1,500 foot decent is already worth it, just for this one sight.

They signal down to me with their green laser pointer. They've got the message that I've reached the cave. Onward.

There's one narrow passageway off this small chamber. I enter. It's so narrow, only about five feet wide. It goes as far as I can see. I follow it. The walls are covered in white crystals that are unlike the giant pillars we saw in the crystal cave. These are roundish, look more like corals and they are mostly the size of cauliflower or broccoli florets. I inspect. It's aragonite. The last time a human being was down here, they wanted to pursue this tunnel, but they couldn't. It was too risky.

I run. I run. I run. And I run some more. Looking at my watch, it's been about fifteen minutes. I don't know what my pace is. I just know it's beyond fast, even by Olympic sprinter standards. I don't know how far I've come. I haven't felt much of an up or downward grade, so the passageway is horizontally pretty flat. Its walls are still covered in the white cauliflower like aragonite. I keep going.

Something just changed. I can feel a breeze on my face, and I know it's not caused by my acceleration against the air in the tunnel. This is something else, more like wind. As it intensifies, it tugs and yanks me forward. It feels like I'm inside a vacuum cleaner's tube. It's so loud. Sounds like a train is moving in parallel with me, but I know it's not. The only things in motion here are me and the wind.

I stop pumping my arm and leg muscles, the human mechanisms which had been propelling my run. I don't need to move myself at all. It's simply pulling me forward. The force changes from a monolith of wind to a braid with multiple strands, each strand yanking each of my limbs in a different direction. It lifts me up off the ground. I pull my body tightly into a ball to try to maintain control. I'm spinning through the air like a well kicked soccer ball.

Faster. Faster. Faster.

Like a bullet, I'm released from the tunnel into a large cavern. Its walls glow like moonlight, softly illuminating the space. I wonder if others would also see this illumination, or if it would look dark to them. As I look down, I see a calm, still body of water about one story below me. Turquoise blue. Not red like the one in the crystal cave earlier today. It's beautiful, more beautiful. I look up and around. I'm exactly in the center of this large round space.

The wind ceases. My spinning slows and stops. My body stretches out and for a few seconds I feel like I'm in zero gravity until—the instant when—I'm falling.

The calm turquoise waters below me morph into an accelerating whirlpool. Did the wind just move into the water? It's pulling me down. Is it the whirlpool's force, or simply gravity? Probably both.

Here I go!

I straighten my body out, feet down, ready for a pencil dive. Seconds later, my toes are in the water in the vortex of the whirlpool. My legs twist tightly together and my arms fly up into the air. I'm spinning like an ice skater doing the climactic spin of her routine. At eye level, it's a wall of water around me, as I'm pulled deeper into the vortex, now up to my waist in water. And—I'm under.

I keep my eyes open underwater. The whirlpool continues to pull me down and I can't see beyond the swirling wall of the vortex.

Down. Down. Down.

I'm not panicking. Remembering my swim in the Charles River the morning after I first saw my crystal blood, I know. I don't need to inhale air underwater. I don't know why that is. Maybe I'm a mutant amphibian who should have been born in the Devonian period. I'm pulled down further and further.

Then, the force of the downward pull subsides. There's an opening in the middle of what looks like the rocky bottom of an ocean floor. I flip, diving down with my arms and head leading, my legs behind me. I swim through the opening.

I'm in a huge chamber. Covering the bottom surface of the space is a layer of rolling hills that look like corals. Each hill is topped by obelisk-like crystals. All clustered together, the obelisks look like buildings in a cityscape. The hills are white, the obelisks transparent, and the turquoise water is the underwater sky. It's brilliant. I feel like I'm seeing beauty for the first time. My heart tingles.

I swim further down to inspect it closely. The hills are actually made of aragonite. They are giant versions of the cauliflower shaped crystals that lined the tunnel which led me here. The building-like clear crystals are quartz and shaped just like the ones in the crystal cave. These are simply smaller versions.

Rays of light are shining down from the hole at the top of the chamber through which I entered this place. As the light hits the quartz obelisks, little sparks bounce off, dance, and play around in the water. I wonder if anyone other than me could see these sparks.

Hundreds of these quartz cities on aragonite hilltops surround me in every direction. I swim from one to the next, to the next. I feel like I'm in a magic fairy garden. It feels bittersweet because I want all of reality to be this beautiful, this enchanted. I feel like I'm crying, but in this water, I can't tell. I touch my eyes. If I have added a tear drop to the water surrounding me, I hope it's bonding me eternally with this place.

There's one city on a hilltop across from me that has a purple hue at the base of the quartz structures. As I swim up to it, the purple color becomes more saturated. One of the many rays of light that beam down the hole at the top of the chamber becomes brighter and moves in my direction. Like a spotlight, it shines on the purple hilltop.

A bubble emerges. And then another, and another. Dozens of them are floating up. Some keep rising, others pop. Tiny sparkles of light are bouncing off the points and edges of the quartz structures. One of these sparkles collides with a bubble. Now the sparkle floats inside the bubble and morphs. A clear, perfectly round pod forms around the bubble which holds the sparkle in its center, making concentric spheres. The sparkle's light is somewhat softened now, within the pod, which thickens to a point where it looks like semi-opaque glass.

Several other similar collisions occur between bubble and sparkle. The same process is happening in each one. The space above this purple hilltop is being populated by sparkles, inside of bubbles, inside of pods. They look like little floating snow globes.

All around me, in waves, other hilltops light up with a faint purple hue. Then, the color intensifies into the same saturated purple I see at the hilltop I've been staring at in wonder. They light up like a time lapsed video of a field of purple flowers opening to bloom. Bubbles, sparkles and collisions rise up to fill the chamber. They emerge in groups like flocks of birds rising off the ground into flight.

The colors are brilliant. White and purple, dotted with translucent light, against a turquoise sky.

The soft popping sound of the bubbles that burst fills my ears. More of them remain intact. They float up and around.

From the pocket of my jeans, I pull out the capped test tube.

I need a sample. I have to find a pod, containing a bubble, containing a sparkle, that is small enough to fit in here and hopefully not burst, or pop, or break.

This is the reason I'm down here.

But at this very moment, I don't need a reason to be here at all. It just feels right and natural. It feels like home. I could simply remain, if it weren't for a few certain humans waiting for me at the top of the Robin Hole.

I twist open the test tube's cap. Over to my left is a quartz city atop an aragonite hilltop that is one of the smallest. The bubbles emerging from it are also smaller. I observe in wonder as a sparkle collides with a bubble and enters it. A pod forms around the bubble and encapsulates it. Mine!

I run the open test tube through the water and towards the bubble. I aim so that the pod will go directly into the test tube without making contact with its edges. I don't want to harm it.

And—I've got it! I fasten the cap back on. My test tube is full of water, with one beautiful specimen inside of it. One. Only one. I wish I had brought two test tubes. What was I thinking? I need to get this into a lab, as soon as I can.

I swim up towards the opening at the top of the cavern. Part of me doesn't want to leave. I look back down. I wish I could have a picture of this for Amanda, for Everett, and—strangely—for Ikal. I wouldn't have gotten here without him. I will describe it to them in such abundant detail that they will feel like they saw it.

Turning back up, towards what I assume is north, or at least surface, I swim to the opening through which light is shining. I enter the upper body of water. It's calm and still. No whirlpool. No vortex. I can see beyond the water's surface to the cave's ceiling. That will lead me to the aragonite covered horizontal passageway and to the Robin Hole for my vertical ascent.

As I swim towards the water's surface, I feel it. There's a buzzing sound. The Impossible Triangle forms and creates an image.

The image I see is a large white octagonal tent, with a conical roof. The tent's exterior walls are decorated in turquoise and gold patterns. This tent looks familiar. Where have I seen it before? I'm staring at it, processing, trying hard to remember. I don't. I can't.

The tent is fading away. I don't know what or where it is. I need to remember! Please don't fade from my sight yet! But something else is now appearing.

It's the face of a woman. Her coloring and features are not unlike mine. She's wearing a pointy silver headdress, embroidered in gold, in the shape of a Hershey's kiss. The wide base of the Hershey's kiss hat is made of white fur and rests upon her forehead. She smiles at me and hums a lullaby.

I remember! I remember where I've seen her before. How could I not have seen her face in my memory for so many long years?

I want to touch her. I want to be in that reality where she is, but I'm not. I'm still here in the water, and I can only see her on the 2D screen. I move my head forward, into the Impossible Triangle, hoping to experience being with her in a 3D reality. I swim into the screen. It retreats further towards the surface of water. I swim towards it, chasing it. As I near the surface of the water, the Impossible Triangle dissolves into the micro-waves and ripples that my movement has created in the previously still water. I rise above the surface and breathe in air.

The sensation of air in my lungs again feels exhilarating.

I look up. Back to the surface I go.

I know this just isn't possible, but Ikal seems happier to see me than Amanda and Everett combined. All three barrage me with questions as we walk back to town. My clothes are wet, cold at my joints, and feel frozen stiff onto my body everywhere else. Everett has given me his sweatshirt to wear. He has goosebumps along his arms, I assume due to the cold, as he wears just his goofy science t-shirt of the day. It's simply the sixth element. In the middle of the t-shirt, a rectangle has a large C in its center, a 6 at the top left corner, and the atomic weight of 12.011 is presented under the C. In big bold letters under that, are the words: *Carbon Based.*

The three of them have been taking turns carrying the sample. Carefully. Very carefully. I don't dare hold it in my hands because I'm shivering. We don't want the pod floating in its water inside the test tube to burst as a result of friction with the tube's walls.

Ikal stops walking. He holds the test tube up against the sky.

"Amanda, your turn," he says and he moves it in her direction. The little sparkle, inside the bubble, inside the pod, inside the test tube, twinkles like it could be one of the thousands of stars visible in the desert sky tonight.

Ikal turns to me. "The sample is yours. For your lab. Now. For me. Where is next?"

"Where is next? What do you mean?" I ask.

"Tikal? Caracol? Copán? Sayil?" He probes, naming some of the cities of ancient Mesoamerica. "You should know now. You have to tell me."

"None of the above. None of the above for me at least. I might be headed eastwards," I look to Amanda for a reaction. Nothing. She's poker faced. "I'm not clear on what you're looking for Ikal. But I . . ."

"What I'm looking for," Ikal cuts me off, pointing his index finger at me. "What I'm looking for is not the results of your lab work. I'm looking for the very source of creation. I believe that place is right around here, and accessible to me, not just to you." His finger moves in the direction of my heart and lands there with a little jab. I get chills up my spine as I recall my studies of the ancient Mayans who sacrificed humans to their gods by cutting out their hearts.

Get. Me. Out. Of. Here.

I move his finger off my heart, the heart I wish to keep inside my body.

"If you're looking for the very source of creation, I'm sure you can see it everywhere," I guide his index finger with mine, pointing at the stars and back down again to Earth in a full 360° circle. I want to distract him from the location he's asking me about. I don't want him following us. I tell him a tall tale, maybe taller than the ones told to him by his ancient ancestors. My tall tale has the foundation of evidence-based science.

"Ikal," I say. "Creation. Thanks to the Big Bang, it's everywhere."

12

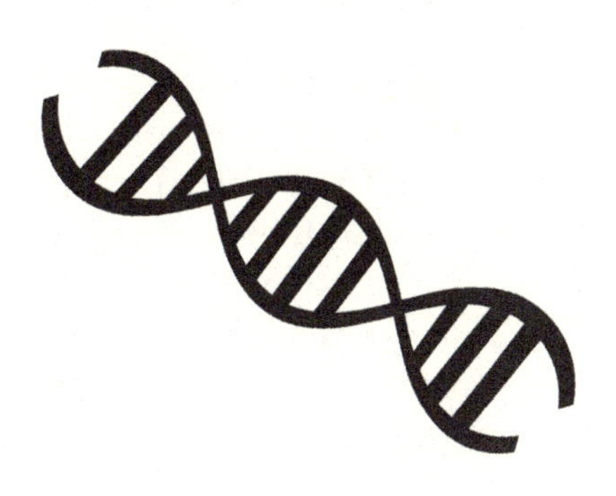

D • N/A

A double helix takes shape as the pencil glides across the paper. It's almost like Everett's hand has nothing to do with it. It's almost like the carbon artist's pencil is taking direction from the person on the other end of the telephone conversation from Everett. It's like Everett is just the middle man in this exchange. The incoming data from the phone enters Everett's brain, is translated, and comes out depicted as DNA on the paper.

"Uh huh . . . yeah . . . OK . . . huh? Oh . . . OK," Everett's end of the conversation is less informative to me than the image each stroke of the pencil reveals. I guess that's the point of images. I didn't know he could draw. I mean, really draw. His drawing is not cartoony and it's not a simple sketch. It also doesn't look like the computer generated images of DNA in my 9th grade biology book.

How would Michelangelo have drawn DNA, if they had known of DNA during the Renaissance? His hands are beautiful. Everett's that is, not Michelangelo's. Maybe Michelangelo's were too, but that is not what is in front of me now. It's like Michelangelo drew Everett's hands.

I make my eyes move from Everett's hands, to the image his hands produce. The shading and symmetry are perfect. It looks like the DNA is going to come off the page and become a 3D sculpture. If it did, it would be about the same size as the DNA sculpture that rests on top of the lab bench adjacent to the one we are at now.

We're in Dr. Collins's lab at New Mexico Tech. This is Amanda's university and she's hosting us here, unbeknownst to Dr. Collins. It's late and Dr. Collins and her crew have already finished their work day here analyzing the three samples they managed to get in the upper chamber of the crystal cave before I violated all safety protocols by entering the lightning shaped crack.

While Everett is receiving data about my sample, my crystal blood, from his friend at an MIT lab, Amanda is doing the same with a trusted colleague of hers down the hall. Redundancy. Only two data points instead of ten, or twenty, or thirty, but at least two is better than one, or none. We don't need any human error in trying to figure out what kind of human I am.

Redundancy is something we won't have, not yet at least, on the two items we discovered yesterday. Item one: the small chunk of red selenite from the previously inaccessible portion of the Cave of Crystals. Item two: the little sparkle, inside the bubble, inside the pod, inside a test tube, that is still intact after its long journey from Naica,

Mexico to Socorro, New Mexico, the home of New Mexico Tech.

The pod floats in its original waters in the test tube, against a backdrop of drab grey counters, cabinets, and equipment lit by fluorescent lights. This is a very far cry from the physical beauty of the place the pod came from, deep below the surface, with quartz cities on aragonite hilltops immersed in the turquoise blue water that is its sky. But I love this lab, and any other lab, no less than I love what I saw yesterday, the underwater secret garden. That's the best way I could sum it up for Amanda and Everett. It's an underwater secret garden. If these locations, the labs and the underwater secret garden, were living organisms, I think they would have the same genotype. The genes coding their purpose are coding them to be a source of creation and discovery. But they would have a different phenotype. Their physical expressions are totally different.

Right when we got to the New Mexico Tech lab this evening, I gently, carefully, took a small sample of the water from the pod's test tube, thinking maybe, just maybe, it will be like amniotic fluid and have some kind of microscopic organic material floating in the water that will tell us something about the pod and its contents. Amanda took the sample of this pod water and the red selenite to the diagnostics lab down the hall, along with a sample of my blood.

Everett now labels the base pairs on the DNA he draws as he mumbles *Uh huh* and *Yeah* many more times into the phone. Starting from the bottom rung of the DNA ladder, which attaches on each side to the sugar phosphate backbone, he's labeling the rungs with either A-T or C-G.

Why is he skipping a rung for every rung he fills in? Everything, every living thing's DNA is comprised of these same nucleotide base pairs, adenine which pairs with thymine and cytosine which pairs with guanine. Just these two pairs strung along the double helix are responsible for the astonishing variety of life.

I put my finger on the blank, unmarked rungs of the ladder and give Everett a quizzical look. I don't want to disturb his focus on the phone call and data download, but the immediacy of my question stomps on my patience.

Everett takes his pencil off the paper, leans back on his lab chair and looks up at me. Keeping the phone to his ear, he runs his fingers through his thick brown curls. He takes a slow steady breath and exhales before putting his carbon pencil back to paper. Everett swiftly fills in all the blank rungs of the ladder with N/A-N/A. N/A-N/A. N/A-N/A. N/A-N/A. Over and over and over again.

"What the heck?" I demand.

"N/A," he answers.

"I can read!" I say, my voice elevating.

He speaks into the phone, "Hey thanks Joel. I'll call you back." He puts the phone down.

"N/A. Not applicable. Not available. No answer. Take your pick. Any and all of these are appropriate," he sighs and hangs his head down. "I'm sorry I don't have the answer." He says, as though this were the first time in his life when he didn't have the answer, the right answer, to anything asked of him.

"I have extra, unknown, unidentifiable base pairs in my DNA?" I ask.

"Yes and No," he responds.

"Well that really clarifies things for me. Thanks," I snap.

Everett puts pencil to paper again. He's drawing out the structural formula of adenine, guanine, thymine, and cytosine. The four elements carbon, nitrogen, hydrogen and oxygen, which make up adenine, guanine, thymine and cytosine, some lines that connect them, and 2 in subscript are all he needs and uses in his diagrams.

"The yes part of my response addresses the fact that, yes, you have two extra sets of base pairs in your DNA," he says.

"Instead of four nucleotides, I have eight?" I say out loud. I didn't mean to say it out loud, since the math is so obvious, I don't want to come off as though I can't do 2 x 2.

"That doesn't exist! It doesn't exist in nature at least. Eight base pairs have only been synthetically produced in a lab," I say, " . . . not in nature."

Without taking his pencil, or his eyes off the paper, Everett responds, "You are standing here in front of me in this room." He looks up at me. "You exist and you are in nature."

"Human error! Who is this guy Joel who gave you this data anyway? He's in error. His equipment is in error." Phrases are shooting out of my mouth so fast, I think I'm turning into Amanda. Not knowing what I am made of is freaking me out.

I stop talking and calm myself. I look down at Everett's pencil.

"And, the no part of my response addresses the fact that, no, the extra sets of base pairs in your DNA are not unknown and unidentifiable, not completely at least. We've identified part of the structure and we're working on the rest," he says.

On a new, blank sheet of paper he makes a table with two columns and four rows. In the left column, in each row, he writes N/A^1, N/A^2, N/A^3, and N/A^4. In the corresponding column to the right, he draws part of a structural formula. Each diagram is different. Some of the bonds and elements he fills in and some he leaves blank. The elements here include carbon (C), nitrogen (N), hydrogen (H) and oxygen (O), just like he used for adenine, guanine, thymine, and cytosine. But here there's one more, silicon (Si).

"Silicon," I whisper.

With a boom the heavy lab door swings open 180° and smashes the wall it is hung upon.

Another boom and it slams shut again. OK. They need some door stoppers here. Other than that, this is a world-class research lab.

"Oh my gosh!!! Alexis!! You're, like, the first silicon-based complex organic life form!!!" Amanda screams and shrieks with joy. Well, I'm pleased I've made her happy today. She runs over and looks at Everett's drawing of my DNA.

"We just got the results on your blood test. Affirmative. Same results! You're the first silicon-based complex organic life form," she repeats.

"Complex being the operative word there," Everett chimes in.

Did he just insult me?

"I'd rather be complex, than a simpleton," I retort.

"Simple can be beautiful," Amanda observes.

"I mean. What I mean is . . ." Everett gets just those words out before Amanda's mouth starts firing away again.

"What he means is for example, one example, is diatoms, a simple, fairly common, single cell, naturally occurring algae that evolved all on its own with a silicon dioxide skeleton. But we don't know of any naturally occurring complex organism that combines silicon with carbon in a molecule," Amanda explains.

"Well, we don't know of any . . . naturally occurring complex organism that . . . on its own . . . makes silicon and carbon bonds," Everett clarifies. "Researchers at CalTech used directed evolution to coax heme proteins to form carbon-silicon bonds. But that's in a lab."

"Heme proteins?" I ask. "As in hemoglobin? As in blood? As in, they combined the red pigment that carries oxygen to the body with silicon? That's possible? Is that how my crystal blood carries oxygen in my body?"

I see two sets of shoulders shrugging, as Everett and Amanda give me a *Who knows?* through their body language.

"Directed evolution, that's like when they intentionally force mutations, in order to emulate the evolutionary process, right?" I ask.

"Correct." "Yep." The collegiate pair responds in unison.

"So if there's no naturally occurring organism that can do this on its own, without the aid of scientists, then did someone use directed evolution to genetically engineer me?" I pause.

My throat starts to tighten, like someone is strangling me. Sam, Ira, and Kan, their faces flash in and out of focus in my mind. I feel like I'm going to throw up. Am I a product of that evil trio? Are they my Frankensteins, and am I their monster?

"Oh no!!!!" I say.

"No. No. There's no evidence of that. No evidence to support that at all," Everett says, and gently puts his hand on my wrist. He places his three middle fingers on my radial artery. I think he is measuring my pulse. My focus on that and sixty seconds of quiet calm me. Everett takes his hand off my wrist and steps back.

"We don't know the answers yet. But we do know science and we do know that science is not at a point yet where it can create . . . you," Amanda says.

"It wasn't hemoglobin they used at CalTech," Everett clarifies. "They tried a whole bunch of heme proteins and found one heme protein, from Rhodothermus marinus that was able to create the carbon-silicon bonds. And it did so more efficiently than any synthetic technique. Rhodothermus marinus. It's from hot springs. In Iceland."

"Iceland?" I ask.

"So, you're making the Iceland part up, right?" Amanda asks.

"Why would I be making that up?" Everett questions.

"Jules Verne. In his book, Journey to the Center of the Earth. That's how they reached the center of the Earth, from Iceland," I say, thinking of the amazing things we've discovered, just a few thousand feet below the surface, let alone the center.

"We've just been relatively deep inside the Earth, and Alexis, the first complex silicon based life form we know of, seems quite comfortable there," says Amanda. "And this Rhodothermus marinus, which can also make silicon-carbon bonds is from Iceland where, at least fictionally, one can go even deeper into Earth than Alexis has."

"Hmmm. Interesting coincidence. But, no. I am not making it up. Look," Everett pulls something up on his phone and shows it to me. It's an article in *Astrobiology Magazine*. He reads, " . . . from Rhodothermus marinus, a bacterium from hot springs in Iceland."

"Weird," Everett says. "But hey, nature is weirder than anything we could invent." Looking back down at his phone, he says, "Take a look at what Prof. Frances Arnold, who led the research at CalTech said. She said, 'My feeling is that if a human being can coax life to build bonds between silicon and carbon, nature can do it too.'"

"Thank you. That makes me feel better," I say. This idea of nature creating weird things like me feels good and pushes the faces of Kan, Sam, and Ira further out of my head. I can stop thinking of them as my Dr. Frankensteins. I figure, "Well. Why not silicon, anyway? It's much more abundant on Earth than carbon."

"Exactly. Almost thirty percent of the Earth's crust is silicon," Amanda assures me.

"And carbon is only a fraction of one percent of the crust," Everett adds.

"It's just plain much more efficient for nature to use silicon instead of, or in addition to, carbon for life," Amanda declares. Together, Amanda and Everett are like parents consoling a young child. At this moment, I don't mind being on the receiving end of this.

Boom—the lab door flies open again.

"I just got the results from the red selenite and that . . . water sample. Anyone interested?" asks a disheveled student with a French accent.

A chorus of "Yes!" belts out of our mouths.

"That water, maybe it was saliva from her?" the student looks curiously upon me. "The DNA from the water is not exactly, but almost exactly, the same as the blood sample."

I grab Amanda by the arm and pull her aside, whispering, "Is he talking about the water from, you know, around the pod? And, you told him that was my blood? Can we trust him?"

"Yes and yes," Amanda answers before she pulls her arm out of my hand. "Anton's a friend. It's OK. Don't squeeze so hard. It hurts." She makes her way back over to Anton.

"How much *almost* the same?" she asks.

"Well, if we just look at the parts that are . . . normal. The segments of the DNA strand from the water that have the standard A-T G-C base pairs; they are 99.9 percent similar to the blood sample," Anton reveals.

"Astonishing," Everett utters.

"That's like, percentage wise, as similar as any two human beings are to one another," Amanda says, looking over at me.

Since all humans are 99.9 percent identical in their genetic makeup. If the DNA from the water surrounding the little pod is 99.9 percent similar to part of my DNA, then, is that little pod a lifeform, like me?

I look at Everett and Amanda. All three of us make a dash for the test tube. We halt before we crash into it. I'm thinking—*LOOK BUT DON'T TOUCH!* It's so delicate. Six eyes, in a semi-circle are staring at the test tube, in reverence.

Without taking my eyes off the pod, I ask Anton, "And what about the part of the DNA with the other two—unusual—base pairs?" I ask. No answer. I take my eyes off the test tube to look back at Anton. He's eyeing the DNA drawing and partially completed structural formulas of the four N/A nucleotides produced by Everett.

"I can't say how similar they are or are not. It looks like we know about as much as you do, and not more," Anton responds, tapping on the structural formulas drawn by Everett.

"And, the red selenite sample?" I ask. "Any organic material in there?"

"In fact, interestingly enough, yes. There was a little air pocket, and in it, we found some bacteria. Rhodothermus marinus," Anton says.

At the sound of those last two French accented words, Amanda and Everett turn away from the pod and let out a joint, "What?"

"What?" Anton asks back.

"That's the stuff that creates carbon-silicon bonds. Isn't that found only in Iceland?" I ask.

"No. It's found in geothermal habitats in other parts of the world too, like deep in the Pacific Ocean in hydrothermal vents. It is merely most accessible in Iceland because it's in a shallow hot spring at the surface," answers Anton.

"Alexis?" Everett sets up his question.

"Yeah?" I respond.

"You told Ikal last night that you were headed Eastward. Did you mean, North-Eastward?" he asks. "As in Iceland?"

"Yes and No," I say. It's my turn for cryptic responses because I have an answer he doesn't, for once.

"Touché," he says. His retort annoys me.

"Are you trying to impress me with your French? Or are you trying to impress Anton?" I ask.

"Everett will need a lot more French than that to impress Anton," Amanda snorts. She looks at me, "It's all about you baby. Go on."

"The yes part of my response addresses the fact that yes, I did mean North-Easterly. And the no part of my response addresses the fact that no, the actual destination is not Iceland," I say.

Everett has followed me and Amanda to Naica and to New Mexico Tech. Now, it seems he may be interested in following us further. I think for science, he would go anywhere on Earth and probably even beyond. Having spent several consecutive days with him, there's a part of me that wants two things. One, I would like it if he were following us, just—or at least, in part—because of me. Two, I would like to confront him and ask him to tell me the truth about his age. But if I did, and if he confirmed he actually is sixteen, then would that keep him from going with us on the next adventure, an adventure which may allegedly be too dangerous for mere minors? It sometimes is no fun living in a world made up of rules that are made up by people who think they know better, simply due to when they were born on the planet.

"Why are you following Amanda and me?" I have to ask, hoping that I'm part of the answer.

"Scientific discoveries with the girl with the crystal blood? Why wouldn't I?" he responds in questions and with a smile so subtle, I can barely call it a smile. I do interpret it as one though, because that's exactly what I want it to be.

I hope I'm not blushing. I can feel the blood rushing to my face. But wait. This is great. I can't blush. My blood isn't red. So, then I wonder if my cheeks look extra silvery or sparkly.

Amanda retrieves me from my thought path, as she declares, "Biz Qazaqstanğa baramız."

Furrowed brows on Everett's and Anton's faces indicate their confusion and a desire to understand what just came out of Amanda's mouth. I don't understand much Kazakh but I do know what she said.

I come to the aid of the confused, "We're off to Kazakhstan." I turn to Everett. "Care to come along for the ride?"

This morning, when I had a few moments alone with Amanda, I told her about the images I saw upon exiting the underwater secret garden at Naica, the images of the white tent and the woman wearing the Hershey's kiss shaped hat, who sort of looked like me. Amanda confirmed my hunch.

She told me, "I have seen that tent. I know that tent. I can take you to that tent."

13

YOUR YURT

I am falling.

The fall awakens me. I look around. It was the turbulence, which has roused a few other passengers out of their slumber. I'm seated between Amanda and Everett, who are both sleeping through this. The airplane lights are dimmed and most people are buried under their blankets during the overnight flight.

The airplane shakes some more, and then, the next drop in altitude awakens Amanda. The turbulence continues, but lessens in severity on our Aeroflot flight which, after a seven hour layover in Moscow, will take us to our destination city of Almaty in Kazakhstan. I think the slower, smoother tail end of this turbulence has rocked Amanda back to sleep. I'm wide awake, but I close my eyes shut in the hope that I will also doze off like everyone else around me.

A sudden sensation of extra pressure around my head and a buzzing sound that overpowers the consistent hum of the airplane startles me. I open my eyes. It's happening again, my Impossible Triangle, but this time, in public. Granted, most people in this public place have their eyes closed. It's floating in front of my face. My eyes dart around. Can anyone see this? The first time it happened, I was in Hannah's room and she was sleeping. The second time, in the Cave of Crystals at Naica, I had my spacesuit helmet and head cam on. Ikal and his friends back in the tent monitoring the cameras couldn't see it. The third time, I was alone and underwater in Naica. Now, out of my peripheral vision, I see a flight attendant walk by. I look at her. Noticing my gaze, the flight attendant simply smiles back at me, nods her head, and continues down the aisle. There is no way she would have simply smiled and nodded if she had seen what I see in front of my face. Apparently, the Impossible Triangle is my own private experience. If only I could control when it happens.

The buzzing sound with which the Impossible Triangle began morphs into the roar of an engine. I recognize that roar. It's the souped-up Cadillac Escalade EXT. It's the sound of Sam, Ira, and Kan's truck. On the screen, I see a blob. It's a white blob against a black background. The white blob moves in and out of frame, then it splits into three. The three smaller blobs change in color through shades of grey and begin to take human form, as the background of the screen goes to white. The three blobs turn into Sam, Ira, and Kan. No more white lab coats. They are dressed in black suits—and I'm there with them. They stand still, facing me, yet their bodies move around me like shuffled cards, seemingly moved by an invisible hand. In unison, their mouths move. They speak to me. Even mute Sam speaks.

"Alexis, we will not let you destroy humanity. We will not let you destroy our world."

They jump towards me, their hands aiming for my throat. My throat burns in pain.

I try to gasp, but it's too painful. I feel like I'm being strangled.

I shake my head and move my hands in front of my face, batting away at the Impossible Triangle. It fades away like it was never there.

I can breathe again. I'm hyperventilating. I grab Amanda.

"Wake up. Wake up, Amanda. Wake up," I whisper. I don't want to make a scene, but I'm freaking out.

"Hmm? What?" Amanda says through the fog of sleep.

"I never want to see that Impossible Triangle, ever again," I say.

"What happened?" she asks.

I tell her what Sam, Ira, and Kan said to me and how they tried to strangle me.

"Don't wish for that Impossible Triangle to go away," Amanda tells me. "You have to be able to deal with the scary stuff, as well as the good stuff, the useful stuff. Trust me on this one. When you get used to seeing the scary stuff, then it's not so scary anymore. It just is."

"I would simply dismiss it as a nightmare, except for the fact that so far, a bunch of things I have seen on that screen turned out to be sort of real," I say.

"Are you afraid of Ira, Kan, and Sam, or, are you afraid what they said about you destroying humanity is true?" Amanda asks.

"Both," I say.

"OK. So, you are getting your info on this, what you call Impossible Triangle. That is a more graphic and therefore more potent way to get your info than the way I get my info. So, I can understand why you would get scared. During the time I've been with Bekzat and the Nomads in Kazakhstan, I was training. I was training to receive information. I get it in the form of thoughts. Those thoughts have a different, I'll say, flavor, than my own thoughts and that's how I know they are not originating in my head. It was through those thoughts that I also received information about Kan, Ira, and Sam not being who they presented themselves to be to our family and I also received the info that they were not to be trusted. I have never, ever received the thought that you are going to destroy humanity or the world. Sometimes, I'll admit, you are a pain in the butt little sister, but world destroyer you are not. Don't let them scare you. Think about it. They drugged you into not knowing your true strengths and abilities. I'm sure they would love nothing more than to have you be too scared to access information that you have a right to access. They would like you to do exactly what you said you want to do, never see the Impossible Triangle again. I mean, what you are able to see, it's like a superpower. Why would you give that up? Because you are scared? Instead of shutting it off, or giving it up, live up to it, Alexis. Fear not."

They gallop away from me. Both of them. Amanda and Everett, on horseback. Their joyful laughter echoes in the valley. The first rays of morning sunlight appear over the mountain peaks in front of me. We are at the skirt of the Tien Shan mountain range in the southeast corner of Kazakhstan. Bekzat, our guide, nudges me again to mount the golden horse. It's a beautiful creature. But my sole reaction to it is fear.

I have always disliked horses, looked away from them, avoided them. I was only five when Hannah gave me a My Little Pony playset for my birthday. When the giftwrap I started to peel away revealed something resembling a horse, I threw the package across the room, horrifying my little friends and their mothers. I don't know why I did that.

Each time Bekzat moves the horse one step closer to me, I take two steps away from him and the horse. Amanda has already derided me for my refusal to get on horseback. She schooled me on how these four horses, hers, Everett's, Bekzat's, and apparently mine, are of the Akhal-Teke breed, the very pride of Central Asia. She tells me I'm insulting the entire local culture, by refusing. The horses' coats are shiny in a way that is almost metallic. The one assigned to me is golden. The other three are various shades of copper and brown. Bekzat is speaking to me in Kazakh, but I just don't understand most of it. Amanda has been our translator. He tries a bit of broken English on me.

"Is OK. You try. You like," Bekzat says. He waves me over towards the horse. I don't budge. Keeping one of his hands on the horse's lead, Bekzat moves towards me again in his gentle and non-threatening manner. This time, Bekzat places his leathery fingers around my wrist, as he pets the horse with his other hand. Bekzat looks to be about fifty, but he may be younger. Living the life of a nomad, as Amanda had explained, he's outdoors most of the time in this high desert, making him look more weathered. I wonder, how often is he on horseback, here in Kazakhstan. Land of the wanderers. That's what the country's name means. Land of wanderers sounds like an oxymoron. I wish he would just wander away from me right now and take the horse with him. Instead, his fingers attached to my wrist, he tries to move my hand towards the golden horse's black mane.

"Gooood horse. Is nice horse," he says, motioning for me to pet it.

"No!" I yank my hand away from his grasp and I bolt. I run towards Amanda and Everett, who are having so much fun on their Akhal-Tekes, they are totally oblivious of me and my equinophobia. They are racing. With each one of my strides, I approach the duo of humans upon horses with greater acceleration.

Amanda's caramel colored ponytail dances as she rides, mirroring her horse's tail of the same color. Everett's thick brown wavy hair is air lifted as well. His head looks like a giant pine cone, bopping up and down with each gallop. But there are no real pine cones around. No pine trees. No trees at all, as far as I can see. Stunning, stark, jagged snow capped rocky mountains, surround a rocky valley spotted with some grassy greens that are still partially frosted from the overnight high desert cold. When Everett and Amanda's parallel gallop lines start to diverge, I step up my pace and run between their two horses. Everett sees me out of the corner of his eye.

"Hey! Wow! What are you doing?" he asks.

"Proving I don't need to mount the horse," I respond.

Amanda hears this and turns her head to look at me. She halts the gallop and hollers something unintelligible to Bekzat, who responds by nodding his head and going into the yurt, the local version of a tent. The yurt is round, almost octagonal in shape, with a conical roof. Its wooden frame is covered in white felt. It is the same shape as the white tent I had seen in my Impossible Triangle when I was in the underwater secret garden at Naica. This yurt is where we spent the night, with the horses. I didn't get much sleep, despite the creature comforts they had for us inside. I prefer seeing the four legged equine creatures in my fearful waking state instead of in my nightmares, where I have less control over outcomes.

In response to Amanda's halt, I've stopped running as well, as I try to decipher what she told Bekzat. Amanda, atop her horse, circles around me. Everett follows her. I find myself in the center, looking up at Everett and Amanda. A part of me feels like stalked prey, stalked by Amanda. Everett is blissfully oblivious of our sisterly spat.

As she circles, she says to me, "First, you may have totally screwed things up for me with Dr. Collins at New Mexico Tech when you fearlessly went into restricted zones in the Naica cave. Now, out of irrational fear, you're refusing the get on the horse. You could mess things up again, and this time by slowing us down."

"I'm sorry about Dr. Collins! I can't undo that, but here, I won't slow you down. I won't mess things up. You'll see,"

I say, confident of my physical abilities. I don't think I've even come close to testing my limits, yet.

"Fine! We'll ride. You run. See how long you last. It will be twelve hours or more before we get there. You need to get past your fear, or the journey stops here. Remember what we talked about on the airplane. You have to be able to deal with the scary stuff, as well as the good stuff."

"You could ride with me," Everett offers. Nice thought, I think. Yeah. But. No. Not nice enough to subdue my equinophobia.

"No." I say to him. "No, thanks," I clarify. Looking at how composed he is, almost regal on horseback. I ask, "Where did you learn to ride like that anyway?"

"Kentucky, as in Kentucky Derby country. I grew up in the outskirts of Louisville and worked around the horse farms," he says. Hearing his response, I realize that other than this, I know nothing about him. I know nothing of his life outside of L-12H in the Green Building at MIT.

"Let's go!" Amanda commands. Being on horseback, the dictator in her really comes out. Eight horse hoofs and my two human feet respond by snapping into motion towards Bekzat and the yurt.

Bekzat, via Amanda, directs us three Americans in western garb, to change our clothing. What we are given is not exactly traditional nomad enough to look like a historical costume, but it's definitely close. Comfortable, layered natural fabrics like cotton, wool, and leather to cover our bodies and fur-lined hats and gloves for our extremities. The tones are grey, brown and tan, to match the rock, dirt, and sand of the landscape. This is clothing made for nomads on foot, on horseback, in a caravan on the actual Silk Road. To me, the clothes indicate camouflage.

All we've been told by Amanda and Bekzat is that we need to be even more discrete after we leave this yurt. No connected devices through which we can be tracked are allowed, Bekzat had said. We were made to leave our mobile phones in a safe deposit box at the airport when we landed in Almaty. Hannah would not like that.

As Amanda and I dress behind a curtain in the one-room yurt, I think about Everett having to part with his goofy science t-shirt of the day, which today is something titled Being Human. It resembles a packing label, listing ingredients including oxygen, carbon, and hydrogen, right next to a UPC code and a message that says: *contents may vary in color.*

Amanda is already dressed and out the door. I am putting on the last touches of my camouflage, donning the outer, robe-like layer that serves as a coat, and a fur lined hat over my one thick braid of hair, which drapes my right shoulder. I wish there were a mirror here. I wonder if I now look any more like Genghis Khan. I'm in the right place to look like him. He did, after all, cross these Tien Shan mountains himself with his army on one of his conquests.

"Knock, knock," Everett says, from the other side of the hanging rug which effectively serves as the yurt's door.

I step to the yurt's entrance and open the carpet door as though I were opening my curtains at home to let the sunshine of the new day into my world. I motion for Everett to enter.

Stepping in, he pauses. His eyes circle from my face, down along my long braid, and back up to my face again.

He smiles. Everett then looks me up and down. Is he checking me out? Sizing me up? Admiring my wardrobe? I don't know. But, his approving smile and nod push those questions out of my mind. So, apparently, as long as he's looking at me, I don't care why.

"Nice look. It suits you," he says. Was that a compliment? I don't know. But I do know a way to keep him looking at me. I prompt him.

"I was wishing there was a mirror in here, so I could see if I look more like Genghis Khan now, in this outfit. That's my nickname on the debate team at school, Genghis Khan. My teammates say it's because of my debate tactics. I think it's because of my Central Asian ancestry," I say. "Since you're looking at me so carefully, maybe you can be my mirror. What do you think?"

"Well, I . . . uh . . . you do look like you are of this region. So, yes, you could say you look like Genghis Kahn. In fact, you could even be a descendant of his, an estimated sixteen million people are. And, and you look, well, you look very pretty. You *are* very pretty."

"Oh, thank you," I say. He says nothing. Then, he breaks the awkward silence.

"Logically speaking, that's not to say that Genghis Khan is pretty. I don't mean to imply that. It's just that, I find you very pretty."

He moves away from me towards a stool on which rests a fur lined hat. "I forgot this," he says, placing the hat on his head. He's wearing a long sheepskin vest over a tunic, and knee high leather boots. He adjusts his hat so that it perfectly frames his face, highlighting his high cheek bones and intense eyes.

As I look at him, I feel a little shaky inside my core and not so stable on my feet. This isn't good, because my back is to the carpet door, not exactly a solid surface that I can lean back into. The word handsome bubbles up in my thoughts. Not cute, not cute geek, and not even hot geek, but handsome. He feels older here, more like a man. I'm nervous. Being alone with him here, in a yurt, in the middle of nowhere, feels very different from being alone with him in a lab at MIT. I don't know what to do with myself, so I mirror him, adjusting my hat.

"You didn't need to do that," he says. "It was perfect before you adjusted it. Just move it back to the left a bit."

I do.

"Your other left," he says with a smile.

Oh. I can't even keep my right and left straight at this moment.

"Here," he says and steps closer to me. He puts his hands on the fur lining of my hat and adjusts the folds. I try to keep my breathing steady, and wonder if the electricity I feel from the tips of his fingers are real or imagined.

"You know how Dr. Ojigwe said you have a brain the size of a planet? Well, exactly how long does it take to grow such a brain?" I ask. I don't want to ask him his age, point blank. This is just in case he would perceive such a point blank question as a sign that I like him, in that kind of way. I don't want to risk embarrassing myself just in case he doesn't like me back, in that kind of way.

"A good amount," he responds.

I take one step closer to him, so that the only thing that could possibly fit between us is a seventeen millimeter diameter test tube.

"Could you be more specific?" I ask. "What is a good amount of time to grow such a brain?"

"Yeah, about that," Everett says leaning in a few centimeters closer to me. "At Naica, when this thing came up about minors not being allowed in the caves . . . minors with an o, not miners with an e . . ."

"Yeah, yeah I got that. Just, go on," I say.

He continues, "I wanted to tell you . . ."

Listening intently to every single one of Everett's words, I feel a cool flow of air coming in from behind me. This is followed by heavy wet breaths against the top of my head. Then, a huge tongue licks the side of my face.

It tickles. I giggle.

Then, I see it's face. The horse. Amanda's horse.

I scream and leap forward, away from the horse who has stuck his head inside the yurt to lick my face. I've jumped into Everett, who catches me with an embrace. I wipe the horse saliva which covers my face onto Everett's sheepskin vest.

"You will be getting on your horse today," Amanda commands from atop her horse. She pulls the animal's head back out of the yurt. The yurt's carpet door closes again. "Everett! Come on out here. Don't tell me you're going to slow us down too! Otherwise, I'll question whether you are non-essential to this mission."

Everett steps out of our momentary embrace, grabs me by the elbow and whispers, "You may think you look like Genghis Khan, but Amanda's the one who acts like him." He pulls me outside with him.

"Yep, here we are. We're ready," Everett says to Amanda. Is he groveling?

"Alexis," Bekzat calls me. He's already on his horse, which is loaded with supplies, mainly food and water, I think. The golden horse, my horse, is attached to Bekzat's.

Everett jumps on his horse. Amanda signals hers to take off. The three other horses, Everett's, Bekzat's, and mine, follow. I'm still standing here, in front of the yurt, watching them gallop off.

It's here in Kazakhstan that Amanda learned to ride horses. With Bekzat and the Nomads, as she calls them, she lived a nomadic life over the past several summers. She learned the Kazakh language, and in her opinion, most importantly, she learned to listen and receive information in the form of thoughts.

My feet start moving before she, Everett, and Bekzat get any further up that mountain, before they go over it and disappear from my line of sight. Amanda is leading the trio. But unlike her vertical ascent in the four-wheel drive Jeep up the hill in Naica, here she's traversing. It's way too steep to approach it any other way. I will catch up to them.

At the underwater secret garden in Naica, the image I saw just under the surface of the water was a woman from here. Somewhere here in Kazakhstan, that much I know because Amanda said my description of the white tent, or yurt as it's called around here, matches one that Amanda knows. The woman I saw with the Hershey's kiss shaped hat looks like me. Once my feet touched soil here in Kazakhstan, I started to remember her. Visual and sensory memories floated back into me. I remember being cradled, held, and sung to by her. Is she my mother? Amanda had told me that I was adopted from this country. When I picture this woman's face, I feel overwhelmed with love.

But if she is my biological mother, why would she give me away? This woman is our destination. My legs move faster.

It's almost twilight. We're headed east. The sun set less than an hour ago, behind the tallest of the snow covered peaks we crossed earlier in the day. Now we're coming up towards the peak of the mountain we've been riding up since early afternoon. They've been riding up, I should say. I'm still on foot and right by Amanda, Everett, and Bekzat's side. They are looking worn out by the high altitude. Amanda had predicted I would have tired out by now and succumbed to mounting the golden horse. Nope. Not going to happen. Going up and down the mountains, the horses got pretty tired too. I still don't like the wickedly beautiful creatures, but I respect their strength.

As we crest the mountain, we all stop to take in the panorama before us. Stunning. Snow capped mountains circle a perfectly round valley. A blanket of dense clouds, above which we stand, appear magically lit by the waning moon. I imagine the moon itself transformed into a cotton ball, came down to Earth, rolled down the mountains, and nestled itself to hide the valley floor from our curious eyes.

Staring at the beauty of this sight, a deep, deep sadness, a sorrow, a grief comes over me. Something lost, something gone, but I can't grasp what that something is. Maybe it's just the elevation affecting my body chemistry. Dizziness. Nausea. I'm swaying back and forth. I know I'm too close to the edge of the peak to be feeling this way, without the risk of freefall. My head is spinning. I'm so, so sad—

I regain consciousness, finding myself falling into Bekzat. He's standing between me and the sharp, rocky descent into the valley below. My head is hanging over his shoulder. I'm looking down into the cloud blanket below. How long have I been out? I turn my head around, to see Amanda and Everett dismounting and running towards me and Bekzat. Not long, is my guess.

"Alexis!" Amanda cries.

"Sit her down," Everett is telling Bekzat.

Amanda says something to Bekzat as well, which I guess is the same thing Everett just said, but in Kazakh. Bekzat carries me away from the edge of the peak towards the narrow plateau at the top of the zig-zag we traversed to get up here. As he's doing this, we take a step, closer than I would have liked by the horses. Bekzat places me down on the ground.

The golden horse's one eye stares at me from the side of his face.

I remember. I remember!

I remember being put on horseback and taken away from her, away from the woman whose face I saw in the underwater secret garden. I must have been about three years old, given my size relative to my environment. I was looking back at her, over the shoulder of the adult who held me so tightly and wouldn't let me jump off while we rode away. The woman, standing in front of her yurt, was getting smaller and smaller as the horse galloped away and up the mountain, this mountain. My three-year-old head hung over his shoulder, like it did just now when he stood between me and the precipice below. It was Bekzat! I look at his face. It's him. It was he who put me on the horse and took me away from her, from here, from home? Bekzat's skin is more leathery and his hair is salt and pepper, but that's him. I remember the boniness of his shoulder, upon which my three-year-old head rested as I drifted off to sleep, exhausted from screaming at being taken away.

I jump up from my seated position on the rocky mountain surface. My fist flies directly at Bekzat's face. My knuckles land on his jaw.

A guttural, animal sound comes out of me that I have not heard before. Then, I scream at him, "You took me away from here!"

I don't know if he can hear me past his vocalization of shock, as my punch sends him backwards, off and down the cliff.

Thud. We hear him land. Not too far down, I hope.

Amanda, Everett, and I get closer to the edge and look down the cliff to see he's landed about twenty feet below, on a dirt patch along the traverse path that leads down into the clouds. He's moving. He appears to be alive. Relief. I didn't mean to kill him. I didn't even mean to punch him. I've lost control.

"You need to seriously chill," Amanda tells me. "You almost killed the guy." She and Everett run down the traverse path to Bekzat's aid.

Her words are meant to cut through me. But there is only one thing on my mind.

The golden horse and I stare each other down. He snorts and neighs. Now he's rearing, standing on just his hind legs, front legs up in the air. He has thrown down the gauntlet.

Well, I accept. I charge over to him and jump him. I land on his saddle while he's still at 45°. He puts his front legs down, turns his head and stares at me again with the one big brown eye that faces me. He nods at me. His thoughts meld with mine. I understand. I don't need to fear him. We are one. We are a team. My fear, in an instant, turns into love for this creature. I grab his reins. We charge down the mountain.

I ride past Bekzat, Everett and Amanda. I don't stop.

Each gallop down the mountain atop the golden horse dissipates the hatred I momentarily felt for Bekzat, dissipates the feelings of sadness, grief and loss that I felt before I fainted and was caught by Bekzat. It's because I'm taking action. Action to restore something lost, to become whole again. I think this action can't coexist with hatred, grief, and sadness.

The golden horse and I ride. We ride. And, we ride, into the white. It's all white. White, cold, and beautiful. The horse and I have descended into the clouds. Diamond-like spots appear all around us. They float. It looks magical. But it's not hocus-pocus. It's real. Snow crystals moving around in a cloud. That's all. Something that happens every day on planet Earth.

The cloud is thinning out as we continue to gallop downhill.

Now, we're in the clear. The cloud is above us. The golden horse stops. I look.

At the bottom of the valley is a yurt. It's the only human-made thing in sight. This yurt is as white as the cloud I just travelled through to get here. Decorated with turquoise blue and gold patterns that look like something from a tribal Central Asian oriental rug, the yurt's conical roof catches a light dusting of snow. The flakes are only apparent against the tribal pattern of blue and gold. On the white, the flakes camouflage. I lean forward and squeeze my legs around the golden horse, signaling him to gallop. The sound of his hooves against the rocky mountain echoes. It's the only thing I hear. Air coming at my face at thirty miles per hour is the only sensation I feel, until we reach the destination.

I'm within ten feet of the yurt. Ornately carved wooden double doors stand between me and what's inside. It's dark out here. A bit of moonlight only occasionally peeks through the cloud blanket. The yurt is glowing with a warm light from within. Smoke drifts up from the opening at its center, the top, of the conical roof.

I dismount the golden horse. He whinnies.

I walk forward and put my hands on the doors. I push them open and step through.

An explosion of colors expresses itself through rugs, pillows, cushions, cloths and tapestries. Reds, blues, purples, greens, and yellows. A fire burns inside of a copper pot in the center of the room. Directly across from the doors, behind the pot of fire, is a low couch padded with cushions. There.

It's her. She sits cross legged, the Hershey's kiss shaped hat on her head. We lock eyes. She slowly, gracefully, stands up and walks towards me, as I stand frozen at the doors. She takes my hands into hers and walks me a few steps further into the yurt.

"Alexis," she whispers, as though she were expecting me.

She looks almost exactly as I had seen her on my Impossible Triangle, just below the surface of the underwater secret garden at Naica. Through our joined hands, I feel a warmth that I didn't even know I needed, until I felt it. She's talking to me in a soft and gentle voice. I can't understand. It sounds like Kazakh. I don't understand!

Is she revealing to me everything I want to know? Who is she? Who am I? What am I? What am I to her? I desperately want to understand her words. I block out the language that I can't decipher and instead I use just my eyes.

I stare more closely at aspects of her face. She looks a little more mature, a little older than what I saw on my visual screen underwater at Naica. She's still talking to me. I still don't understand. She squeezes my hands tighter. The warmth becomes heat.

It feels like when I understood the golden horse's mind. When I realized he's on my side and I have nothing to fear.

Like the burst of bold colors that exploded onto the cones of my eyeballs, as I walked into the yurt from the grey rocky exterior, a flood of images pour into my mind.

I was here. I was here for three years before I was taken away. I remember. As a baby I was being held by her, fed and sung to by her. I was fed from a bottle, lying in her arms, looking up into her face and hearing her talk to me. I was walked outside of the yurt, cradled in her arms as I looked up to the stars in the clear night sky. In my memory, I understand some of the words she used to say to me.

Then, in a later memory, I was sitting upright and was fed soft, mushy food. I can understand more of the words she says to me in my memory now. I used to crawl around the yurt. My little hands stroking the tribal rugs, I would make my way, on all fours, over to the door and crawl outside. I would sit myself down and look up at the stars of the Milky Way galaxy.

Later, I was sitting at the table with her. A round, low table a few feet off the ground. That table is still here today. She and I used to both sit, legs crossed, as I spoke with her, back and forth, in Kazakh. Now I remember and I understand all of the words she said to me when I was a young child. I would run outside. Fast, very fast. She couldn't catch me. I would run the circumference of the valley and start to climb at the base of the mountain.

"Not yet. The world is not ready yet," she would tell me.

I snap back into the present moment as I hear the words, in Kazakh, that flow from her mouth now. I understand all of her words in this moment.

"Child. Child of mine. Child of Earth. Child of creation," she says. "You remember."

I respond in Kazakh. "Yes. I remember," I say.

It's just automatic. A part of me is here and a part of me is observing this happen wondering how this can be. It's like I just got a software download for the Kazakh language. I can express whatever I feel, without thinking, just like I can in my native tongue, English. But now, I don't know which is actually my native tongue.

"You have a lot of questions, and some will be answered," she tells me.

"Are you my mother?" I ask the question that's been with me since I saw her image under the surface of the waters in Naica.

With a whoosh, the yurt's doors fly open.

"Well, I'm glad you found your yurt!" Amanda says. Flakes of snow waft in behind her. "Meanwhile, Bekzat's jaw is dislocated, thanks to you. He needs help, like now."

Right behind Amanda, in walks Everett helping a bloody and bruised Bekzat who clearly is in pain.

I feel awful. I did that. Then, I left him behind as I galloped down the mountain.

"I'm sorry. I didn't mean to," I tell Bekzat, in Kazakh. The three new entrants into the yurt look at me in astonishment.

"What?" Everett inquires, trying to decipher my words.

"You're a quick study," Amanda comments.

"You are forgiven," Bekzat replies in his native tongue. I still feel awful about what I did to him.

The woman, whose name I still don't know, who told me I'm a child of hers, puts my awful feeling about hurting Bekzat into perspective as she takes my hand, pulls it towards her, and jabs her long pointy thumbnail into my wrist.

"Bloody hell!" I yell out, in English, as my crystal blood reveals itself to her.

She now answers the question I had asked just before the yurt doors flew open.

"No," she responds. "I am not your mother."

IES

The sky has just fallen, on top of me. That's how it feels. I'm an orphan all over again. She's not my mother. Who is? Where do I come from, if not here? When I saw this yurt, I thought it was my destination, the repository of answers that would make my life make sense.

"Please step back," says the woman of the yurt, directing all four of us by pointing to the interior circumference of the yurt. The three of us who understand her language immediately obey. Everett looks at us, takes our lead, and is the fourth to step back from the center of the room.

The woman with the Hershey's kiss hat fixes her eyes on the fire, which burns inside the large copper pot in the middle of the yurt at the center of a large round red oriental rug.

She opens her mouth. A frequency of sound comes out of her that I have never before heard. I would say it almost sounds synthetic, digital, but it's so raw, so animal, I think its source could only be biology, not machine. The sound frequency morphs into a song. It's half chant, half tribal song. The round red oriental rug moves up from the floor. Flames in the copper pot intensify. The oriental rug, rising, would look like Aladdin's magic carpet, if it weren't for the shiny stainless steel and glass cylindrical tube beneath it, pushing it up, as the woman continues to sing.

"Woah . . ." Everett utters.

A large steel cylinder, whose top is the exact size and shape of the rug, continues to rise, we see blond hair. The hair is smoothly, neatly combed over a forehead. Then, under it, a chiseled masculine youthful face rises. This is followed by the man's broad shoulders. I realize what this cylinder is.

"It's an elevator," I whisper.

The semi-circular half of the elevator facing us is glass. The back half looks like stainless steel with a sheen, a luster, that's new to my eyes.

I now see all but the feet of the young man riding up the elevator into the yurt. He's wearing a charcoal grey monochromatic jumpsuit. It looks like a uniform. Form fitted, as simple as can be, with no visible seams, it looks like a second layer of skin made of fabric. The most notable part of the garment is a small round emblem, maybe four inches in diameter, located over the center of the man's chest. The emblem is composed of three horizontal stripes, white, blue and red, from top to bottom.

When the floor of the elevator meets the floor of the yurt, the elevator stops moving. The glass semi-circular half of the cylinder opens, silently, rotating to the interior of the stainless steel half. Witnessing this glass door rotate open, I notice three letters etched into the stainless steel half of the elevator, behind the man's head, located right across from me, at eye level—IES.

The man in the elevator doesn't step out.

"Welcome," he says, in an accent that I'm pretty sure is Russian. "Please, step in." Those three additional words, combined with the fact that his accent matches the emblem on his chest, a round version of the Russian flag, confirm it.

Bekzat waddles into the elevator, his hands covering his dislocated jaw.

"We will get you fixed up very soon, my friend," says the man with the Russian flag in Kazakh, as he pats Bekzat on the back in a very familiar way.

"Seats please," the Russian elevator man continues in his accented English.

Five vertical white cushioned rectangular shapes rise from the floor of the elevator. Bizarre. The elevator floor previously looked perfectly smooth, with no seams indicating anything was underneath.

The five rectangular protrusions, evenly spaced in the circular elevator, look like airplane seats, but are upright. Bekzat steps to one of them and rests his back against the white cushioned surface. The Russian's voice command was *seats*, but it looks like five people will be standing.

Still inside the elevator, the Russian addresses the woman of the yurt. He nods, puts his hand over his heart, right over the Russian flag emblem, and gives a slight bow in her direction.

"Sofia," he says to the woman, who I briefly believed was my biological mother. That's her name, Sofia.

"Ivan," she says, bowing back to him. Even in her bow, the Hershey's kiss shaped hat stays on her head. It looks like it's made of silver and would therefore be heavy enough to just fall off. But—hmmm—I wonder if it stays on due to a tight fit, or is there some kind of chocolate or caramel adhesive in there?

"Please, step in," he invites, looking at me, Amanda, and Everett, as he steps aside within the elevator and points to the vertical seats.

I have had it with going to great lengths and still not finding the final answers. Who am I? What am I? Who gave birth to me?

"Why? Where do you think you're taking us? Who are you? Why should I trust you?" I demand.

"Stranger danger . . ." Amanda chimes in.

"My name is Ivan," Ivan says.

"Wow. That takes care of it. Now that we know your name, we'll just enter your vehicle, just like that," Amanda says, rolling her eyes and crossing her arms. She looks at me. "I know Bekzat. I don't know this guy."

Everett is inspecting the elevator, without stepping into it. He runs his hands across the glass and stainless steel surfaces. He kneels down to the ground and reaches in to touch the place where one of the seats, the one closest to the door, just sprouted out.

"There's no seam. It's like the seat just grew out of the floor. That's some serious materials science. How?"

Everett questions the Russian guy with a tone of wonder and reverence.

"Everett, if you want to see how that's made, come on in. It's just a quick ride down. I'll take you to our engineering lab," says the Russian. Ivan knows Everett's name. How? Ivan also knows Everett's magic word, *lab*. Everett looks at me and Amanda. We both shake our heads no to him. He shrugs his shoulders and walks into the elevator anyway. Everett takes a vertical seat next to Bekzat.

I turn away from the elevator and towards the woman of the yurt.

"Sofia? That is your name?" I ask in Kazakh. "I didn't remember that, from when I was very young."

"You didn't call me that," she responds.

"I called you . . . mother. Didn't I?" I ask for confirmation to validate my memory.

"Yes," she says. "That was until the time came for you to enter the world beyond this valley. I couldn't go with you. My place is here. I would have cared for you, in person, every day, for the rest of my life, but I couldn't leave this location and you had to go. Instead, I care for you, from a distance, every day, for the rest of my life," Sofia explains with a nurturing softness that should be dissipating the anger rising inside of me. But it doesn't.

"So, you turned me over to people who didn't tell me I was adopted, people who allowed me to be drugged into not knowing what I am, people who preached to me that I'm weak through all their *be carefuls* and *don'ts*!" I accuse.

"Alina and Dale, your mother and father, only know what they've been told and they have not been told the truth. They are kind, normal people who loved and protected you," Sofia responds to my anger with firm, calm, solid strength.

She turns my palms up so that we both see the spot on my wrist where she had cut into me with her sharp thumbnail. Nothing but smooth skin now.

"Healed, already," she says. "Just like you healed, almost instantly, from the conditions under which you were raised."

"Why did you cut me?" I ask.

"In my heart I know who you are. I had to see your blood to prove it to my mind, before summoning Ivan to take you," she responds.

"Ladies," Ivan looks at me and Amanda. "We're waiting."

"You need to go with him," Sofia tells me and Amanda.

"Why would I trust you? You gave me away!" I screech at Sofia.

"She already told you, she's not your biological mother. Just accept it," Amanda whispers to me.

"That doesn't matter! Then, it's like giving away your adopted child," I say.

"Please, trust them," Bekzat chimes in, pointing to his jaw which is turning a darker shade of purple. "Amanda, you know better," Bekzat adds.

I grab Amanda and interrogate her, "And just how much do you know? According to Sofia, Alina and Dale were not told the truth. Have you been told the truth? Whatever that is?"

"The limits of what I know stopped at the entrance of this yurt. I had only heard of Sofia and not met her. I heard what I thought were some tall tales and imagined her more a sorceress, like the good witch of Oz," Amanda looks

Sofia over. "But, really, she's quite average looking, even for this region," she continues in English with a snort.

"Amanda," Sofia interrupts. "I understand your English, so be careful with your words, as you are about to offend me," she says in Kazakh.

"I'll stop speaking like you aren't in the room, then," Amanda says to Sofia and turns to me continuing in English. "I have seen this yurt before, from the top of the mountain on a clear day. I was told that Sofia lives here and that so did you, with her, during your first years." She points her thumb at the elevator behind. "This sub-magic carpet tube, elevator thingy, with the Russian dude . . . never seen it. Never heard of it. Each summer, when I came to visit Bekzat and the Nomads, the ancients as we call them, I learned more, about you and about me. Most of what I learned, I wasn't exactly told. It was more like I received thoughts, like I told you before. The more of the truth I knew, the harder it became to function at home, with you, Mom and Dad, three clueless human beings."

"Why couldn't you inform and enlighten us three clueless human beings?" I ask Amanda.

"They, Bekzat and the Nomads, told me that I could not interfere with your choices, and that I could not tell you what I know, until you directly asked me. They told me I could do nothing to stop your trio of doctors from so called . . . treating . . . you. Even though they assured me that it would be alright, it was the hardest part, sitting back and watching my parents believe Ira, Sam, and Kan, and letting them drug you, damage you, and . . ." Amanda is cut off by Sofia who has been tracking our conversation.

Sofia protests, "Does she look damaged to you?"

"No. You're right," Amanda concedes to Sofia and then turns to me. "I was told that I was to remain by your side, until the time came when you discovered what you are. I think that discovery started when you saw your blood. I remain by your side until you fully answer that question, of what you are. They said, at that point . . . we would just both know."

"Know what?" I whisper, as I feel little sparks and chills fall upon the top of my head. They feel like snowflakes. I look up. Of course not. We're indoors. There are no snowflakes falling on my head. The sparks feel sharper as they make their way down my entire body. This is like what I felt the first time I saw my blood.

"Our purpose," she says.

My throat feels hugely expansive. I know she's telling me the truth. Remembering to pay attention and notice what happens with my throat, I now have my own internal truth barometer.

"Ladies, I must insist," Ivan prompts us again. "Bekzat awaits medical treatment. You two appear to await more answers."

"Amanda, the Council is waiting for you," Ivan says.

Amanda spins around on her heel and asks Ivan with incredulity, "The Council? The Council is at the other end of this elevator's path?"

"Yes. They are at the other end of this capsule's path. We call it a capsule, not an elevator. The Council is waiting for you to take your place in their circle," Ivan confirms.

Amanda taps her foot. I see her processing. Deciding whether to believe him, or not.

"Alexis, our guest of honor. Do you want to go to your birthplace? Your home?" Ivan asks me.

How can I say no? Every cell in my body says yes.

Amanda and I look at each other. Simultaneously, we leap into the elevator. All four of our feet land at the same instant, right in front of Ivan.

"Amanda," he says, as he bows and takes her hand. "May I?" he asks, slowly moving her hand towards his mouth. While my mind is processing a guy, in what looks like a post-modern futuristic jumpsuit, behaving like a 19th century European nobleman, Amanda has already blurted out her answer.

"Yes!" she says.

Ivan kisses her hand, then, gently lets it go. He turns to me.

"Alexis. May I?" he asks.

I give him my hand.

"You're . . . just going to kiss my hand, not cut me to see my blood? Right?" I find myself having to ask, now that both Ikal and Sofia have cut into me before granting me access to their prized locations.

"Dear Alexis, I am not a vampire. I am simply a gentleman. I trust you will be gentler with me than you have been with Bekzat?" he enquires before his soft lips meet my knuckles.

"Well. That. I didn't mean to do that," I say, looking at Bekzat's jaw. Ivan releases my hand.

"Please, take your seats," Ivan says, as he steps back into his white vertical cushioned seat. "A question for each of my three guests today. The last time you were on a roller coaster, did you hold onto the handrail, or did you let go and throw your hands up into the air?"

"Oh, I always let go," Amanda answers with pride.

"I . . . held onto the handrail," Everett says like he's just admitted a sin.

"I've never been on a roller coaster," I say, rolling my eyes. "Because I was allegedly too fragile."

"Everett, please keep your hands by your sides. Same for you today Bekzat. Amanda and Alexis, arms up!" Ivan says as he lifts both his arms into the air to demonstrate, just like a good flight attendant.

"Straps please," Ivan says. At his command, four wide white elastic straps, pop out of the right side of each vertical seat, cross our bodies, and snap into the left side of the seat. Within a second, we are wrapped like mummies. Four bands cross our shins, thighs, torsos, and chest.

Everett looks alarmed and tries to move, wiggle out somehow. Nope. Not happening. Amanda can't help but mock Everett. I see her snapping her fingers, doing silly dance moves with her arms.

"Sorry, Everett," I say apologizing for Amanda's behavior. To compensate, I rest my arms across my chest, mummy style, joining him in solidary by retiring use of my arms.

"Sofia," Ivan nods to the only person remaining in the yurt and brings his hands down by his sides.

As she looks not at Ivan, but directly, and only, at me, Sofia emits a sound very similar to, yet lower pitched than, the one we heard when the red oriental magic carpet had started to rise, revealing the capsule. Her sound morphs into a different chant-like tribal song and the elevator slowly descends, until I can still hear her voice, but I only see her pointed slippers. They are the foot covering version of the Hershey's kiss hat, with cute little conical points at the toes, topped with a little yarn ball at the end.

And then, total darkness. We have submerged.

Within seconds, a series of dim lights turn on, giving only a soft illumination to the interior of the elevator. Brighter lights point outwards, granting us a view out the glass half of the elevator. I wonder, based on my recent experience, if I could see what's outside without the benefit of the artificial light. That would depend on whether there is crystal in the rock.

We're going down. Fast. The pace of our acceleration is evident in the speed at which we see layers of rock, sediment, and clay pass by through the glass. This feels more like a spaceship than an elevator. But they call it a capsule?

Faster! Faster! Faster!

As my body is pulled, deeper into Earth, my arms, which were folded across my chest, mummy style, unravel and fly up into the air. Ivan's and Amanda's arms also fly up over their heads and shoulders. Everett and Bekzat's bodies remain strapped in tight, arms and all, like they are inside of a burrito.

Bekzat is the first to scream. Is that the sound of pain? Maybe the force of our speed is pushing his jaw up, making it hurt even more. But there's something of a laugh mixed in with his scream. He has given the rest of us permission.

"Whooo . . . hoooo . . . oh . . . yeah!" Everett cracks a giant smile. Our ultra-rapid descent moves his skin up and tight around his skull and lifts his hair up into the air. Oops. There go his tortoiseshell framed glasses. My eyes follow the spectacles, which fly up off this face, hit the ceiling of the capsule, and now appear glued there. Everett's jaw looks pointy and his head becomes triangular. His skin looks a mix of pale green and white, indicating he may be the first to barf. He looks like a cute version of Batman's Joker. I didn't think that was possible. But yes, only in this case can the Joker be cute.

"Wheeeeeee . . ." Amanda screams out.

"Wheeeeeee . . ." I echo her. I can't help myself. This is fun.

We've gone through layers and layers of Earth. Instead of peeling back the layers of the onion, we're moving through it. And now, water!

"Wow!" I exclaim. "Aquifer? Sea? Ocean?"

"Yes," Ivan answers. This really isn't an answer, but I'm having too much fun to care.

"Love that glass wall," I yell. "Going through all those layers. It's like going through Earth's history," I shout. Then I scream louder, "I totally! Finally!! Feel like a geologist right now!!!"

"Yes," Ivan says softly. "But you don't need to yell."

Of course. There's something strange about the breakneck speed of our descent inside this capsule. It's silent. So why was I screaming? Maybe it's an innate human response to speed.

"Seems like there's no friction," Everett points out. "Is it a version of maglev?" he asks Ivan. Well, it makes sense. Trains that use opposing magnets on the train and the tracks make the train levitate, as though through magic. Yet it's not magic. It's science, simply the properties of Earth and its elements at work. The trains can reach speeds close to 400 miles per hour.

"Something like maglev coupled with pneumatics," Ivan explains.

"Like those pneumatic tubes they use at banks and some stores to move money around?" Amanda asks.

"Yes," Ivan responds.

"Is that why you call this a capsule instead of an elevator? It's like those capsules inside the pneumatic tubes that go up or down, right or left?" I ask. Out of the glass door I see the water we have been travelling through turn into rock again. I feel the capsule take a sharp turn from vertical, to go horizontal.

"Whoooaaa . . ." comes out of we three Americans for whom this is a virgin voyage. Ivan and Bekzat are quite blasé. Everett's glasses dislodge themselves from the ceiling of the capsule and fall on the curved wall behind Amanda.

"That was . . ." I begin, before we take another sharp turn into what I assume is a vertical descent again. But I can't even complete my sentence because we're, horizontal, diagonal, vertical, over and over. If the capsule isn't spinning yet, my head certainly is. Everett's glasses have flown up, down, and all around. The broken pieces of his spectacles fall to whichever surface of the capsule leads towards the center of the Earth. At least, with the help of those pieces and gravity, we have a clue about which way is up.

"I get it. It's a capsule, like when a person takes medicine in an enteric capsule through their mouth, and it travels vertically down the esophagus into the stomach, and then it goes in all directions through the intestines before it breaks down," Amanda says, speculating on the choice of labels for the vehicle that, despite its many directions, is definitely, net, net, taking us down.

"Seems like we're pretty far down the intestines of Earth," Everett makes his observation. "Are we going to disintegrate, like an enteric capsule, in the bowels of the planet?"

"Not to worry my friends," Ivan assures us.

"So we're friends now?" Amanda enquires.

"All admitted to the IES are friends, forever," Ivan answers. OK, Russian dude, I think. BFFs? Really?

As the capsule continues its moves, diagonal, horizontal, and vertical, Everett is turning a different shade of pale green.

"Your tunnel boring technology must be out of this world," posits Everett.

"You could say that," Ivan affirms.

"Are we there yet?" Amanda asks, "Because, I really need to pee."

"I really need to barf," Everett adds.

"I really need to see where I come from," I state.

The capsule decelerates. Through the glass, I see light and a vast open space. No more rock. No more water. Just empty space. We are about five stories above a mesa. About 300 feet away from us is the mesa's edge. Below that is an underground vista, a cityscape, both futuristic and organic. Steel, granite, and marble, merge with vegetation, waterfalls, and animals, populated by people, dressed in different shades of the same jumpsuit that Ivan wears. From this distance, I can see the emblems positioned on their chests are also different colors and patterns.

The capsule descends and lands softly in a foyer. The white bands that had kept our bodies strapped to the vertical chairs release themselves. We're free.

"Welcome to the IES," says Ivan.

"IES?" I ask, eyeing Everett and Amanda. "As in, I'm guessing now . . ." and before I can say my next word, Amanda cuts in.

"International . . ." Amanda says while doing the pee dance, with her newly found freedom of movement.

" . . . Earth . . ." I continue.

" . . . Station . . ." Everett concludes, looking like he's about to vomit.

The capsule door rotates open.

"Restrooms are to your right," Ivan directs Amanda and Everett. They bolt out. Looking at Bekzat, Ivan uses his voice command, "Medics please."

The medics show up, instantly. They are a young woman, who looks about my age, in a navy blue jumpsuit decorated with the emblem of the Argentinian flag, accompanied by a robot. It looks like version 3.0 of Tin Man from the Wizard of Oz. It wears a funnel on top of its head and has a cylindrical torso. Before they enter the elevator, the robot's torso flattens out like a table and moves into a horizontal position over its legs, as wheels pop out of its feet. The robot becomes a stretcher, upon which Bekzat lays, and he is taken away.

I exit the capsule and track Amanda and Everett. Amanda enters what I presume is the ladies room, because on its door is an illustration of a cavewoman, part Wilma Flintstone, part shapely savage. Everett enters through the door that bears an illustration of a caveman, wooden club and all.

"Nice," I say, turning to Ivan, who I think is trying to assess my reactions.

"A picture is worth a thousand words?" Ivan asks. "That's the expression in English right?"

"Yes. Thanks for confirming that we are, after all, in a cave," I say. I walk out of the foyer where the capsule and cave men's and cave ladies' rooms were and I look out to the cityscape below. With each step towards the edge of the mesa, I am granted a better view.

The people of Earth, in all their variety of race, ethnicity, and age, appear to be represented here, though a majority of them look like they could be high school or college students. Hundreds of people are moving about the city. Some sit on park benches, others walk their dogs. A couple walks hand-in-hand having a private conversation. Some walk briskly in and out of structures, the purpose of which I can only guess. The quality of light illuminating the city feels very sun-like. The sun-deities have not been forsaken in this futuristic underground. As we continue to walk towards the edge of the mesa, I look up. The sun, on a giant screen covering every inch of the ceiling, is enough to make me potentially forget my location. The sun is positioned at high-noon, as a few wispy clouds float by it. It was nighttime when we left the yurt. This feels like a different time zone, adding to its otherworldly reality.

"The metropolis below you is IES City," Ivan says.

"This exists. This actually exists," I utter. "And this is where I come from? Why underground?"

"Two reasons. The Cradle and secrecy," Ivan answers. "I'll start with the latter, secrecy. Everyone knows of the ISS, the International Space Station. The ISS is serving its purpose, showing that all peoples of Earth can work together to advance knowledge and advance into a new frontier. But this, here, goes a few leaps beyond the ISS. If we built this somewhere on the surface, or even if we built something like this in space today, which is more feasible than people on the surface presume, we couldn't do it with the level of secrecy it requires. If you would indulge me, let me use one of your American expressions to describe the state of satellites today. Everyone and their brother has one. The only place to hide something on this scale is below the surface."

I step closer to the edge of the 500 foot sheer cliff of smooth grey, silver and pink granite, which looks like the kitchen countertops at Alina and Dale's house. I'm tempted to just jump down into it, to join it.

I pick up my foot. I'm going to move it past the edge of the mesa and then I'll decide if I'm going to jump. Something stops it. There's something solid there. I put my hand forward. It too, at the point exactly parallel with the edge, stops.

"Glass?" I ask.

"Yes. We wouldn't want people to fall off. You'd probably be fine, but not the rest of us," Ivan says.

"But I can't even see it. It's totally clear," I say in wonderment.

"Like your friend, Everett, said, we have some serious materials science here," he reminds me.

"And, can we return to the other reason, the first reason why the IES is located underground? The cradle?" I prompt, thinking that might have something more specifically to do with me.

"Yes. The Cradle. Your birthplace. It's located here. Shall we proceed?" he asks, with a broad, slow wave of his arm presenting IES City below. He's like a gameshow host presenting me with a prize.

"Yes. Yes, we shall," I exhale.

15

SANTA AND THE NSA

The waters of the wudu can be any color I desire and can be delivered unto me in any form I choose. This is what my audio guide has told me upon entry into the wudu, my private spa-like washing and dressing room. Private, that is, with the exception of the female voice that guides me through my choices.

Ivan directed me, Amanda and Everett to enter our own assigned wudus, so that we may be purified of potential contaminants from the surface before entering the main space of the IES. Apparently, the mesa where we landed, and upon which we still stand, is a receiving port, and one must clean up and get into a uniform jumpsuit before being granted access to move further into the IES. I recognized the word wudu, which is the Islamic practice of washing oneself in order to purify. When I asked Ivan about it, he pointed out that most religions have some form of ritual washing, but that the person who designed the spa-like dressing and washing rooms of the IES is in fact of the Muslim faith, and therefore, that designer got to name the wash rooms as he pleased. Ivan went on to point out that belief systems aside, there is indeed proof that cleanliness is useful to survival and evolution. None of this mattered to me, because I have two days' worth of dust and sweat on me, my hair is oily, and I really, really need a shower, so enter the wudu I did.

"Please select a color," says my pleasant audio guide. The water, which pours down from the ceiling in rain-like drops in a corner of the spa, is clear, standard looking water. This is already so inviting I just want to walk into it, but the digital screen on the wall adjacent to the rain corner presents to me an interactive color wheel, which I can manipulate, to choose one of what seems an infinite number of hues. I move the wheel to lavender. The water drops coming from the ceiling instantly change color. They look like liquid lavender petals as they fall onto the white marble floor. I try brown. Nope. Looks too dirty. I know it's not, but I can't get past that visual. I try red. It looks like blood, but less viscous. A part of me wants to recoil, like I would have in the past at the sight of blood, but that part of me doesn't recoil. Something about this appeals to me.

"The red is good," I respond to the other voice in the room. I figure, since I don't have red liquid coursing through my vessels, then I'll just have to have it pouring over my body.

"Do you prefer rain, showerhead, fountain, waterfall, or bath mode?" the voice asks me, as the water takes shape with each of her descriptors. The red rain drops, which had been falling evenly from the ceiling, concentrate into a standard showerhead formation. Next, showerhead disappears and water bursts out from the floor, like a fountainhead. Then, the water pours out of the wall, like a waterfall. Last, water rises up, out of the marble floor, in the form of a bathtub. But there is no tub that I can see. The water appears to be holding its form without the benefit of a solid containment vehicle. Not only do they have some serious materials science here, they also seem to have advanced the science around the states of matter.

"Bath tub mode, please," I say. I have to explore this one. I remove the local clothes I've been wearing since early this morning and place them on the counter under the color wheel screen. Rearranging the clothing so that the softest items are on top, I create a cushion, a safe spot for it.

It—the test tube containing the precious pod.

The pod, which I took from the underwater secret garden in Naica, which we tested in the lab at New Mexico Tech, and which Amanda and Everett believe still remains in Dr. Collins's lab. The pod is now in fact a stowaway on the IES.

Well, I couldn't just leave it there. As we were exiting Dr. Collins's lab, Amanda hid the pod away in a crevice, behind a large cabinet in the main storage closet of the lab, where she said no one would find it, until Amanda herself returned. When Amanda and Everett went out to grab a snack, I raided the storage closet and took what's mine, the pod.

We don't know what it is, but its DNA is like mine and I feel responsible for it because I removed it from its home in the underwater secret garden. Unbeknownst to anyone, I've had it securely tied into the center panel of my bra since we left New Mexico Tech. When I couldn't find a test tube protector in the lab to protect the pod for the duration of its journey, I went out and purchased a box of super-sized tampons with cardboard applicators and used the cardboard as a protective sleeve for the test tube. Even though we're restricted from bringing liquids past the TSA checkpoint, the tampon trick worked. The TSA agent lady at Albuquerque International Sunport who did the extra pat-down on me noticed what appeared to her simply to be a super-sized tampon, and she just smiled at me and told me to have a nice day. Female to female, it was the right thing to do. She probably didn't want to add to my presumed PMS by interrogating me about a tampon stored in my bra. Since I never got my period, this was my first purchase from the feminine hygiene section, so I had a new experience which made me feel a little more grown up, and the pod has travelled across the world. Overall, the super-sized cardboard tampon applicator protector has been a win-win.

It occurs to me now that the pod and I seem to be in a safe place. I remove the test tube from its protective cardboard tampon sleeve. There it is, a bright sparkle, inside of a bubble, inside the pod. It looks just like a tiny snow globe that holds one little star. I lay the test tube down on my clothes.

The tub of blood-red water is ready for me. I step into it and lie down. There is no visible bathtub container here, but the outermost layer of water molecules seem to have solidified, and certainly not into ice.

"May I have soap and shampoo, please?" I ask my audio attendant, wondering if the red water will leave some color on me after I've exited the tub.

"No. You may not," the lovely voice in the room responds, prompting me to think they may need to improve their customer service in this wudu. But, the voice continues, "The water is infused with cleaning, rejuvenating, and moisturizing agents. Please submerge and you will be clean. Then, please walk through the dryer," she says. Upon the word dryer, golden god rays appear, shining down from the ceiling just a few feet away from the tub.

I do as I'm told and submerge. Opening my eyes underwater, I look around the tub and all I see is red. Instead of evoking the thought of blood and the emotion of fear, this little container of crimson makes me feel like I'm floating in and out of poppy petals in an infinite poppy field.

Poking my head out of the red bath, I see the golden god rays await me. I step out of the tub by stepping through it, and walk to the rays which had appeared when she said the word dryer. Indeed. I am now totally dry. My skin. My long hair. All of me. Instantly cleaned, rejuvenated, and moisturized, just as my guide promised. Wow. I would like to import this technology up to the surface, for the benefit of humankind. In particular, for any young adult males who don't prefer to shower daily, and the girls who like them, would be prime beneficiaries.

"Please select your jumpsuit color," says my guide.

A door shaped image lights up on the wall, to the right of the color wheel and the counter where my clothing from the surface still cradles the pod. I see the color wheel is not just for water. I move my finger over the wheel and zoom in on the vast selection of blues available. I choose a shade of turquoise that most evokes the underwater secret garden of Naica.

"Please select your emblem," directs the voice. The color wheel disappears from the screen and a rotating map of the globe appears. Countries, as they exist today, are outlined, yet not labeled. Over each country is a small emblem, a round version of its flag.

I put my finger on the screen, onto the U.S. and the image of the globe stops spinning. The American flag emblem enlarges the longer I keep my finger on the U.S. I remove my finger and the globe returns to its rotation. This American emblem would have been my obvious choice, just a few days ago. But no longer. Things have become complicated. As the globe spins to Central Asia, I put my finger on the Kazakh emblem and notice that the flag is almost the same shade of blue I chose for my jumpsuit. Maybe there's a reason why blue is my favorite color. Yet, just today, in the yurt, I learned that I was born here. Here in this cave. I don't even know what country we are in, or under, as the case may be. The yurt we departed from is located in the Tien Shan mountain range in the southeast corner of Kazakhstan. However, we travelled so fast in the capsule, in so many directions in addition to down, that at this moment, I don't know in which country I would end up if I just bore a hole directly up to the surface. The IES, or at least the part of it in which I stand now, could just as well be in the northeastern corner of Kyrgyzstan or the northwestern edge of China. Placing my finger over each of these nations' emblems, I ponder. This does not lead to an answer. To the pondering I add my heart, since it is over my heart that the emblem will be placed. I connect my feeling to my brain. As the globe on the screen in front of me rotates, my finger moves to land on the U.S. of A. This wasn't a random, pin-the-tail-on the-donkey kind of landing on a spot. This was the most intentional choice, made by me.

"Is that your final answer?" asks my audio guide.

"Yes," I affirm.

"Please take your undergarments. Your jumpsuit will be ready shortly," the voice says. The door shaped image, which had lit up on the wall previously, now slides open. A robotic clothing rack emerges from the opening. The robot's frame is made of a silver colored metal. Its red velvet covered arms and hands present me with new underwear and a bra. The rack retreats back into, what I'm guessing, is a closet. I put on the undergarments. They fit perfectly. The robot rack reemerges with my jumpsuit and a selection of matching footwear. I put on the jumpsuit and choose the wedge heeled boots. The rack retreats again. The door slides closed and the rectangular space that used to be the door now becomes a mirror.

I take a look at myself and like what I see. My skin no longer has a concrete grey pallor, as it has for most of my life when I was being dosed with drugs by Sam, Ira, and Kan. It's my natural honey-olive porcelain now. My long black hair drapes loose over my turquoise jumpsuit which is beyond comfortable. My feet feel pampered in the matching turquoise wedge heeled knee high boots. At the center of my chest, over my heart, is a round emblem, about four inches in diameter, in stars and stripes of red, white and blue.

"Please join your party," the voice in the room tells me. Before I go, I take the test tube containing my pod and nestle it, like before, between my skin and the center panel of my bra.

I exit my wudu and see Amanda and Everett, to my left and right, doing the same. We look each other up and down and huddle together. Everett is in a grey jumpsuit. The color works for him, making his navy eyes appear an even deeper shade of blue. Amanda is in her favorite shade of light brown, which she calls caramel. Her hair, were it not tied up in a messy bun, would camouflage on the jumpsuit, because the bun looks like a caramel covered cinnamon roll. All three of us wear the same emblem on our chests. Clearly, these two had no question about which one to pick. USA.

"That was an interesting hygiene experience," says Everett.

I notice he must have shaved. The stubble that was prominent on his upper lip is now gone.

He continues, "I was given options on many things. But for other things, there were no options. They just knew what I needed and the little robot rack handed them to me with its red velvet hands. They knew my eyeglasses were shattered in the capsule. That's obvious enough, but the glasses were shattered beyond the point at which one could decipher the prescription."

Everett looks at me and Amanda intensely.

"They knew my exact prescription," Everett says, pointing to the new eyeglasses on his face.

"They knew my favorite shade of lip gloss," Amanda says, pointing to her shiny caramel colored lips.

"They knew my bra size," I say, pointing to my chest. Amanda stares at my boobs as Everett appears uncomfortable and looks away. Oops. I put my finger down.

The three of us disperse our huddle and march over to Ivan, who stands at the edge of the mesa, overlooking IES City.

"Aha. The suits suit you," Ivan says to us.

"Very interesting," Everett says, looking at Ivan and pushing his new black framed eyeglasses up the bridge of his Grecian nose. "Three pairs of glasses, in a variety of colored frames, black, red, and tortoise shell, with my exact prescription, were ready for me. How . . ."

"Yes," Ivan interrupts. "I see we may have pleased you with the variety of frames. You've switched from your prior tortoise shell to black."

"The black frames work for you," I say. "It's sort of more Clark Kent."

Everett takes his glasses off, looks at them. With more of his face exposed, I see I may have possibly made him blush. He puts the glasses back on again.

"How did you know my prescription?" Everett asks.

"We know a lot of things. My colleague and friend here at the IES, keeps us well informed," Ivan says raising his hand towards a large white tube that is extending towards us, at eye level, over the city below.

I hadn't noticed it before, but there's another mesa on the other side of IES City. The white tube extends from the opposing mesa, about a football fields' length away from us. There's a man standing inside the tube. In his white jumpsuit, he would totally camouflage in there if it weren't for his cream colored face and ginger blond hair.

He's staring intently at us. Actually, as the tube extends closer and closer, I see he's staring solely, exclusively at Amanda.

The white tube merges with the glass barrier at the edge of our mesa. The glass barrier dissolves and the young man in the tube steps towards us, onto our mesa. His emblem informs us that he's an American.

"My friends, meet James," Ivan says.

James briefly nods to me and Everett to acknowledge our existence, and immediately returns his gaze to Amanda. He steps in front of her and motions for her hand.

"May I?" James asks her. Amanda puts her hand out and James holds and kisses it.

They have some weird social etiquette around here, I think, putting my hand out, expecting that, like Ivan, James will want to kiss both ladies' hands. Nope. He doesn't even notice me.

"Wow. I thought this hand kissing was a Russian thing. Are all the guys so gallant here at the IES?" Amanda asks.

"Not at all," Ivan chuckles. "I only kissed your hands in the yurt because James asked me to."

James glares at Ivan.

"James wanted me to do it, so that when he kissed your hand, Amanda, it would not seem so strange," Ivan explains. "You see, James has, what you call in English, a crush on you."

I see Everett's eyes are darting between Ivan and James. Then, his observations move to my hand, which is still out, waiting for James to kiss it. Everett moves my hand down, and away from James, as if to protect me from the man in the white jumpsuit. "How is that possible? He doesn't even know Amanda," Everett pauses, then asks. "Or does he?"

"Oh. He knows her. We know her. We know all of you," Ivan clarifies.

James takes this further.

"Behavior, strength of character, physical dimensions, eyeglass prescriptions, IQ, and . . ." James's eyes gaze from Everett, to me, and back to Everett again, ". . . date of birth."

"Date of birth?" I ask.

Everett looks away from me. I wonder, when and if, he will confirm what Dr. Ojigwe told me back at the lab, that he's a sixteen-year-old grad student, not a twenty-something.

"Yes," James confirms. "We know everything, including who's been naughty and who's been nice. Just like Santa Claus."

"Oh. I love Santa Claus!" Amanda says, nearly jumping up and down. It's more of a subtle bounce she does, with her feet not leaving the ground, but her knees slightly bending and straightening instead. I don't know if it's James's talk of Santa that's appealing to Amanda, or the fact that his face seems to get more handsome the more you look at him. I think Amanda's curious about him.

"Or, more like the NSA than Santa Claus," Ivan informs us.

Amanda pulls her hand away from James's gentle hold. Her knees lock and her body stiffens. "I love Santa Claus, but the NSA, not so much."

"Former NSA," James clarifies.

"He's been watching you for years," Ivan says to Amanda. "Massive crush."

"Watching me? How?" Amanda asks. "Sounds creepy."

"It's my job!" says James with an air of professional authority. "And it's only been two years. Only since I've been working here, I have monitored and observed. I don't watch. I'm not some kind of weirdo stalker."

His weirdo stalker comment erases the professional authority he had temporarily commanded.

"Right . . ." Amanda rolls her eyes.

"Come. I'll show you," James steps into the white tube, motioning us to follow him.

Everett follows him, "Yes, please do show us."

"This was not on the schedule and we're expected at the Council," Ivan says.

But I think it's too late for Ivan's schedule because Amanda and I join James and Everett in the tube. We're ready to see what James has to show us. Resigned, Ivan joins us in the tube.

The white tube pulls away from the mesa we had been on and slowly retracts back towards the mesa it came from. Standing inside of it, I feel like I'm in a straw. I look down the open end of the straw, at the city below. Every shade of human skin tone on the surface of Earth is represented here. These shades are only outnumbered by the variety of jumpsuit colors. It's a human kaleidoscope.

"Please, take one," Ivan invites, opening his palm to reveal three small ladybugs. They don't look alive and are very shiny. Maybe they are candies or mints.

"Place it either on your earlobe," he says to me and Amanda. Then he looks to Everett. "Or, if you prefer not to be wearing a ladybug earring, you may place it behind your ear, as I have done." He folds his ear forward to show us where his ladybug resides.

"We call it the babel bug," Ivan says.

"As in, babel fish?" I ask.

"As in, Google Pixel buds for translation?" Everett asks.

"Yes, in a way, both," Ivan affirms. "We've miniaturized the technology to a state where the real-time translation device is smaller than a babel fish, the fish you would stick in your ear if you lived in *The Hitchhiker's Guide to the Galaxy*. And, we've advanced the technology far beyond Google's, so that our babel bug is consistently accurate and does simultaneous translation of nearly 7,000 Earth languages. So, please," he motions for us to take them.

Amanda and I each put one on our earlobes. Everett goes for behind the ear. I can feel the little ladybug lodge each of its six little legs into the flesh of my earlobe.

"You can't imagine the amount of diplomatic grief this bug has saved us," Ivan says, without the Russian accent. "We don't have to agree on a common language. And, you don't hear my accent anymore because I'm speaking in Russian and you are hearing me in English through the babel bug."

With this invention, I wonder if I really need to keep taking a foreign language class in order to meet college admissions requirements.

Our white tube has reached its destination. It fully retracts, into the glass wall of this mesa, until the tube looks like a giant white donut. We step onto the mesa and see a large sign in English that hangs from the ceiling—Santa's Observatory.

We follow James towards a large door with a different sign attached to it—Only the Nice are Admitted.

"This is where you do your weirdo stalker spying?" Amanda asks James. "Please. Don't ruin Christmas for me. It's my favorite holiday."

James hangs his head low for a moment, then recovers. He explains, "I was with the NSA only briefly, after I dropped out of college. I agreed with most of the good things they asked me to do and I did them willingly. But there were a few things they asked me to do, which I refused, because they weren't good, in my opinion. So, I came here to the IES, where so far, I have agreed to do everything they have asked of me, including the task of staring, for hours on end, at the most beautiful woman in the world." He stares at Amanda.

Amanda appears not entirely displeased right now. She opens her mouth and no words come out. I jump in to save her before she says or does something stupid.

"So, you don't have to agree on a spoken language thanks to the babel bug, but the signs are in English?" I ask Ivan, pointing to the Only the Nice are Admitted sign.

"An American created this section of the IES, so she got to name it," Ivan responds. Then he adds under his breath, "And you Americans think we're the spies."

James leads us into Santa's Observatory. It's basically a planetarium. We're standing inside of a half sphere. The interior surface of the sphere, from floor level to its uppermost point, is a screen. On this giant dome shaped screen, we see—it must be thousands of—tiny smaller rectangular screens which show individuals around the world going about their daily lives, both outdoors and in interior spaces. Some of these rectangular screens zoom larger for a while and then recede back into their prior smaller size.

At the center of the observatory floor, a team of about twenty people sit in low, round beanbag seats that rotate. These people, in various colored jumpsuits and bearing different emblems from around the globe, appear to be taking notes on their digital pads. They write, type, and speak their observations into their devices.

"And this is where we identify future members of the IES," says James.

I desperately need to know right now. Is there anyone else, observed on this dome, who has crystal blood? My eyes scan all the screens, both little and zoomed large, that cover the dome like a quilt. Is there anyone out there like me?

Everett interrupts my thoughts with a different question for James, "So, you're saying that the IES has been observing me, and Amanda, and Alexis for years and that we've been admitted here, because . . . we're nice and not naughty?" He sounds incredulous.

"In accordance with the IES's definition of naughty and nice, yes," James confirms.

"Meaning, I'm not here by sheer random coincidence as a result of meeting Alexis at the lab, discovering that she's a biological anomaly with crystal blood, and deciding to follow her to . . . well . . . not the ends of the Earth, but to . . . the innards of the Earth?" Everett asks.

"Random? Listen to yourself? What about that sounds random?" asks James. "It's not random. Very little is random. You were selected following careful observation. A boy genius who left his family home in Kentucky to do his graduate work at MIT at the age of fourteen, that's rare enough; but your integrity and character put you over the top."

"Or, under the ground, as the case may be," Ivan chimes in with a snicker.

"Fourteen? Did you say he's been at MIT since he was fourteen?" I ask James, wanting confirmation of what Ojigwe told me back at the lab.

"Fourteen," James confirms.

"How long have you been at MIT?" I ask Everett. He's shifting his weight from one foot to the other, looking at me and then at James. I wait for Everett to confess. He says nothing.

"OK," James says, with a broad, broad smile on his face. "Coming from a linguist. That's my background, I'm a linguist. That's what I was studying before I dropped out of college." He continues, now talking to us as if we may have trouble hearing or understanding him. "Let me do the arithmetic for you science and math geeks. Alexis and Amanda, your friend Everett is . . ."

Everett blurts out, "Sixteen. Alexis, I'm sixteen years old, like you,"

I fake gasp. "You hadn't told me! You were misrepresenting yourself," I accuse.

"Technically, I was not misrepresenting myself. You never point-blank asked me my age. When you first started interning at the lab, I guess you just assumed, just like everyone else, that I was an average grad student. I almost told you when we were at the mountain top at Naica, before we went into the crystal cave, but then I thought Amanda might back out if she knew she had two people under the age of eighteen on her hands. I almost told you a second time, in the yurt, before you got slobbered upon by Amanda's horse. I tried. But look, at MIT, only the professors know. I didn't volunteer my personal information to other students and researchers on campus, because—because I wanted to fit in. All I wanted was to belong and feel normal. I've never fit in, not even with my own family. But, I thought about telling you . . . I am telling you now . . . because with you, I feel like I fit and belong."

We are standing facing each other, close to each other. I want to tell him I've known his age since that day at the lab when Ojigwe told me. I want to tell him I'm mad at him for pretending to be my senior.

But—oh my gosh. He steps even closer to me. Mirroring grins take over our faces. I see him leaning in towards me. He places his lips onto mine. They are so soft. He gives me a kiss. Then, after a moment he gently pulls back.

I look around. Everyone is staring at us, including the twenty people working at Santa's Observatory.

"I figured, here in this room, or there on the screen, it would not have been a private moment either way," says Everett. "You know what I am now, so I figured, it's time now."

"I confess, I have known your age since the day I discovered my crystal blood. I was just waiting for you to fess up," I say.

"Sneaky," he says, leaning in to give me another kiss.

Private or public, I don't care. He kissed me. He's sixteen!

16

MAYFLOWER

"Is there anyone else out there like me?" I ask, vocalizing the question in my mind that has been competing for attention with my new thoughts about Everett, whose lips just met mine. I rotate 360° in my spot, looking up at the thousands of individuals on thousands of tiny screens being monitored by James and his friends here in the giant dome of the IES's Santa's Observatory.

"Are there others like me, with crystal blood, out there?" I ask pointing my finger around the dome.

"You are the first," James responds. Finally, an answer, but not the full answer.

"That didn't answer my question. Am I the only one alive on Earth today with crystal blood?" I ask pointedly.

"Yes," James answers point blank.

"The rest of this conversation is for the Council," Ivan insists. "Alexis and Amanda, please follow me." Ivan moves towards the door.

"What about me?" Everett asks.

"You may come to the Council, if you wish, though the lab may be of greater interest to you," Ivan says walking further away from us and closer to the exit. I can't budge quite yet.

My eyes are scanning the screens, each featuring a person. Screens expand and then retreat back into the thousands of smaller screens from which they emerged. It creates a pattern that looks like visual music. I wonder what it would sound like. I'm not very musical, but now, I can almost hear a rhythm that rhymes with the visuals.

"Why do the screens expand and shrink?" I ask James.

"We've programmed the screens to expand when the subject being observed is displaying behaviors that are of interest to the IES," explains James.

Then, I notice one specific screen that is enlarging. It's about 30° to my right and about twenty feet up from floor level.

"Noah? That's Noah!" I say. "Look Amanda! It's Hannah's little brother."

"Wow. It is," Amanda confirms. "AKA Captain Underpants," she adds under her breath.

"How are you seeing him in his house, and these other people who are in interior spaces?" I ask.

"Santa's Observatory creates composite video imaging by combining data from our satellites which have advanced technologies to see through walls, with images that we capture of exterior spaces, and what we hear from connected devices in homes," James says, as though this should have been obvious to me.

"See," James says. "His screen is expanding because he's doing something of interest to the IES."

Noah is opening a giant LEGO box. The box for the Millennium Falcon indicates it has 7,541 pieces and is made for those aged sixteen and up. And there he goes. He's doing what he usually does with his LEGOs. I've observed this many times while hanging out at Hannah's house. On the screen, I see him in his living room dumping out all the little LEGO pieces from all the plastic bags. Then, he grabs the instructions. I know his next step. He stands up. Our view of him zooms out. He goes into his mom's home office, walks to the paper shredder, and carefully feeds the LEGO Millennium Falcon building instructions through the shredder's sharp teeth.

On the screen, we see Noah is now building his version of a spaceship.

"That right there," James points to Noah. "Throw away the instructions and do it differently, do it better, that's of interest to the IES. He's a good potential Do-Something."

"You're observing people of all ages and I noticed people of all ages down in IES City. So, you don't mind that Everett and I are both under the age of eighteen?" I ask James.

"Of course not. We don't practice age discrimination here at the IES," he confirms.

"Enough for now, James," Ivan says and signals to us. "We must go."

As Ivan is leading us out, in the corner of my left peripheral vision, I see an enlarging screen that stops my feet from moving another inch. I spin my head around to watch it, both my eyes locked to the person the IES is apparently observing.

"Josh!" It's Josh and he's doing nothing. So, why is the IES observing him and why is the screen expanding? What could be interesting about Josh laying on the grass in his yard, under a tree just staring off into space?

I call out to James, who is on the other side of the exit door with the rest of our group.

"James, why are you observing Josh?" I ask. "Look. The screen keeps getting larger and larger the longer he just lays there on the grass doing nothing."

"Exactly," is James's response.

"Exactly what?" I prod.

"He has great potential as a Do-Nothing," James says.

"That sounds like an insult. Are you mocking my friend?" I defend Josh. "I actually haven't seen him space off like that in a long time."

"He does it more than you see. He has learned to control it," James explains.

"Control what?" I ask. "Doing nothing?"

"Very few humans have that kind of ability to, at their own will, disconnect from their specific point on the space-time continuum and then return when needed," James explains.

"Where I come from, we call that daydreaming," Everett says, taking steps towards us.

"That's exactly why he doesn't do it in public much anymore. Now that he's older, he doesn't want to be perceived as lazy, or as spacing off," James says.

On screen, a red-orange leaf departs from the maple tree, under which Josh is laying, doing nothing. The autumn leaf falls into Josh's long blond mop of hair, which looks like a pillow under his head on the grass.

"When we were younger, some kids used to call him an airhead," I say, not wanting to trash talk Josh, but simply to confirm that Everett's not the only one who would see this act of doing nothing as useless daydreaming. "Often in class, he would just stare off into space and look totally disengaged. Then, the teacher would ask him a question, trying to bust him for not paying attention. It never worked. Every time, Josh answered the question fully and the teacher ended up wondering what the heck just happened."

"That's what I mean. He's able to pull himself back into the current moment from wherever it was he had wandered off to. Wandered off in a non-physical sense of course. We suspect he has a dual track awareness, sort of can be in two places at once," James delivers his hypothesis.

"Since the rest of us can't be in two places at once, I insist we immediately go to see the Council, who await us," Ivan is trying to get us out of Santa's Observatory. He points to me, Amanda, and Everett, and adds "Pulling you three away from these screens is like pulling children from their digital devices."

"Technically speaking, two of us are not yet legally adults, so that's entirely appropriate behavior for us," Everett says to Ivan, and then turns to me, grinning. I can't help but grin back.

We follow Ivan out of Santa's Observatory and walk towards the edge of the mesa where we can again see IES City below us. Ivan guides us into an elevator, which is a glass sphere. It lowers us down into the city. As my eyes take in the underground metropolis that looks like future Earth, my mind processes the odds that out of the billions of people living on Earth today, me and four people I know, Amanda, Everett, Josh, and Noah, are all either already in, or candidates to be part of, the IES. That can't be random.

"James, the people you are observing, in Santa's Observatory, out of the billions of people on Earth today, how can five of them be people from the greater Boston area who know each other?" I ask.

"We've detected a clustering pattern. We don't know why yet, but the people we end up observing are not randomly dispersed over the globe. Boston is a cluster zone, as is Timbuktu, Auckland, and some others," James answers, as our glass sphere elevator approaches the park on the ground level of IES City.

I expect our elevator to stop. Nope. The elevator is not slowing down. A circular labyrinth at the center of the park slides open and our elevator sinks below it.

The space we are sinking into is bright, big, open.

We are descending into the center of an equilateral triangular prism. There's a bowl-like receptacle at the bottom center of this space. The receptacle looks like it will receive our glass sphere elevator. The three square shaped walls of the triangular prism are reflective, black and look like an opaque glass.

"The walls, obsidian?' I ask.

"Correct," Ivan confirms.

As our elevator lands into the receptacle bowl, I get an eye-level look at three doors, each located at the bottom vertices of the triangle. The vertex directly across from us has a door that is round and made of carved wood in the pattern of a mandala. I turn 120° to my right and face another vertex of the triangle. This one has a square door that looks like a clean sheet of stainless steel. I turn another 120° to my right to see the third vertex. Its door, a triangle, is a plant wall covered in small, five-petaled white flowers that grow in clusters of green vines.

"Mayflowers," I say.

"Yes," says Ivan as he puts his hands gently on my shoulders and turns me back around another 120° to complete the circle and has me facing the carved wooden mandala door again. The elevator door opens and he nudges me forward out of the glass ball.

"Proceed, please," he directs.

The five of us, me, Amanda, Everett, Ivan, and James walk towards the round door which opens by itself when we get close to it. We walk into a cavern.

"The Council," Ivan presents.

The cavern has walls of shiny green selenite. The space is lit by a pillar of fire that emerges from a hole in the center of the room. Around the fire are nine evenly spaced seats and one low platform that looks like a mini-stage, together creating a circle. In eight of the seats are IES members in various colored jumpsuits and bearing their respective emblems. One seat is empty.

Ivan nudges us to move forward and step up onto the low platform directly in front of us. The IES member seated directly across from us, from the door through which we just entered, stands up. She's so tall.

"Mayflower," she says looking directly at me. "We've been waiting for you." She adds with a cold, stern manner that makes me feel like I'm in trouble. "Come forward," she commands.

She looks like a Nordic Viking goddess and maybe this is what creates an air of chill that I sense in the cavern now. Her white jumpsuit bears the emblem of the flag of Norway.

"My name is not Mayflower. My name is Alexis," I say with a bit of defiance. I step off the platform, walk into the center of the Council's circle and stand by the pillar of fire.

"A glory filled creation," says a bald man from Vietnam who looks like a Buddhist monk. "It doesn't matter what we call you. All that matters is that you are, and that you have found your way here."

The Nordic Viking goddess sits back down onto her seat and addresses me again.

"Mayflower. It's not such a bad name is it? Epigaea repens. The flower's scientific name literally means creeping and running on the Earth. They grow in clusters," she says.

"I thought the codename had to do with the Mayflower Society," Amanda interjects.

"Codename? I have a codename?" I say. I'm no longer offended by the Nordic Viking goddess not addressing me by my real name. Something is uber cool about having a codename.

"Mayflower Society you know, because we're . . ." then Amanda looks at me and stops. "I mean . . . I am a descendent of the 102 people from England who arrived in North America on the Mayflower ship 400 years ago."

"Indeed. That is another reason we use that . . . codename as you call it," says the Nordic Viking goddess. "Brave humans taking a large risk to seek a better life, that's what the people aboard the Mayflower did. They left behind what they thought was a corrupt world and travelled to a New World. In the seventeenth century, they did that through a change in geography. In the twenty-first century, creating a new world is happening through a change of biology, and its cascading effects. So, our first Mayflower," she looks at me, and then turns her gaze to Amanda, "and sister of our first Mayflower, did you know that the mayflower plant was the first flower of springtime that your," she points at Amanda, "biological ancestors saw after they survived their first winter in North America, thanks to the help of Native Americans?"

Amanda and I look at each and shake our heads no. Well, I guess I missed that botany fact in my history classroom in Massachusetts. I am being schooled in American history by a Norwegian. I don't know if I like this.

I look around the circle at the other Council members. Are the others more friendly? Immediately to the Nordic Viking goddess's left is an empty seat. The thought runs through my mind. Is that seat for me? I have to know.

I point to the seat and ask, "Is that sea . . ." before I can finish getting the word out of my mouth, Amanda shoves me aside, in the familiar way only she can, and runs for the seat. Are we playing musical chairs here?

"Bekzat and the Nomads, as well as Ivan, have told me I may now take my proper place in your circle," Amanda says to the Council with an abundance of enthusiasm as she approaches the empty seat. But I know this tone of hers. It's a little more over-the-top than usual, even for Amanda, so I know this means she's doing a sales job. She's really not sure of where she stands here. But apparently, she doesn't plan on standing for long, because she heads straight for that empty chair and places her butt on it.

"No. Not for you," says the monk from Vietnam, who sits on the other side of the empty seat. Amanda ignores him. She looks around the circle to the other Council members, seeking their approval.

"Darling, Amanda," the Nordic Viking goddess says. "We are very pleased to meet you in person. But, that is not your place. Not yet, please return to your group." Dejected, Amanda rejoins our group on the platform.

The rest of the eight Council members include a young Haitian girl with dreadlocks who looks only twelve years old or so, a middle-aged man from Australia who could easily be a stock photo model of a businessman, an elderly Brazilian man with mocha skin, a thirty-something Spanish man sporting a goatee, a young woman from Japan who has the doll-like face of an anime character, and a mature woman from Mali with the biggest white afro I've ever seen.

As I look at each one of them, all of the Council members are staring at me. Before today, this might have made me feel self-conscious, but instead, here and now, I feel entitled.

I enjoy the warmth that emanates from the pillar of fire, beside which I stand. The hole from which the pillar of fire emerges is much wider than the fire itself. I look down into it and observe that it goes down so deep, its source is not visible.

"The fire comes from the very center of the Earth," says the woman from Mali. "We've designed the column of air around it to manage the flame."

"I've got to see this. May I?" Everett asks the Council respectfully.

"Please," says the Spaniard.

Everett walks towards me and looks down to seek the flames' origin.

"Like the twisting stripes of a candy cane, one stream of air twists and moves up while the other twists and moves down. This contains the flame at the level we desire," the Spaniard explains as he runs his fingers through his goatee and observes the curiosity on Everett's face. He gives Everett a bit more to chew on. "Nano-particles of opposing magnetic charges make the stripe," he says.

"This pillar of fire, the capsule that brought us down here, and everything else here at the IES, how did your science advance so far past what we know . . . up there?" Everett asks pointing up.

The Spaniard shrugs his shoulders. "There's no reason scientists and engineers on the surface can't do the same. After all, we all have access to the same ingredients, the same periodic table of elements."

The Council members all look at each other and burst out laughing.

I think they are laughing at Everett. He looks dejected. Not cool. It's the first time the Nordic Viking goddess has cracked a smile, and it's at Everett's expense. I'll get them to sober up.

"What am I?" I ask her sternly.

"You are the next step in the evolution of the human species," the blond from Norway says.

The monkish looking man from Vietnam adds, "Earth has decided it is time for humans to take a giant leap in evolution. The planet is doing this by giving birth to humans like you, Alexis. You are the first to emerge directly from Earth's womb."

Earth's womb? I let that sink in and imagine what this might mean.

"Everyone else around you, including us, including Amanda, and Everett," says the young woman from Japan. "Especially Amanda, we are all here to support this evolutionary transition. The planet has called us to help, and we have responded."

"You are sort of a beta-test. We will learn from you and then, hopefully, others like you, waiting to be born, will emerge," the man from Australia says.

"Why do I have crystal blood?" I ask.

The Haitian girl who looks like she's twelve answers me. "Think about the molecular structure of crystal. The unit cells are orderly, periodic, creating an invariable lattice. This order gives power to your body, to enact your thoughts. Your blood is a form of crystalline silicon, a material that otherwise, in the world up there, conducts electricity and light, turns sunlight into energy, and strengthens the cell walls of plants. These are useful qualities for humans. Alexis, you may have discovered you have certain . . . abilities that other humans don't."

"Super powers would be more accurate," Everett suggests.

"These abilities, or superpowers, call them what you will, will soon simply be part of human nature. Hyper-fast healing, physical strength and speed, the ability to visualize where you need to go and what you need to do next on your own Impossible Triangle 2D screen that feels like a

3D reality, that only you can see, these will all be human nature soon," says the Brazilian man with the silver hair.

"Historically, human biology has changed and evolved, but not only to survive. We have indications that the prime driver of human evolution is beyond survival. The prime driver is the very basic desire to improve, to be better humans than we were yesterday, to strive to know ourselves and our role in the universe," the woman from Mali tells me.

"Alexis, does this have the ring of truth for you?" the Nordic Viking goddess asks me, as she stares at my throat.

She knows, I think, about my throat. As my throat gets that expansive, tingling feeling, that I now know to be the feeling of having heard or thought a truth, it occurs to me this is a bit like a ring of truth indeed. If the tingling sensation in my throat could be measured as sound vibration, the vibration may match that of a metal bell that has been rung.

"Yes," I say.

"Imagine if just that one ability, just that one ability of yours to tune into your body and know what is the truth and what is a lie, if all humans had that ability, life on Earth would be fundamentally changed," the woman from Norway tells me.

I know it's true. I can feel chills in the core of my body.

"But . . . so many structures would fall apart," I say. I get a flash of realization. "All of those institutions, all of those relationships that are based on lies, would just fall away. Some governments would topple. Some companies would go bankrupt. Some belief systems would crumble. Humans would see right through falsehoods and walk away from lies." The feeling of chills in my core move up my body and morph into a heat sensation the shape of a vice grip tightening around my skull. I'm dizzy from the pressure.

"Unveiling truth, at least in the short term, could lead to total chaos," I say softly.

A few of the Council members look disturbed.

A few others turn their gazes to the empty ninth seat of their circle.

17

DO NOTHING OR DO SOMETHING

They are still staring at that empty seat. The Council is silent.

Everett breaks the chill in the subterranean air. "You know an awful lot about Alexis's abilities. It appears to go beyond the intelligence gathering at Santa's Observatory. You almost sound like you've . . . bioengineered her?" he prods the Council.

I turn to him. "So I used to be a mutant, and now I'm what? Bioengineered artificial intelligence? You told me before there was no evidence of that."

He whispers into my ear, "It's just, now that we've seen more of their technology, I wonder. Maybe they have advanced science enough to do that here. But, Alexis, no matter how you came to be, I'm so into you."

I look at his face and for a very brief moment I don't care how I came to be.

"We haven't bioengineered Alexis. The planet has. And there's nothing new about that at all," says the woman from Mali, as she picks a fallen strand of her curly white hair off the sleeve of her cherry apple red jumpsuit. "Everything on Earth is the planet's creation, isn't it? We are all made of the same ingredients. Home-made. Think of it this way: the planet is trying out a new recipe, to create a more delightful dish. New and improved."

The monk-like man from Vietnam adds, "What we know about you, Alexis, is what the planet has told us. But we also need a seriously long talk with you to get the details of your personal experience."

"The planet told you?" Amanda chimes in from behind me. She's still back with the group, standing on the platform, awfully close to James I see. "You sound like Earth is a person or something," she adds.

"It's time to take a walk," says the Nordic Viking goddess as she stands up. She's so tall! The rest of the Council follows.

The large round wooden mandala of a door opens for us. I feel like someone should have said Open Sesame! or something magical like that. But no, this ancient looking door must have a modern sensor. We exit the Council's chamber and walk back out into the giant triangular prism. Six of the Council members sign off with us and enter the glass sphere elevator. Ivan and James join them. Up and away they go.

"The Prism," says the Nordic Viking goddess. "We call this space the Prism and my name is Freya. This is Huy," she says formally introducing me to the bald monkish man from Vietnam.

Freya and Huy lead me, Amanda, and Everett, along the long wall of black onyx to our right towards the vertex where the triangular door covered in mayflowers opens to receive us. As we walk by the door, I touch the flowers. They are real and growing on the door's surface.

We step into a small receiving foyer. A pane of glass separates us from the rest of this enormous chamber.

In front of me is a mountainside peppered with IES people in their jumpsuits and emblems. They could just as easily be mountain goats.

Some rest in a meditative posture, with their eyes closed, on small grass covered plateaus. Others lie down along a ridge staring off into various directions. One man in a green jumpsuit bearing the emblem of Costa Rica hangs upside down from the limb of a tree that juts out of the mountainside.

At the peak of the underground mountain is a man who sits, staring at us, through us, and beyond us. He looks to be perhaps from the South Pacific islands, but I can't tell, because he's the only person I have seen at the IES who isn't wearing the uniform jumpsuit. He's naked, with the exception of cloth over his private parts.

None of these people on the mountain are talking. In fact, they all appear to be doing nothing.

"Welcome to the chamber of the Do-Nothings. Some of the most important work of the IES happens here," Huy says. "This is where your friend Josh can make a huge contribution one day."

My eyes scan the mountainside and come across a man who could easily be Josh fifty years from now. This man is simply laying there on the ridge, staring up into the screen on the ceiling which emulates a daytime blue sky.

"Oh, when Josh is in his spaced out state, he'd fit right in alright," I say.

"These are the listeners and watchers. They communicate with the planet. They do nothing, nothing other than listen, and those with their eyes closed or staring off into space also watch. Each one receives information through their senses. This is how the planet guides us, gives us information, so we can have the choice to participate in its future," says Huy.

"Or not, as the case may be," Freya adds.

"What if we weren't listening?" I ask.

"We certainly don't have to. The planet doesn't need humans. But humans, given our current technological capabilities, or restrictions would be a more accurate way of putting it, need the planet," Freya answers. "We're not quite ready to colonize Mars, or any other planet, just yet."

"Is this a two-way conversation?" I ask.

"It mostly involves listening, but yes, the IES members do pose questions, questions that we have all collectively agreed upon. Then, they do nothing, nothing but listen and observe," says Huy.

"Why is that man," I point to one at the mountain's apex, "not in an IES jumpsuit and almost naked?"

"He's the original. He is the Do-Nothing with the strongest signal. He identified this location for the IES a long time ago and has been here ever since," Freya reveals.

"How long?" I ask, wondering when this place was established and when people started to think they could communicate with a planetary body.

"That I can't say. But, he claims to be 183 years old. Says all the doing of nothing keeps him young. Doesn't look a day over thirty-five does he?" Huy asks me.

As I'm staring at the man on the mountaintop, trying to gauge his age, I feel someone's eyes upon me. It's someone from the other side of the glass. I scan the mountain side. It's him!

"Ikal!" I hadn't noticed him before. But his eyes have since opened and are shooting like laser beams at me.

"Uggh . . . what's he doing here?" Amanda asks.

"Nothing?" suggests Everett.

"After helping you in Naica, he earned his place here," Freya says.

"But he thought we were headed someplace that was an important city in ancient Mesoamerica," I inform Freya.

"Ikal didn't know about the IES at the time," she says. "What he knew was the oral history his ancestors handed down to him, combined with a feeling he lived with all his life. That feeling was an inner itch that told him he needed to be in a very specific place doing a very specific thing. And he has now discovered, this is it."

Ikal flashes a smile at me. The smile is so bright that it erases my prior thoughts of him tearing my heart out and sacrificing it to his gods at the top of a pyramid in Mexico. With that thought erased, I sort of like him.

I smile back. The look of satisfaction across his face morphs into contentment and he closes his eyes again.

Amanda chimes in, "This looks a lot like the exercises Bekzat and the Nomads have had me doing. I didn't know I was communicating with the planet. I also didn't know what the purpose was, but I kept wanting to do it because I was getting information about Alexis and my family."

"The purpose was to find out if you are a Do-Nothing or a Do-Something," says Huy. "It turns out you are divinely suited to do both. Just as we suspected, you are one of a rare breed that can do both."

"Everett," Freya says. "Would you like to see the Do-Somethings?"

"Yes," Everett says. "I am a Do-Something. And I'm proud of doing things. But is this fair, that these Do-Nothings, seem to have a pretty easy go of it? I mean, they're just sitting around doing nothing."

"It's actually not that easy," Amanda informs us.

"Try it and see," says Huy. "Come, you three." Huy motions for Everett, Amanda, and me to follow him closer to the glass wall that separates us from the mountain of Do-Nothings. He places his palm against the glass. The outline of a door shape lights up and then the door opens. We follow Huy in. He whispers to us, "Find a spot. You may sit, lie down, or hang off a tree, like our friend from Costa Rica. Find the position that suits you and then, listen. If that doesn't work, watch with your eyes closed or open. Come. Try." Huy gives a little extra encouragement to Everett who looks reluctant. While Amanda and I find places to sit, Everett does not budge. Huy nudges him and asks, "If it's so easy to do nothing, why the resistance?" Everett nods his head and lies down in a grassy spot. Huy exits back out the glass door and joins Freya to watch us.

I keep my eyes open and listen. It's so silent. I am hearing silence and silence has a sound. I know this sounds like an oxymoron, but I think it's not. I believe I can hear molecules moving around outside my ears. I hear my blood coursing through the blood vessels in my ear. I'm not hearing a planet talking to me yet though. What does that even sound like?

I remain quiet for a long time. But still, mother Earth is not talking to me. I hear a new sound. It's not the sound of silence though, it's someone snoring. I look around.

Everett! Wow. He has totally fallen asleep, mouth gaping, he snores. I glance at Amanda who has her eyes closed, and her body posture indicates she is alert.

Since the listening technique alone is not producing results for me, I want to try making my Impossible Triangle appear on demand. With my eyes fully open, first I visualize the triangle in front of my face, then I imagine the three beams of white light coming from each of my eyes and the middle of my forehead, then I visualize the rainbow colors on the screen. This feels quite different from the prior times, when it just appeared spontaneously, because I'm not literally seeing it, like I did before. It's just in my imagination. How do I make it actually appear?

I feel like I need to concentrate harder, to move any other thought out of my mind. I start over. I focus exclusively on imagining the three beams of white light. Using my mind, I push them forward. I extend them and stretch them. The triangle pops up! I push the three beams into the vertices of the triangle.

Now I hear a soft buzzing sound. It's the same sound I heard the very first time the Impossible Triangle appeared to me when I was sleeping at Hannah's house. Completely on their own, without me forcing it, the three merged beams of white light blend into one rainbow colored spectrum on the triangular screen. Now the buzzing sound gets really, really intense and I feel a buzzing sensation in my body along with it.

And—it appears. I see an image on the screen. It's real. The buzzing sound and sensation quiet away.

I see Earth spinning on its axis. Then, as though through an X-ray machine, I can see into its core. The very center of Earth looks like a star. It pulses. I hear a beat. It sounds like a heartbeat. It starts softly and then gets louder. I see the pulsation of small, what look like particles, emanating from the core of Earth to its surface. The pulsation of the particles matches the sound of the heartbeat. A wave of tingles moves through me, from my bottom where I have physical contact with the Earth, all the way to my head. The pace of my heartbeat changes, slowing to match the heartbeat of the planet. I feel like I am a part of Earth, an extension of it, like the branch or root of a tree. I belong. This feeling of belonging erases the bad feelings I had at home, feelings of not belonging, feelings of shame for thinking something was wrong. My feeling at the square root of forever, which was bad has just changed to good.

The screen disappears. I change my focus and look around. Amanda's eyes are open. Everett is still snoring. Huy comes in to get us. Huy nudges Everett awake and silently motions for me, Amanda and Everett to follow him out.

"So, easy?" Freya asks us. Then she looks at Everett. "Nice snoring."

"I tried. I tried to listen and watch for incoming messages. But, instead, my mind just kept going back to trying to figure out how you've advanced technology here, and then I got tired, and then I guess I just fell asleep. Sorry."

"It takes a lot of determination and focus to remain very active and alert and Do-Nothing," explains Huy.

"It wasn't easy, but I was able to make the Impossible Triangle appear for me," I say. I feel sad and happy at the same time and I feel a crack in my voice as I continue to speak. "I experienced something new. I feel like I belong now. I feel like I belong on this planet, anywhere on it, not just in a science lab." My eyes are watering and I take a deep, slow breath, not wanting to cry because this feels more happy than sad. "I want to keep this feeling forever. I want it to not go away."

Silence. Everett reaches over to hold my hand. His hand is so warm and strong around mine. My hand belongs in his, just like I belong here on this planet. Huy and Freya look at each other with an expression of satisfaction on their faces. The silence continues until Amanda talks.

"I got thoughts, like I usually did when hanging out with Bekzat and the Nomads on the steppes of Kazakhstan, on the surface. But here, the thoughts became more vivid images when I closed my eyes. I saw the physical structure of a bunch of elements and their isotopes. They combined in ways I didn't know were possible. I could decipher this because I know science. But what about others here who may not know science? Would the message get lost?" Amanda asks, looking up at the other IES members who are Do-Nothings.

"Every one of these Do-Nothings spends part of the time here each day in the IES-SEI," says Freya. "The International Earth Station-Science of Earth Institute. They need to understand the basics of how Earth works, so that they can better decipher what the planet is trying to tell us."

"So basically, they are going to school, learning some pretty hard core science, in addition to staying awake and alert, while doing nothing," Everett sums it up.

"Yes. Indeed. So, the label Do-Nothing is a bit misleading is it not?" Huy asks.

"Yeah. It would not meet the standards for truth in advertising laws," Everett says.

"Good thing we are not bound by such laws here," Freya says.

I wonder what other laws on the surface of Earth they do not abide by here at the IES.

"Follow me," Freya tells us, "to the Do-Somethings."

She leads us out past the triangular door covered in growing mayflowers. Out in the Prism, we turn to our right and walk along the third wall of black onyx that leads to our next vertex, at the end of which is a square shiny steel door.

I expect it to open, just like the round carved mandala door and the triangular mayflower door, but this one does not. Freya walks ahead, into and through the stainless steel door.

She just disappeared into it.

"What was that?" Everett and I say, at almost the same instant.

Confirming what we think we just saw, Huy simply vanishes through the door as well.

Amanda, Everett, and I aren't budging.

"Behind that door, do you suppose it's the lab?" Everett asks me and Amanda. We shrug our shoulders.

Everett looks at me. He looks at Amanda. He faces the square stainless steel door and puts one foot in front of the other.

He holds his hand out and cautiously places it on the door.

"It doesn't feel solid," he says. "But, it does have a texture." He pushes his hand through. It's no longer visible to us. Everett turns around and looks at me and Amanda, his hand still consumed by the door.

"Doesn't hurt or anything," he shrugs his shoulders. "What the heck."

He walks through, and out of our sight.

"I'm next! I'm next!" Amanda announces and runs through the door.

I am left alone.

I proceed. I don't run through like Amanda. I don't test the door like Everett, not with my hand, nor my toe. I walk exactly halfway into it. The front side of my body sees what's on the other side of the door. It's the lab, alright. Full of people. Lots of IES people, busy doing a lot of things. It looks like they are doing experimental things, using machines I have not seen before. I feel like a Neanderthal who just strolled into Tony Stark's R&D lab.

The back half of my body is still on the outside of the stainless steel door. I turn my head around and look back into the Prism. It's still there. I'm in both places at once and I'm split by this door. The longer I stay here, the more I can feel and hear the door. I don't see the door vibrating, but just where it cuts through me, I can feel every cell in that thin sliver of myself oscillating. I hear a high pitched sound. I have felt and heard this somewhere before. The sensation is not new.

"Please keep moving through," Freya says. "The door was not designed to have you stand in it."

"Normal people rush through," Huy says.

"I'm not normal. I'm weird," I respond.

I can't budge yet because I want to remember where I have felt this strange oscillation before. Freya doesn't have patience for this. She grabs my hands and pulls me into the lab until I'm standing right between Everett and Amanda.

Mouths gaping wide open, necks bent way back, Everett and Amanda are speechless, staring up. My eyes follow their line of sight to discover what it is that has them paralyzed in this ridiculous posture.

I look up. Up there hangs a ginormous periodic table of elements. But it's different.

"They have . . . an eighth row?" I utter.

"And . . . they have a ninth row," Amanda whispers.

Everett looks at the Council members, who stand below the periodic table that hangs above them like a flying banner.

"You've reached the island of stability, haven't you? You've reached the magic number," Everett says. "That explains the materials science here."

I realize that also explains why the Council laughed when we were in the chamber, when Everett asked how their science is so advanced and the Spaniard had said we are all working with the same ingredients, the same periodic table of elements—Not!

"Yes," Freya says. "While on the surface the latest elements discovered, or created shall we say, are increasingly unstable, our team here at IES has created the next several dozen elements and reached the island of stability. Some of these elements are very stable and therefore we can do some extremely exciting things with them. Welcome to the Do-Somethings. I believe you'll be right at home here, Everett."

Huy motions for Amanda and Everett to move their eyes from the periodic table to him, as he explains, "Discoveries of the new elements and nearly all of the other inventions made here would not be possible, without the contributions of the Do-Nothings. There is intense collaboration between the Do-Nothings, who receive messages, ideas, and even solutions, while the Do-Somethings work diligently to make these ideas a reality in the world."

"And these discoveries will see the light of day," I point up. "Up there, when?"

"When the population has evolved enough to not weaponize them," responds Freya. "Our probabilists, or you might call them statisticians, are finding there is still too high a chance these technologies could be weaponized. The numbers are moving in the right direction though. Alexis, you and your kind are here to accelerate that move."

She points at my chest and then opens her palm.

"Hand it over," she says.

"What?" I ask, looking at her open palm. What is she talking about?

"One of your kind. In the test tube," she says, staring at me.

"Oh. Oh that," I say. They know about the little pod, in the test tube, in the cardboard tampon sleeve, in the center panel of my bra. The only time I took it out of my bra here was in the wudu.

I look at Freya, "Santa's Observatory has cameras in the bathrooms? That is creepy and pervy and not nice!"

"No. There are no cameras in bathrooms. Actually, we know about that test tube because you had it out in the open at the lab in New Mexico Tech," Freya responds.

"Oh. Oops. Oh yeah," I say.

"Test tube? New Mexico Tech? Did you take that little pod thing with you? We agreed to leave it there. You don't go taking samples around the world like that, all willy nilly," Amanda schools me. "What if it got damaged or lost?"

I place my hands over my chest and shake my head no at Freya. One of my kind? What exactly did she mean by that?

"Follow me," she commands and she walks right through the square door that I now know only looks like it's made of steel. Perhaps it's made of element number 124, or 148, or 174, of the new and improved periodic table of elements.

I obey Freya, as does everyone else.

We exit the chamber of the Do-Somethings and follow her towards the center of the Prism. I turn around 360° and take in the enormity of the space and admire the walls of shiny black onyx.

Freya faces one of three walls and says, "Clear, please."

I hear a humming sound, but only in my left ear. It tickles. I put my finger in my ear, wondering if something's gotten in there. Maybe my babel bug has crawled up from my ear lobe and wants to play some percussive music on my ear drum. But I can't feel anything in there. I look at Amanda and Everett.

"Do you hear that?" I ask.

"Hear what?" Amanda asks. Well, that answers my question.

"Do you see that?" Everett asks me. The wall is turning from shiny black onyx, to a smoky grey, to clear glass. Behind the glass is where the little pod in the little test tube fastened near my heart clearly belongs.

"Astonishing," Everett says.

"Beautiful and enchanted," Amanda adds.

It's an underwater secret garden, just like the one I swam in at Naica.

"Oh my . . . I didn't know more than one existed!" I say. "I'm so excited you two can see this!" I'm jumping up and down, as excitable as Amanda can sometimes be. "Isn't it just like I described?"

Clusters of mini quartz crystal obelisks are scattered across the aragonite landscape. Little pods with bubbles and sparkles in them float, bounce, rise and spin. Each pod, like a firefly is lit from within.

Huge, huge, huge grins expand across Amanda's and Everett's faces.

I pull out the neckline of my turquoise blue IES jumpsuit, reach into my chest, and take the test tube out. I remove the cardboard tampon sleeve.

"A cardboard tampon sleeve? Really?" Amanda asks. Everett looks away, in every direction, except for at me. Wow. He really is sixteen. Can't even look at a tampon sleeve.

"Well, it worked," I say, presenting the glass test tube and little pod intact. "A cardboard tampon sleeve, genius technology."

"I will be happy to place this back into that water garden, if you tell me exactly how this," I hold up the pod in the test tube, "is one of my kind," I offer Freya.

Freya stares at the test tube, getting closer and closer to it. "I have not seen one so . . . close up," she says, looking at the pod in the test tube, from every angle she can manage.

Huy waves to get my attention. A mischievous grin on his face, he points to another wall of the Prism. "Clear, please," he says to the wall.

Just like the first wall, this second one shifts from black, to grey, to clear. It's another underwater secret garden. But this one is different. The pods are huge and the bubbles inside them are larger than any I've seen. They don't float. They hover low over the aragonite hills and remain near the bases of the quartz crystal obelisks. I stare at each large pod and begin to see they look like embryos. Oh my.

Huy turns his back to me and towards the third wall. "Clear, please," he says to the wall.

"Alexis, this is where you came from," he says.

Shiny black onyx moves through grey and into clarity, revealing what is behind this third wall of the Prism. Unborn children in wombs. Infants, inside of clear, thin skinned bubbles, cradled on aragonite. Quartz obelisks create an ovular crib around each womb.

Eyes closed, the infants are breathing in and out, their chests and backs expanding and contracting with each breath.

I take steps, walking closer to this wall. I can't take my eyes off the infants, but I sense Freya is following me every step of the way there. These infants are of every race on the face of the Earth.

"This is the Cradle," Huy says.

"This is where I come from. I was one of them," the words flow from my mouth. It's a statement, not a question.

I look around to put my eyes on Amanda and Everett. A memory is resurfacing within me now.

"I remember it," I say. "I remember floating up to the top, to the surface of this water which is in an upper cavern of this cave. I was still in the womb, in the bubble which felt thick and fleshy. I saw her. It was Sofia. She reached down into the water to pick me up. Her face was the first face I ever saw. With my little fingers, I tore open the bubble womb. She took me and held me."

Sofia's words to me up in the yurt echo in my mind now. "Child. Child of mine. Child of Earth. Child of creation," was what she said. This is what she meant by child of Earth.

I scan this entire wall to count dozens of unborn infants.

"There are so many. I don't remember seeing others in wombs when I was floating up to the surface of the water," I say. "You were here then, right? Were there others? Did you see?" I ask Freya and Huy.

"We were not here," answers Freya for both of them. "We rotate our positions serving on the Council and leading the Council. It was Bekzat who led the Council when you were born. But we all know the story of your birth," she adds.

"You were the only one. As you have survived and grown, up there on the surface, they have done the same down here," Huy points to babies in their wombs. "Their rate of growth has significantly accelerated since the day you cut your finger on the meteor at the lab. We were surprised. The Do-Nothings had not received any message about that dynamic from the planet."

The test tube containing the pod from Naica is still safely in my hands. I hold it up to the wall of water in front of me. The pod now looks tiny compared to the infants it will grow into.

"It's time to return this to the water isn't it?" I ask. "Will it be OK here, since it originated in Naica?"

"Oh yes," Huy says. "That one was destined to be a traveler." His face lights up. I notice Huy smiles with his whole face, not just his mouth. Wrinkles around his eyes meet his rising cheeks.

I sigh. "Alright then."

I walk across the Prism to the wall where the smallest little pods are dancing about in the underwater secret garden.

"Here," Huy directs me to stand with him in a specific spot halfway along the length of the glass wall. Then, he steps back. "Open airlock chamber," he says.

The part of the floor I am standing on becomes a separate platform and descends, taking me down with it.

"This will take you to an underwater airlock. A few sets of doors and you'll be in the water," Huy says.

I descend about ten feet and the platform comes to rest on a lower surface. In front of me is a doorway. It opens automatically, and I walk through it into a small room. The door closes behind me and the room starts to fill with water rising through a pattern of small holes that dot the floor upon which I stand. If I didn't know that I can breathe underwater, I'd be getting nervous right about now. The water has reached my knees, topping my wedge heeled IES boots, which I've come to really like. I hope the water doesn't damage them, or the jumpsuit.

Water fills the entire room. When the H_20 reaches the ceiling, the ceiling slides open. Test tube in hand, I swim up. Here I am, inside an underwater secret garden again. I look out the glass wall to see my dry friend and sister on the other side. I feel like a fish in an aquarium. This feels so right. I like it.

I uncap the test tube. The pod floats out, joining the thousands of other pods. It floats up and away from me, leaving me. I feel an attachment to it. I'm not quite ready to let go of the little pod so I swim up after it. But like a person blending into a crowd on a busy urban street, it's gone.

Turning around to look back out to Amanda, Everett, Huy, and Freya, I'm halfway up the height of the Prism. I look down at them and see they are looking up, not at me, but at the glass sphere elevator that is descending.

Three figures stand inside of the glass elevator. Three figures I have not seen in person in many days, when they last tried to shoot me up with flurazepam to keep me from knowing what I am. As the elevator descends, the three of them are at eye level with me. They are dressed in black suits. They appear exactly as they did when I saw them on my Impossible Triangle on the airplane, when they told me that they would not allow me to destroy humanity and destroy their world. At this moment, they are looking at me like they want to terminate me.

Worse. They shift their gaze, down to the bottom of the Prism, at Amanda and Everett with the same look.

NO!

18

ROCK THE CRADLE

The glass sphere elevator glides smoothly into its bowl shaped receptacle.

The power goes out.

We would be in complete darkness if it weren't for the thousands of points of light emitted by the tiny pods that surround me in the underwater secret garden.

Amanda looks up at me. I see the physicality of her scream. She's illuminated, not only by the tiny pods that surround me, but also the bigger pods and the wombs that live behind the two other glass walls of the Prism, in the Cradle. I can't hear Amanda through the glass that separates my underwater haven from her, Everett, Freya, and Huy, in the Prism.

Sam, Ira, and Kan jump out of the elevator. Freya and Huy react to them with recognition and horror.

Recognition? Horror?

It was not long ago that I blindly trusted these three fake doctors with my health and my life. I took comfort in how different they were from most people, their oddities, which made me feel relatively normal.

How was I so wrong about them? How was I so naïve?

Freya says something to Amanda and Everett. In response, Everett and Amanda each run towards one of the vertices. Everett charges towards the square steel door of the vertex of the Do-Somethings, through which we had all walked earlier. After unsuccessful attempts at moving his hand through the door, he pounds his fists on what has morphed into a solid barrier. The door won't open. Amanda is at the triangular mayflower covered door at the vertex of the Do-Nothings. It's not opening either.

Swimming down towards the underwater airlock through which I entered, I see Huy and Freya charge at Sam, Ira, and Kan. I have to get out to the Prism and help them.

With his white walking cane, blind Ira strikes Huy's shiny bald head, knocking him unconscious. Freya kicks Ira in the chin with a swift forward thrust of her long leg. Ira falls back, landing next to Huy's collapsed body.

Silent mute Sam nods to Kan. She leaps onto Freya like a monkey onto a tree, digging her sharp black fingernails into Freya's neck. Sam reaches his hands into the pockets of his black blazer. Like a double fisted gunman, Sam pulls out two loaded needles, and jabs the one in his right hand into Freya's throat. Freya drops like a dead weight onto the floor next to Huy's body. Ira gets himself back up, kicking Freya while she's down. Huy stirs, moves, opens his eyes, and tries to get on all fours, only to be put down again when Sam stabs his carotid artery with the needle in his left hand.

The last thing I see before I submerge below floor level, towards the underwater airlock, is fake-doctors Roman charging towards Amanda and Everett.

I swim into the airlock chamber, down past its ceiling level. I look at the little holes on the floor through which water had risen. How do I get the ceiling of this little airlock chamber to close again? How do I get the water to drain back down through those holes and open the door that leads me back into the Prism? The sensors are not responding. I look around. No buttons. No control panel.

In disabling the power, Sam, Ira, and Kan must have disabled whatever Open Sesame technology was powering all of the doors in this place.

I swim back up to floor level where I can see out the glass wall into the Prism again.

Red rubber tourniquets, like the ones Kan had tied around my arm thousands of times since I was three years old, before injecting me with the needle, are now tied around Amanda and Everett's necks.

I push hard against the rock surface at the bottom of the underwater secret garden and shoot myself up like Superman. I'm flying up through H_20. The floating tiny pods look like a meteor shower as I speed past them. Swimming faster than I knew possible, I head up towards what I hope will be an opening to an upper cavern, like the one in the Cradle that I swam up into when I was born.

I stretch my arms further and further, propelled by my kicking legs and feet, until my hands feel air, not water. I've reached the surface.

It's dark up here.

I hear voices, panic, alarm.

A hand reaches down towards me. Whose is it?

Faintly lit by the glowing tiny pods beneath the surface, I see the hand belongs to Bekzat. I almost don't recognize him, his broken jaw bandaged up, out of his nomad garb and in his silver IES jumpsuit. His hand grabs mine.

"Bekzat! Which way?"

I'm lifted out of the water. I don't know if it's me jumping out or Bekzat pulling me up, but right now we are as one, running in lockstep. His hand still firmly gripping mine, he leads the way.

As we run through several series of narrow rock tunnels and wide open caverns, an increasing number of lights turn on.

"They are getting the emergency power systems up," Bekzat utters through a healing broken jaw. That's my fault. He's nearly breathless from our sustained sprint pace through yet another tunnel. A very bright light beams in towards us from the tunnel's end. We run out of the tunnel and into IES City.

"The entrance back into the Prism, I see it!" I say to Bekzat, releasing his hand. I run past him towards the park and onto the labyrinth through which we had descended into the Prism before. Cutting over its well-defined winding paths, I stand in the labyrinth's center, looking for a clue on how to open it.

"It's jammed," yells James running towards me with an anthropomorphic robot shadowing him. James turns to the robot's torso, which is a large computer screen, and gets coding.

"We've regained control over everything outside of the Prism. But this, we can't get in. We've tried everything,"

James explains. He looks at me, "Amanda's down there. Samirakan won't spare her. He won't."

"Samirakan?" I ask.

"Sam. Ira. Kan," James clarifies.

"You refer to them in the singular? Who are they? Are they . . . from here?" I ask.

James nods his head yes.

"So much for Only the Nice are Admitted, huh?" I prod.

"The Samirakan breakout predates me. But still, I had to observe what he did to your family and I had to not interfere," James says. "Now," he looks at me, "It's time to interfere."

"Get the thing open!" I yell at James and the robot. The robot inches back on its wheeled feet, as though offended by my outburst. Or maybe he's inching back because, if we actually get the labyrinth to slide open, we'll be falling down into the Prism. I'm prepared for the fall, but James and his little robot buddy may not fare so well.

"Damn digital device," James keeps coding on the robot's screen. The robot continues to inch back, as he's poked in the torso by James's coding fingers. The sudden sound of heavy machinery coming from behind me amplifies.

"You haven't tried good old reliable low tech," Ivan hollers at us over the sound of the skid-steer he's driving, which is outfitted with an auger drill. At the sight of this, James's robot speeds up its wheels and scurries away.

Ivan aims the tip of the auger drill right over the center circle of the labyrinth, which is made of white marble and is about the size of a manhole cover. On it are carved the words—As Below So Above. Ivan lowers the drill's tip into the marble and bores through. Chips of marble spiral out from the spinning drill, forming a pattern like the arms of the Milky Way galaxy. Reversing the drill's rotation, he pulls the center circle out, revealing a hole plenty large enough for me to jump through.

James and I drop down to the ground and stick our heads into the hole. We look down. It's a five story drop.

At the bottom of the Prism, Freya and Huy are sprawled on the floor, looking lifeless. Amanda and Everett sit on the floor, back to back, bound to each other by red tourniquet. Their hands, and worse, their necks are tied tightly to each other by the thin red rubber hose.

"Samirakan! You horrendous, incompetent probabilist!" James throws his words down like spears upon Sam, Ira, and Kan.

A third head joins me and James in the manhole. It's Ivan.

"You were off limits to us at the surface, Samirakan, but here, you're all ours," Ivan threatens.

Blind Ira looks up at us, takes his dark glasses off and shows us his wicked eyes of white. No pupil, no iris, just white. It's freaking me out as much as the first time I saw his eyes at home in Wellesley.

"James and Ivan, pleased to meet you. Come down and join the party, won't you?" Ira says pointing towards Freya and Huy splayed out on the floor.

Everett sees my line of sight, as I search for signs of breathing and life in Huy and Freya. How lethal are Sam, Ira, and Kan? I wonder. They could have killed me a thousand times over in the past thirteen years when they were pretending to be my doctors. But they didn't.

"They're breathing. Must have been a tranquilizer," Everett says looking up at me, forcing the words out past the red tourniquet decorating his neck.

"Don't talk," Amanda tells Everett. "When you talk the noose gets tighter around my neck."

"You, don't talk! Same thing happens to me," says Everett.

"You, don't talk," Amanda retorts.

"James and Ivan," Ira says, "Bring Alexis down with you. She's the one we want. She's the reason we've left the glorious United States of America to come to this rotten pit. She's the reason we are three."

Kan sticks her fingers between Everett's and Amanda's necks and tightens the red tourniquet that binds them, trying to silence them both.

Amanda works even harder to grunt out at me, past the tightening stranglehold on her neck, "You just had to call ICE didn't you? They could have still been in jail in the U.S."

"What?" I respond. She's blaming me for getting Sam, Ira, and Kan kicked out of the U.S.? "It was Hannah's idea," I remind her. "And you and Everett prodded me to do it!"

"Own . . . your . . . decisions!" Amanda says, gasping for breath. She's right.

But she really needs to stop talking. I think I know how to shut Amanda up at this moment, for her own good.

"Amanda! I forgive you! I forgive you for not being my biological sister and I forgive you for not telling me we weren't biological sisters. I forgive any slight you have ever made against me, imagined or real. And, you're the best sister in the world! And, please, please shut up!"

"No elevator cable?" I ask Ivan and James, looking to my left and right, at their heads which hang down the hole like mine, minus the long mane of wet black hair that extends from my head.

"No. It's a toned down version of the technology used by the capsule that brought you down from the surface," James explains.

I look down at the five story drop and turn to the two other heads in the manhole. "Would you mind pulling back please? I need room."

They pull their heads out and step back.

I jump down into the Prism, sticking the landing like an Olympic gymnast.

Upon my landing, little points of light emanating from the three glass walls of the Prism pulsate, on and off, in a pattern. First the tiny pods, then the bigger pods, and then, in the Cradle, the wombs.

"You called it a party. I brought the strobe lights," I say to Ira.

Oops. I've tipped blind Ira off to my location. He charges at me with his white cane. I dodge it with a quick move to the left.

"We will destroy you, before you and your kind," Ira says, pointing his white cane at the unborn babies in the Cradle, "destroy humanity."

Sam gives me his silent nod and charges at me. I make a quick decision to use the Freya kick-your-opponent-in-the-chin-with-your-long-leg move. My foot meets his face with the sound of a whack. Sam's head leads the rest of his body in a backward fall onto the silver granite floor, culminating in a thud.

Ira's white cane strikes the small of my back. Owww. That sort of hurt.

"You know the truth. You know what will happen," Ira taunts me from behind. "You know the most probable outcome of your kind emerging in mass numbers up there, on the surface."

I turn around to give Ira some payback. Payback for the whack of that cane just now, yeah, a little. Mostly, I want payback for thirteen years of fake doctors Roman shooting me up with drugs that prevented me from knowing how strong I am, knowing what I am, knowing who I am.

"Shut those wicked . . ." I say as I punch Ira's left eye ". . . white . . ." and then I punch his right eye ". . . eyes . . ."

His eyes bleed hemoglobin-rich red blood. I shake his blood off my knuckles and wipe my fist on his black jacket. Eewww! I want none of his bodily fluids on me.

Sam has peeled himself off the floor and comes at me again. I give him two quick punches in the stomach and he collapses like an umbrella.

I hear the sound of choking behind me, and turn around.

Everett and Amanda are both at the mercy of Kan, who rings the red tourniquet tighter again around their necks.

"That's right. Keep fighting us. Their death certificates will state asphyxiation as cause of death," Kan informs me with a grin.

Sam straightens back to an upright position and reaches into his blazer pockets again.

"Asphyxiation by more means than one. We have a tasty cocktail of pancuronium bromide and potassium chloride for them," Kan says as Sam shows me two needles. It's the three-drug lethal injection used in capital punishment, minus the anesthetic.

Kan narrates Sam's actions. It's like a ventriloquist show, a very good one. They are totally in synch. The Prism continues to pulse with light emanating from the new forms of life behind its three walls of glass.

Sam holds up one of the two lethal injection needles, and pushes the plunger up ever so gently. A tiny drop of the deadly cocktail spurts up from its beveled tip.

"We did promise a party didn't we?" Kan says as she and Sam cock their heads up simultaneously to the manhole sized opening which Ivan and his auger drill created for us. "Your IES friends seem to have abandoned you. Maybe they just don't have the stomach for this kind of party," Kan mocks.

Ira stalks towards me.

"Look at the beautiful red blood," Kan says, gazing at Ira. The white of his eyes are no longer visible, hidden behind swollen lids. Blood drips from under his eyelids, down over his lips.

Ira opens his mouth, licks his lips, and says to me, "The rise of you, the children with the crystal blood, will mean the fall of human civilization as we know it."

"You don't want that, now do you?" Kan asks, maintaining her tightening grasp on the red tourniquet around Amanda's and Everett's necks. Sam, needles in hands, steps closer to them.

"Look at these beautiful red-blooded Americans," Kan says, scratching their faces with her black pointy fingernails, drawing blood from Amanda's cheek and Everett's forehead. "They are the product of the institutions, structures, and belief systems currently on

Earth. You wouldn't want to destroy something that produced these two lovely young people, now would you?"

"I am not here to destroy anything . . ." I tell her, ". . . but you." I charge towards Kan and Sam.

"Stop. Unless you want to witness their last breath," she threatens as she tightens the tourniquet further. Everett's eyes droop and close. His head hangs down like he's nodding off to sleep.

"Everett!!!" I scream. He lifts his head up a bit and manages to partially open just one eye. He looks at me like a one eyed pirate squinting into the sun.

I freeze.

"Loosen it. Loosen it! I'm stepping back. Look," I say, as I take several slow steps backwards.

"You know the truth," Ira repeats his earlier statement. He's inching closer and closer to me, bringing with him the stench of sweat, blood, and the pus that is oozing out from around his eyes. Ira's words come from a mouth and teeth dripping in blood, blood that continues to flow down from his swelling eye sockets. "If more humans had the ability, like you, to tell the truth from a lie, then how many institutions, organizations, governments would crumble? What would happen?"

I had essentially thought and said the same in the Council's Chamber earlier.

"Chaos," I respond.

"That's right," Kan affirms, as she loosens the red tourniquet around Amanda and Everett's necks a bit. They inhale.

"Combine," Ira says through a thickening flow of blood pouring over his mouth. The words that reach my ears sound muffled. He pauses. He half drinks and half wipes the blood off his mouth, snorts and continues. "Combine the collapse of current institutions and belief systems, with your physical strength and ability to see certain things, and your kind will have the power to dominate and enslave standard humans. Humans like Amanda and Everett."

I see Everett and Amanda sitting there, bound up, unable to stand up for themselves. In a way, I had done the same thing for thirteen years. I had not stood up for myself.

"Your kind, with the crystal blood, will become like gods walking the Earth. Dominating. Enslaving. Taking over. It's simply Darwinian evolution. Survival of the fittest in the animal kingdom. Your kind will survive," Ira says.

"They will perish," Kan points at Amanda and Everett, standing over them, her high heeled black boots on their backs. With a kick, she knocks them over. They lie there, bound up on the floor.

I feel my neck tightening as though the red tourniquet around Amanda and Everett were also tightening on me.

That won't happen! I think and I try to say it out loud, but I can't. I am feeling asphyxiated. I put my hands around my neck, but feel no tourniquet there, just my bare neck. I am silenced.

Ira puts his hand to his ear. He steps closer to my mouth. "I don't hear a thing. So you don't disagree with us. You know it too." He places his hand, inches from my head exactly where my Impossible Triangle usually appears.

I can't get words out. I shake my head no.

No! No! No!

Sam nods at me.

"Ira, my dear, she's agreeing with us. She's nodding her head yes in affirmation," Kan lies to Ira who can't see me.

"I told you she would recognize the truth once we explained it to her. She's a smart girl," Ira says. He reaches his bloody hand towards my head, finds it, and strokes my hair.

"The probability analysis shows it's the most likely outcome. But they wouldn't believe me. The Council wouldn't believe the data. They just sent you up into the world, just like that," Ira goes on.

The pulsating lights from the pods and wombs in the waters of the Cradle intensify in both speed and brightness.

"And they let us drug you and keep you down," Ira adds.

There's a twisted hint of honesty and sincerity behind the nurturing way he strokes my black hair with his blood red hand.

"Why didn't the Council stop us? You must have asked yourself that. They didn't stop us because deep down inside, they know. They know we are right about you," Ira says.

My neck continues to feel tighter. I feel the way Amanda and Everett look. I have had this feeling of a tightening sensation around my neck before when I had heard lies, but it's never been this bad.

"Wrong!" Ivan's voice booms from above.

"As a probabilist, Samirakan, you just . . . SUCK!" James's voice trails right behind Ivan's.

I look up.

Like Batman and Robin, they descend down upon us, by way of ropes. I look up at the manhole and almost expect to see a bat shaped grappling hook.

"Go to HELL!" Kan hollers at James and Ivan as their feet hit the ground.

Upon that word—HELL—I can feel it forming, the Impossible Triangle pops up. There it is. I look around in the Prism. No one around me reacts to the screen in front of my face. It's exclusively my window into knowledge.

On the screen, Kan, Sam, and Ira, like three monkeys, cling onto my back as I jump into the pillar of fire at the center of the Council's Chamber. I see us descend together, fake doctors Roman and I. To where? To hell? To the center of the Earth? I don't know. All I know is what I need to do next. I shake my head, dissolving the Impossible Triangle.

I am back fully in the present moment.

I grab Ira's hand, halting its continuous stroking of my hair. I place my other hand on his upper arm and lift his body high into the air, over my head. He feels as light as an empty carcass. I thrust him down with a slam.

Droplets of blood bounce off this body and onto my face when he hits the floor.

Sam moves to unload the lethal cocktail from his needles into Amanda and Everett. I lunge at him, knocking his body back up high against the wall behind him. He slides down the wall. I jump on top of him, nailing him to the floor.

Ivan appears next to me.

My hands around each of Sam's wrists, I squeeze. I squeeze until he can grip the needles no longer.

Ivan grabs the two lethal needles. He smashes them under the heels of his IES boots.

Ivan pulls Kan off of Amanda and Everett. He turns her over to James. Amanda and Everett gasp breaths of relief as Ivan removes their tourniquets.

James has Kan on the ground.

"Behind you! Ira!" Amanda warns me.

"Sam, incoming!" Everett adds.

Like monkeys, Sam and Ira jump onto my back. I grab and toss them off, only to have them charge and leap on top of me again.

"I'd never hit a woman, but Kan, you're no woman!" James says as he punches her on the ground.

Kan's black claws reach for James's face. Ivan lunges, grabbing Kan's arm and bends it back behind her.

"Let her go!" I yell, charging towards Kan, with Ira and Sam, still on my back.

Ivan and James look at me with incredulity.

"Trust me," I say.

They let go of Kan.

I pick her up by the collar, lift her over my head and throw her onto my back.

The strobe of the Cradle's lights cease. We are now bathed in the calm, warm light of the tiny pods.

I charge towards the circular wooden mandala door at the vertex of the Council's Chamber. Running across the floor of the Prism, I remember the power is still down. The door won't Open Sesame. As I approach the door, I lunge into the air and roll up like a ball. The monkeys on my back serve as cushioning, cushioning I don't need. But, I figure I'll make these three hurt a little. Like a cue ball across a billiard table that takes flight, we break through the door, which scatters into pieces. We land on the floor of the Council's Chamber.

In my peripheral vision, I see sparks of light. Is it from the crash and fall? I also see three heads looking up and around.

Sam looks at all the empty chairs, nodding.

"Council's Chamber," Ira says, minus the menace that was in his voice earlier.

"It's been . . . so long . . ." Kan whispers.

My legs pump faster and faster towards the pillar of fire in the center of the chamber.

I dive into the circumference of air that surrounds the pillar of fire within the hole. Looking down, the hole appears to go on to infinity.

As we free fall, I can feel us moving through stripes of hot and cold air. Each cold patch bumps us up and the hot pushes us down. Then, I remember what the Spanish Council member with the goatee had told us— "Like the twisting stripes of a candy cane, one stream of air twists and moves up while the other twists and moves down. This contains the flame at the level we desire. Nano-particles of opposing magnetic charges make each stripe."

More sparks appear and disappear in my peripheral vision, like fireflies.

I picture the candy cane in my mind. I want to take the Romans down. Down into what they believe is hell. I figure it's just as likely to be the very center of creation for this planet. Who knows? It's not like any humans have been in there. In the years before the Mayflower crossed the Atlantic to North America, some explorers feared being eaten by giant hungry sea monsters or sailing off the edge of the flat Earth. They didn't know. It was uncharted territory. I figure, let's go ahead and explore.

I move us into the hot, magnetic stripe of the candy cane and we stay in there. Swirling down, our descent accelerates. It's getting hotter. The view on the way down has not changed. We're still looking into infinity.

Boom, boom! Boom, boom! Boom, boom!

I hear a low beat. It sounds like a drum, or a heartbeat.

Ira, Sam, and Kan intensify their grabbing, repositioning, jostling for position on my back. Do they hear the beat? Are they responding to it?

Sam grabs onto my right arm, swinging in front of me. He's nodding at me. That nod, which I've seen thousands of times before, now looks different, because he opens his mouth. A wild roar emerges from his throat. The roar morphs into words. The first words I've heard him speak.

"Alexis!" he says. "Save us."

The sparks in my peripheral vision are getting brighter and larger.

Ira grabs my left arm, pushing Sam aside, and gets right into my face. Heat has dried the blood that was pouring down his eyes to his chin. Dry flakes of red peel and fly up and off his skin as we descend. Ira lifts his puffy lids, revealing his eyes. Milk chocolate colored irises surround black pupils, that regard me with acceptance instead of hate.

"I see. I see a beautiful creature," Ira says to me.

"Do you hear it? I can hear it," Kan says from behind me, placing her head next to mine. She can hear.

"Yes. Yes I hear the beat," I say.

"Listen . . . close," Kan whispers into my ear.

The pounding beat turns into the guttural sound that had emerged from Sofia's mouth up in the yurt, the sound that had opened the world of the IES to me. This sound is overtaken by a very high pitched ringing in my ears. It's so loud! Sam, Ira, and Kan must hear it too. They cover their ears. Their faces cringe in pain. Sam opens his mouth. He creates a high ring tone that matches the one I hear in my ears. The sound changes again.

Now, it sounds like an echo emerging from beneath us. It sounds like the song of angels. Electricity runs up and down my spine.

"That's it," Kan says softly. "That's the sound."

She lets go of me. We're falling together now, side by side, unattached. Ira looks at Kan. He lets go of me and grabs onto her.

"Farewell," Sam says to me, as he jumps from me to Ira and Kan. The three of them grasp each other more tightly. Closer together, they intertwine, like a braid.

The song of angels amplifies.

One of the sparks in my periphery moves towards them and lands on them.

An explosion occurs around them. I see nothing but white light as I continue to fall.

Stretching forward in their direction, searching, I feel nothing but empty space.

A bodily mass slams into me and pushes me into the cold magnetic stripe that rises up around the pillar of fire. The blinding white light is gone. I see I'm not alone. Pushed up with me, along the cool stripe of buoyant air is a man. Aspects of Kan, Ira, and Sam are visible in his physical form.

My mind processes seeing this one person, who appears to embody the three people who have been harming me for most of my life. I feel fear rising in my gut. The fear delivers a question to my mind. Is this a united front by my enemy? That fear dissipates when he speaks to me.

"My name is Roman Samirakan," he says. He regards me with acceptance, with the eyes I have only seen on Ira down here, those milk chocolate irises. His voice is that of Sam's which I heard for the first time when he uttered my name a few minutes ago, asking me to save them.

"My purpose was to help, protect, and care for you. To help give birth to you and your kind." His words ride through the magnetic nano-particles to me on a wave of nurturing that feels feminine. I sense this is the part of this man that is Kan. As we continue to move up, around the pillar of fire, I feel weightless, like I no longer have a physical body, like I am just my thoughts and emotions. He reaches for my hand and continues.

"I got confused. I got lost. In the face of change, I could only see the potential for evil. I'm sorry."

19

EVOLUTION UNSTOPPABLE

Repentant. Ashamed. A touch of the cat-that-ate-the canary. These are the expressions making waves across his face during his so-called trial, as Roman Samirakan sits in his golden bird cage. A cage, with bars made not of metal, but of gold colored lasers. He and his cage are in the exact spot within the Council's Chamber where an empty chair used to be. The ninth chair, positioned between Freya and Huy, the chair which Amanda had assumed was meant for her upon our first entry into the Council's Chamber earlier today. In fact, the empty seat had belonged to Samirakan before he lost his way, or maybe his mind.

This is really more a Socratic seminar than a trial, in my opinion. Samirakan is a full participant in the discussion about how a nice probabilist turned into three very naughty people and inflicted pain and hardship on the first Mayflower, me, Alexis Allerton. Because I was the primary victim of his crime, I get to decide his punishment. I stand in the center of the Council's circle, warmed by the pillar of fire.

"Alexis, your decision please?" Freya urges. Her voice sounds a bit groggy, but she's pretty coherent considering she was knocked out by a tranquilizer earlier today. The IES medical staff shot up Freya and Huy with yet another needle that woke them with a jolt out of the unconscious tranquilized state into which they were put by Samirakan, when he was still Sam, Ira, and Kan.

"Take your time," says Huy, who in addition to sounding groggy like Freya, is growing a bump on his bald head, courtesy of Ira's, well, actually, Samirakan's white cane. The bump looks like it wants to become a mini bald head on top of Huy's already bald head.

I want to decide, I do. If for no other reason, just to end the longest Socratic seminar of my life. At school, Socratic seminars came to a natural end when the bell rang. No being saved by the bell here. Thanks to the skills I've honed on the debate team, I've kept track of the blow-by-blow, all the facts that weigh upon the case. But I need one more thing before I decide. I need to hear it all summed up by Samirakan, from his point of view. I need to sense the feeling in my throat—truth or not truth?

"Roman. May I call you Roman?" I ask him.

"You may call me whatever you like," Roman responds. I think of a few words I'd like to call him, but those aren't words I would say in front of Alina and Dale, so I don't say them at all.

"Roman, let's make this more like a real trial. Give me your closing argument," I say.

"Very well. As a probabilist, a statistician, I have failed. James is correct about that. Fire me. Don't execute me. The mathematical model and simulation I created produced data that showed only a very, very, very small probability that you, and the evolution that you represent, would oppress, and then wipe out humans as we know them today. Instead of remaining objective and rational about the existence of risk, I let fear consume me. That's when I decided I needed to go up to the surface, find you and stop you. I believed that if I could sabotage you, without killing you, if I could cause you to stray from your path, if I could cause you to never wake up to what you really are, then the planet and the IES would see that Project Mayflower is not the path of progress. It's a dud. A waste of time and resources." Roman looks not at me, but at the other eight Council members of the inner circle of nine. His eyes dart to the outer circle, composed of sixteen additional IES members, Ivan and James among them, plus Amanda and Everett. These two, Amanda and Everett, have decided to position themselves on either side of Roman's golden bird cage. Amanda's and Everett's body language tells me they think they are being bailiffs. Not that I need the protection, but their intention is sweet.

"They could have stopped me," Roman points around the room. "Thirteen years ago, when you were just three years old, the IES members who served on the Council could have prevented me from ever reaching the surface. Back then, the other probabilists on my team warned them I was losing my mind. They should have stopped me. Take a lesson from this."

"Noted," says the Australian Council member who looks like he's spent more time in corporate board meetings than in this chamber. "While the other eight Council members deliberated, you acted."

"Acted on the knowledge that he alone is no match for a three-year-old girl!" the Haitian Council member who looks like a twelve-year-old girl herself mocks Roman.

I watch his face for signs of—repentance? Nothing. I keep watching. Hmmm—the face of shame emerges, then recedes back into nothing.

"It's true. That's the point. I was no match for a three-year-old girl. That's why I dipped into the candy jar at the vertex of the Do-Somethings," Roman confesses, the expression of the cat-that-ate-the-canary emerging from his face again.

Nuclear fission. That's the candy jar to which he refers. That's how he split himself into three. One of the newly created elements, which resides on one of the two new rows the Do-Somethings of the IES have added onto their expanded periodic table of elements, behaves like U-235, uranium with an atomic mass of 235. Like U-235, this fission-friendly new element splits into three when one neutron hits its nucleus. When it splits, it throws off a whole lot of energy and three more neutrons, which hit three more, creating a chain reaction in multiples of threes. When this fission-friendly new element attaches itself to any other element, for example, all of the elements that comprise the human body, then, all of those other elements come along for the fun fission ride.

"When I entered the nuclear fission reactor, along with a healthy dose of the new fission-friendly element discovered by the Do-Somethings," Roman says, "I set out on a mission to multiply myself, thereby multiplying my power."

"You strayed from your purpose. How could you? We did move to stop you," the woman from Mali says.

"Stop me? Hardly," Roman scoffs.

"We did minimize the damage," the girl from Japan says.

"The reason only 3 Romans emerged from the nuclear reactor instead of 9, or 27, or 81, or 243, or 729, or 2,187, and so on, is because the Do-Somethings did something, Alexis," Huy tells me "They realized what Roman was doing and stopped him."

"Not before I, or should I say we, because at that point I was already three. We used the excess energy created in just that one cycle of fission to power our way up to the surface before the IES could do anything about it," Roman says. "Once I split into three, well, then I really got crazy. Each part of me became less rational, more paranoid, more likely to see and be evil

"So, multiplying yourself did not, indeed, make you more powerful," the Council member from Spain points out.

"But this is only clear to me now, now that I have reunified. I could even claim a defense of insanity here, I believe," Roman says.

"Don't go there, Roman," I say. "Crazy or not, you're still responsible for what you did."

"All of you, sitting here today, could have acted at any time by coming up to the surface and removing me," Roman looks again, not at me, but at the people in two concentric circles that surround me. "You let me lie and manipulate this child's parents. I even managed to convince them not to tell her she was adopted. They were going to tell her. But I changed their minds. Really, it's almost criminal that the IES didn't interfere," he says looking at me now.

He's not totally wrong on this one. It really wasn't very nice what the IES did.

The adoption agency here in Kazakhstan, a front for the IES, had told Alina and Dale that I had hemophilia, and that a condition of my adoption was that I needed a good, safe home where my medical needs would be met. They even recommended a hematologist who practiced in Boston. This was an actual good, real, doctor and member of the IES. The plan was that this good doctor was supposed to care for me and not drug me with flurazepam. This doctor would keep up the hemophiliac cover story until my family and I found out I was different. Then, this doctor was going to coach me and my family through dealing with my special abilities, without letting the rest of the world know. None of us would be told anything about the IES and how I was really born. The plan was, when I turned eighteen, I would be brought to the IES and told the whole truth. As an adult, I would decide how to proceed.

Maybe all their probabilists here at IES are very bad at their jobs, or just a little. Because clearly, that's not how it unfolded. Well, at least I'm glad I beat their estimated time of arrival at the IES by two years.

Instead of what was planned, Sam, Ira, and Kan landed in Boston, took on the names Dr. Sam Roman, Dr. Ira Roman, Dr. Kan Roman and showed up at Alina and Dale's house saying they were sent by the adoption agency. This was just hours after Alina and Dale arrived home with their newly adopted daughter, me. So, Dale and Alina never called the good, real, IES member doctor who was set up for me. Once Drs. Roman entered the picture, the good IES doctor was not allowed to interfere. He had to stand down.

Roman is right. It is almost criminal that the IES simply stood down, didn't interfere. The Council has repeatedly stated today, in their own defense, that they were not permitted to interfere, per the rules of the planet and the IES.

"The Council and the IES bear equal responsibility. I should never have done what I did. It was wrong and I'm guilty. But they could have and should have stopped me at any point over the past sixteen years, since the day you were born, born of the Cradle of Earth," says Roman. "I rest my case. Give me whatever punishment you will."

I take this in. I feel the center of truth through my throat's expansion. I decide.

"Roman. You believe you are expressing your own truth. But I disagree that the Council and IES bear equal responsibility. Responsibility lies within the individual. I don't yet understand why the Council didn't act to stop you. I also don't yet understand the reason for this rule of non-interference. But I see the result. There has been no irreparable harm done. I have survived. I found my own way to the IES. I didn't have adult mentors guiding me. I discovered what I am and what I can do on my own. And . . . I did it two years ahead of schedule. I'm sixteen, not eighteen, and today I declare myself an emancipated adult. Emancipated of Dale and Alina Allerton and, more importantly, emancipated of the Council and the IES."

A wave of gasps from the two concentric circles in the Council's Chamber alert me that I may have alarmed them with my statement of emancipation.

I've gone rogue.

Amanda snorts. She follows it up with her hyena laugh. Her laugh used to annoy me. Right now, it warms my heart.

I think she's as amused as I am by the concern on the Council members' faces.

Roman, the cat-that-ate-the-canary, chimes in. "You let the genie out of the bottle," he says to the Council.

"Don't worry. I'm going to work with you. I'm not going to dominate and eviscerate you. I love where I come from and how I've come to be. I'll just work with you . . . on my own terms," I say.

"It was supposed to happen this way!" Ikal declares, running into the Council's Chamber. "The entire Do-Nothing population received the same exact message at the same exact time. I believe this has never happened before," he looks around seeking confirmation from the Council.

"That's correct. Messages usually come in pulses to different Do-Nothings at different times," says the young female Council member from Japan.

"I got it. We all got it, at the same instant just a few minutes ago. The planet had intended it this way all along. It was sort of a test. And apparently we, the members of the IES, were also subjects of this experiment," Ikal reveals.

"We're guinea pigs?" asks the grey haired Brazilian Council member.

"We've been used like lab rats?" asks the Spaniard, pulling at his goatee.

"The first Mayflower, Alexis, was put in a position to discover what she is, by her own will, in the face of opposition. That meteor, the one in the MIT lab that cut her finger, was a spark provided by the planet. From that point on, Alexis had dozens of key choice points in which to choose between returning to living a life in denial or pursuing the truth. Because she showed that a Mayflower can find its own way from seedling underground, to flowering in sunshine, the future Mayflowers that are in the Cradle today won't have to go through the same test," Ikal explains.

"So, Alexis passed the test," says Freya. "What about the rest of us?"

"Oh. Well. We didn't get any information about that," Ikal says.

He looks at me. They all look at me.

What? Did I just become the authority in the room?

"Freya, none of you on the Council are on trial. You're all fine. As for Roman Samirakan," I walk up to him and look at him through the golden laser beam bars of his birdcage. "I think you should remain right here, in your seat on the Council. You have a point of view that I think is useful for the rest of the Council. I'll check in with you and your state of mind in the future. Until then, you shall remain locked in your golden bird cage. Your assignment is to think about how you can help the children born on the surface of Earth as well as those born in the Cradle."

"I assume I am welcome to visit my place of birth?" I ask the Council.

The Council rises. They nod their heads in unison, signaling an affirmative.

"Alexis, Amanda, and Everett, on behalf of the Council, the entire membership of the IES, and the Planet Earth, I officially offer you membership in the IES. Do you accept?" Freya asks. She stands there, so tall and regal, and all she's missing is a sword in her hand to knight us.

"Yes!" Amanda blurts out first.

I look at Everett.

"Yes," he says, as he pushes his glasses up the bridge of his nose.

"Yes," I say.

Sun. Air. The surface. It feels like heaven.

Rays of sunlight from across my solar system and an untamed breeze of my planet's air feel like kisses on my cheeks and nose. Standing outside of Sofia's yurt, I gratefully accept planet Earth as my home.

Bekzat and the horses are ready to guide me, Amanda, and Everett on our caravan over the mountains and across the desert valleys of the Tien Shan Mountains in the direction of the closest international airport, Almaty. Out of our IES suits, and back in our local nomad garb, we're in camouflage. Bekzat hands the reins of the caramel colored Akhal-Teke horse to Amanda and my golden horse to me. I stroke the horse's long face. He rubs his head and long neck against my body. The golden horse is behaving like a cat. What would a horse purr sound like? Maybe a deep, low, rumbling version of the heart beat sounds I heard deep down in the fire shaft in the Council's Chamber.

I mount the golden horse. Interesting—the saddle is more like a pillow or carpet, than the more conventional saddles on the other horses. Bekzat gets on his own horse, which steps beside Amanda on top of hers.

Everett looks at us. Shrugs his shoulders and walks towards his horse, still tied to its post by the yurt. Maybe only the females get horse delivery service around here and it's self-serve for the males.

"No, no. Horse stay," Bekzat says with his limited English that is further limited by his healing jaw. He helps himself by gesticulating. "Sofia need horse." Without the aid of the IES's babel bugs, we're back to the reality of broken English and limited communications. I could translate in Kazakh, but first I want to see what Everett can manage on his own.

"Me no stay," is Everett's retort. Oh. Is he being rude to Bekzat? "Me go."

"How many languages do you speak?" Amanda jabs Everett.

Everett holds up one index finger. But he does this like he meant to use his middle finger.

"Yeah, so cool it," Amanda adds.

"You," Bekzat points at Everett. "Go this horse," Bekzat moves his finger to my golden horse. When Bekzat turns his horse around to face me, his horse's tail gives Everett a gentle slap across the face. Bekzat winks and smiles at me. Is he setting me up? Oh, I think he is, and that's why he didn't put a conventional single rider saddle on my golden horse.

"Well," I say to Everett, removing my foot from the stirrup. "Need a ride?"

No answer. Just a grin. Then, his foot's in the stirrup, his body's spooning mine, and his arms reach around me to grab the reins.

Sofia, standing just outside her yurt door, waves goodbye to us.

Everett signals the horse, squeezing his legs around it. And we're off, leading the charge up the mountain. On foot, I'm faster than Everett and any other human, at least for now. I can't comment on the growth of human potential in the future. But on horseback, Everett equalizes the playing field with me.

We reach the crest of the mountain, fast. Bekzat and Amanda are trying to catch up. I turn the golden horse around to take another look down into the valley, at the center of which is a white yurt accented by a turquoise blue and gold tribal pattern. Sofia's yurt. My yurt.

"I am not born from another human being," I say to Everett. "I'm born from a planet."

Everett's long fingers comb through my loose hair. He drapes my mane to one side, exposing my neck to his face. He kisses me. I turn to look at him.

"I'm different. And you don't mind?" I ask.

"Not that different." he says. "In your birth, you just, sort of cut out the middle man, and the middle woman. Maybe it's a more efficient form of creation." He seems to be convincing himself more than he's convincing me, as he talks. "Not that different." He repeats.

"One. We're the same age," he says.

I nod my head in agreement.

"Two. We are made of the same exact elements of Earth," he adds.

"Yes," I agree again.

"Three. Our DNA is up to 99.9 percent identical," Everett says.

"99.9 percent," I say and then I add "Up to." The number could be much lower than that. We don't entirely know yet about the four extra base pairs of my DNA.

His fingers lead my face closer to his. He kisses my lips. I close my eyes. I can hear my heart beating louder. Then, it's drowned out by the increasing volume of hooves approaching us.

Hearing a momentary pause in the hooves, I keep my eyes closed. I don't want this moment disturbed. The sound of Amanda's hyena laugh, which I know is directed at me, also graces the far reaches of the Tien Shan Mountains. Then, the sound of hooves again fade into the distance as they descend the other side of the mountain. Unhurried and undisturbed by the hyena laugh, the kiss comes to a natural stop. I open my eyes. Everett is staring at me. He signals the horse, and we're charging down the mountain, catching up to Amanda and Bekzat.

Hours later, crossing a desert valley, we slow our pace, giving the horses a walking rest.

"I wonder," I say. "If Sam, Ira, and Kan would have merged into one if I had not been there."

One of the tiny sparks that I saw in my peripheral vision had jumped over to them, just before the flash of light that merged three beings into one.

"Your quartz crystal blood being right next to them could have impacted their magnetic field and been a catalyst for their merger," Everett posits. "A study conducted at the Tokyo Institute of Technology published in *Nature* magazine had some interesting findings. It's possible that from a liquid alloy made up of iron, silicon, and oxygen swirling around in the core of Earth, some silicon and oxygen is merging to become solid SiO_2 crystals. This crystal at the core of the Earth could be powering the planet's magnetic field."

"So, you mean my crystal blood could have created a magnetic field that brought Sam, Ira, and Kan together close enough to merge them into one?" I ask.

"Well, it's sort of logical," Everett says. "So, it's sort of possible."

"Hmm . . . deep thought," I say.

"Further research is required," Everett concludes.

Welcome to Boston's Logan International Airport, reads the large plasma screen overhead, as Amanda, Everett and I walk towards passport control. We had shed Bekzat in Almaty. I'll miss that sweet man and hope to see him again. I hope his jaw bone will be fully healed when we next meet. Amanda's phone rings. She answers and bolts over to the wall of windows that overlook Massachusetts Bay. She looks up to the sky, waves and continues her phone conversation. Everett and I wait for her to finish whatever it is she's doing.

Arriving passengers ahead of us split into two directions, one into the line for U.S. citizens and permanent residents, and the other into the line for non-citizen visitors. The composition of people going into either line looks the same. The U.S. citizens line could just as well have been the line into the IES. A kaleidoscope of people, whose ancestors originated from a plethora of points across the surface of the globe converge here, entering the country that matches their passport. I like the IES. I like the U.S.

Amanda returns to me and Everett with a broad smile on her face, her phone back in her bag.

"So?" I prompt.

"So," she says. "James told me which way to look to be in his line of sight. Between the IES's satellites and the phone, we'll remain connected until I get to see him again."

"Oh joy," I say. "Santa's Observatory is still at work."

Amanda, Everett, and I make it past passport control and walk towards the passenger greeting area, where I'm told, Alina and Dale will be. When I last saw them, I had just been informed by the triad I now know to be Roman Samirakan, that I was adopted. It was Ira who revealed, "You do not belong to them and they do not belong to you." My anger, fermenting into hatred, I had jumped the black wrought iron fence of the house in which they raised me and I ran, ran fast away from them.

Everett squeezes my hand. He's been holding it through passport control. "You OK?" he asks. I must have spaced off recalling that last night with Alina and Dale.

"Yeah, I'm OK," I say. But the words coming out of me are apprehensive, unconvincing. In answering the question, I realize, I just don't know how I'm going to react to seeing them. Do I want them as my parents? I am not biologically of them. I have a choice. So do they. They made the choice to take me when I was three years old. They didn't know the full extent of what I am. Maybe they don't want me anymore. I'm not exactly a standard daughter with standard problems.

The sliding doors open. I see them. My feet cross the threshold into the airport's public space.

Alina runs towards me first and grabs me. She pulls me tightly into her embrace and strokes my hair. Everett lets go of my hand and steps back. Dale joins me and Alina. I am held by them both.

Before we left the IES, the Council invited me and Amanda to call Alina and Dale and tell them about me, my blood, my origin, my purpose, and to offer them very, very limited information about the IES, on a need to know basis only. Amanda took them up on that offer. I did not. I allowed Amanda to do the telling because they deserved to know. I wasn't ready to talk to them yet. I felt strongly that I needed to see them in person to decide, decide what role we would have in each other's lives, if any.

At this moment, standing in Dale's and Alina's embrace, I feel like a young child, like a three-year-old.

A longing emerges in me to have these people to take me and keep me. The feeling has caught me off guard.

"We are yours. We are made of flesh and blood and we are yours," says Alina. My mother.

"Would you be ours?" says Dale. My father. "Would you forgive us for what we didn't know? Would you also forgive us for what we could have known but didn't? Would you forgive us for what we did know, but didn't tell you?"

I pull away from Dale and Alina's tight hold of me. Not because I don't want them, but because I need to see their faces. I need to see their faces, not as Dale and Alina, but as my parents, again and for the first time.

"You know I'm . . . different," I say.

They both nod.

"Would you be ours?" Dale asks again.

I am in the very unique position of choosing my own parents.

"Yes, Mom and Dad," I say.

The waning moon hangs in the morning sky over Wellesley. It's October 11th.

Per my consensual agreement with the powers that be at the IES, I have agreed to *act normal* up here on the surface and keep my crystal blood and its powers a secret, until I turn eighteen, at which time, I will decide if, how, and when to reveal. Per the agreement, I will return to the IES for the next two summers during my school breaks for "R&D". The powers that be at the IES are further encouraging me to stay focused in school and go to college. So, really, not all that much that is observable has changed in my life. Fortunately, Amanda has kept her position as research assistant with her professor, Dr. Collins, at New Mexico Tech. We turned over to Dr. Collins the red selenite I had taken from the previously inaccessible far reaches of the Naica cave. It was a peace offering to her after I *endangered my life and the lives of others,* as we have been reminded. Dr. Collins and the Naica people still have not figured out how I managed to survive in there, but they are now distracted enough analyzing their red selenite specimen.

I go to school each day. I hang out with Hannah and Josh. And, I still don't participate in PE, lest the school administration and entire student body find out I have superhuman physical abilities. The days I go to the MIT lab after school for work are still my favorite. It's not the escape it used to be, because I don't need an escape from home now. It is my time to experiment, learn, and hang out with Everett.

One very welcome change, the black wrought iron fence that used to secure the perimeter of my home has been taken down. Now, the house at the corner of Sterling and Temple is really a home.

I step outside of my house. Brown autumn leaves crunch under my wedge heeled boots. These boots aren't quite as fabulous as the turquoise ones I wore at the IES, actually not even close, but they'll do for now.

"Alexis," Josh calls from next door.

We meet on the sidewalk. He takes my hand. We skip to meet Hannah at her cross street. I turn Josh over to Hannah. They hold hands and I walk beside them. As we continue our walk to school, Josh recites poetry to both me and Hannah.

"Treasured third-wheel," Josh looks at me. "This trio triumphs together through tough times to taunt trepidation of abandonment, tossing this terror towards termination."

Since my return, I've decided there's nothing wrong with being a third wheel. Like being the front wheel of a tricycle, I remain an essential part of our dynamic. So what if Hannah and Josh have a special relationship of boyfriend and girlfriend, of which I am not a part? I am happy for them. They can have that boundary and it doesn't diminish who I am to them and vice versa. I am putting more of my thoughts and efforts into maintaining my own new boundary, of which they cannot yet be a part. That boundary is built to protect two secrets. One, is my knowledge that Hannah's little brother Noah, and Josh himself, are candidates to become members of the IES. Two, is my knowledge of the existence of the IES, period. Although Josh and Hannah both now know about my crystal blood, at this time, neither can know about the IES.

As we walk onto campus, my first agenda item, before Period One, unfortunately, is meeting with Vice Principal Montgomery about the Earth Science Club. While I was away, Hannah hustled and helped me get more club members, and upon my return I added a few more, but I'm still only at eleven. Mr. Montgomery had made it very clear that we needed twelve members to make the club a club by October 11. That's today. Today, I'm going to ask for an extension. I walk into his office.

"Welcome, Alexis," he says to me.

"Good morning Mr. Montgomery," I say. "Because I was out for a while recently, on . . . uhmm . . . family business, may I please, please have an extension on the deadline to get twelve members for the Earth Science Club?" I ask.

"No," he responds.

"Mr. Montgomery, please?" I plead.

"I'm saying no, Alexis, because you don't need the extension. You just got your twelfth sign up earlier this morning," he informs me.

"I did? Really? Who and how?" I ask.

"A new student enrolled yesterday afternoon. Just moved into the school district. He specifically asked what clubs we had on campus and he signed up for two clubs. The Comic Book Club and the Earth Science Club. He seems like a very nice, bright young man. You ought to meet him. He's finishing up some registration paperwork next door," says Vice Principal Montgomery.

I jump out of my seat.

"Thank you Mr. Montgomery," I say, shaking his hand.

I pop my head into the office next door.

"Everett Evans!" I say.

"Hello, Alexis Allerton," he says.

"What are you doing here?" I ask.

"Do you remember what I said to you last week at the lab?" he prods.

"About . . . ?" I ask.

". . . about, the only thing that could make me happier . . ." he says.

"Oh. Oh, yeah, that. You said the only thing that could make you happier, post-IES, would be if you could just be an average teenager going to high school," I say.

So, this is his way of having a high school experience? Even though due to having a brain the size of a planet, he skipped some of middle school and all of high school already? I guess.

"I do remember," I say. "Welcome to high school. You belong here."

He smiles at me. He adjusts his t-shirt, coaxing my eyes to look at his goofy science t-shirt of the day. I suspect this one is custom made.

The formula on his t-shirt is $(SiO_2)A^2 + E^2 = \infty$

THE END . . .

. . . but, if you're Infinitely Curious . . .

. . . visit https://mirhouse.net/science-behind-the-book for links to research, articles, videos, and books on the science behind the story.

We are stardust brought to life, then empowered by the universe to figure itself out—and we have only just begun.

Neil DeGrasse Tyson

If you enjoyed *Alexis Ascending*, we invite you to visit www.mirhouse.net and sign up to receive special offers and updates on new releases.

Reviews from readers like you on your favorite book retailer's website are appreciated and serve to help other readers find this book.

Thanks for your time and for taking this journey with Alexis.

ALSO BY DILEK MIR:

Picture Book:
When Echo Met Shadow

COMING SOON BY DILEK MIR

A Young Adult Novel:
The Travels of Mackenzie McDougall

Audio Books:
Alexis Ascending
The Travels of Mackenzie McDougall

Picture & Audio Books:
Baby Palm
Little Palm
Young Palm

ACKNOWLEDGEMENTS

A very heartfelt thank you goes out to my young beta readers: Angelina Todorov, Alyssa Duren, and Kylie Duren.

Your feedback gave me encouragement to move forward with this and my other books.

Made in the USA
Monee, IL
27 November 2020

49775142R00194